Praise for

# SCARLET
## and
# IVY

"This is one of the best books I have ever read. It was exciting, funny, warm and mysterious." **Lily, aged 9**

"The whole book was brilliant… after the first paragraph it was as though Ivy was my best friend." **Ciara, aged 10**

"This book is full of excitement and adventure – a masterpiece!" **Jennifer, aged 9**

"This is a page-turning mystery adventure with puzzles that keep you guessing." **Felicity, aged 11**

"A brilliant and exciting book." **Evie, aged 8**

"The story shone with excitement, secrets and bonds of friendship… If I had to mark this book out of 10, I would give it 11!" **Sidney, aged 11**

SOPHIE CLEVERLY was born in Bath in 1989. She wrote her first story at the age of four, though it used no punctuation and was essentially one long sentence. Thankfully, things have improved somewhat since then, and she has earned a BA in Creative Writing and MA in Writing for Young People from Bath Spa University.

Now working as a full-time writer, Sophie lives with her partner in Wiltshire, where she has a house full of books and a garden full of crows.

### *Books by Sophie Cleverly*

### *The Scarlet and Ivy series*
### *in reading order*

THE LOST TWIN

THE WHISPERS IN THE WALLS

THE DANCE IN THE DARK

THE LIGHTS UNDER THE LAKE

THE CURSE IN THE CANDLELIGHT

# SCARLET and IVY

## The Curse in the Candlelight

# SOPHIE CLEVERLY

HarperCollins *Children's Books*

First published in Great Britain by HarperCollins *Children's Books* 2018
HarperCollins *Children's Books* is a division of HarperCollins*Publishers* Ltd,
HarperCollins *Publishers*
1 London Bridge Street
London SE1 9GF

The HarperCollins *Children's Books* website address is
www.harpercollins.co.uk

Text copyright © Sophie Cleverly, 2018
Illustration copyright © Manuel Šumberac, 2018

7

978-0-00-821831-7

Printed and bound in England by
CPI Group (UK) Ltd, Croydon  CR0 4YY

**MIX**
Paper from
responsible sources
**FSC™ C007454**

*For Theo and Willow, who are tiny and new*

## Chapter One

## SCARLET

It was the worst birthday I could remember. And considering I had spent my last birthday locked up in an asylum, that was really saying something.

I ran into what had once been our bedroom, slamming the door shut behind me. I flung myself down on the dusty sheets and beat the pillow with my fists, sending clouds billowing into the air.

It wasn't long until I heard light footsteps gently treading the stairs, and the creak of someone pushing the door open. I knew it was my twin, Ivy.

"Scarlet," she whispered, somewhere near my ear.

"No," I said, my face still in the pillow.

"No what?" she asked.

I pushed myself up and stared at her, my arms folded. "No, I'm not going back in there. And no, I'm not going to apologise!"

She sat down on the bed beside me. "I wasn't going to say that. I don't blame you at all. I think *she* should apologise. But I know she never will."

We hadn't wanted to go to our father's house that summer in the first place. We'd spent most of the holidays with our scatterbrained Aunt Phoebe, in her cosy cottage. It meant cleaning and tidying and cooking because our aunt could barely remember to do that for herself, let alone us as well, but we didn't mind. Aunt Phoebe's house was always filled with love.

Father's house, on the other hand, was filled with the stepmother who hated us, and our three hideous stepbrothers. I couldn't bear it. I missed Father sometimes – or maybe I just missed the way he had been. The rest of them were a nightmare. I hadn't wanted to go back.

But in a rare moment of remembering that we

existed, Father had turned up at Aunt Phoebe's the day before our birthday, asking to bring us home. Aunt Phoebe had thought this was a "lovely surprise" and so here we were now. I would rather have caught the plague, to be quite honest.

Unfortunately, we hadn't had a choice in the matter. We had waved goodbye to our aunt and sat bundled in the back of Father's motor car, dreading what would lie ahead at the end of the journey.

Our stepmother, Edith, had greeted Father warmly, and given us a greeting colder than ice. That was typical. Ivy had tried to say hello to our stepbrothers, but they had just ignored her and carried on playing with their model trains.

Dinner hadn't gone any better. Our stepmother had given us the smallest helpings of everything, and then called me greedy when I had asked if there was any more. Her boys got portions the size of mountains, *and* she gave them seconds. I glared at them one by one, but they were too busy stuffing their faces to notice.

We'd spent a chilly night in our old twin beds. I spent most of it staring through the crack in the curtains at the black night sky, hoping that if I stayed awake long enough it would delay the arrival of morning. But soon my eyes slipped shut, and I woke up to the weak, watery sun rising on our fourteenth birthday.

Ivy rolled over sleepily in her bed. "Happy birthday," she mumbled to me.

"Happy birthday," I said back, without much feeling. I peered over at her, through the dust spiralling in the light. She was smiling. "What?"

"Well..." She sat up and hugged her knees. "You have no idea how much it means to hear you say that."

"Sorry," I said to the ceiling. "I know I should be more grateful not to be 'dead', but I'm not. I still hate that I was left there." The time I'd spent locked in an asylum while our nasty headmistress had told the world that I'd died was never far from my mind. "And I just have a bad feeling about this birthday too."

The bad feeling was sitting in my stomach, weighing me down. I climbed out of bed, my bare feet heavy on the old wooden floorboards.

Ivy sighed. "It can't possibly be worse than last year."

I hoped she was right, but I still wasn't convinced.

We got dressed, putting on matching dark blue dresses that were some of the few clothes we owned, and headed downstairs. It was early in the morning and the house still hadn't warmed up, even though it was the last day of August.

"I suppose a birthday breakfast is too much to hope for," Ivy whispered.

It was. We arrived in the chilly kitchen to find our stepmother lazing in a chair, a glass of something pale and unappetising in her hand.

"Oh," she said when we walked in. "You're up. Well, make yourselves useful, then. Get the fire swept and lit."

I looked at her in disbelief. "I'm not your servant," I muttered under my breath.

Ivy gave me a wary look.

Edith stood up and slammed her glass down on the empty table, sending the drink splashing from the sides. She must have heard me. "When you're in my house," she said, pointing a finger at us, "you live by my rules – understood?"

I was about to protest further, but that was when Father walked in. "Good morning," he said, rubbing his eyes with one hand, the other tugging on his tie. "Everything all right?"

It was like someone had flicked a light switch. The murderous expression evaporated from our stepmother's face and was replaced with a calm, serene look. "Quite wonderful, dear. The girls had just volunteered to make a fire for us, *hadn't you*, girls?"

I had a good mind to set fire to her pinafore just to spite her, but that definitely wouldn't have gone down well with Father. Ivy obviously didn't fancy getting into trouble either, because she went over to the fireplace without a word and began sweeping it out. I muttered a few choice words under my breath and went over to help her.

When we'd finished, Edith told Father that we'd also volunteered to make everyone breakfast. Father just yawned and smiled, his eyes staring somewhere into the past.

I couldn't take much more of this. "You know it's our birthday, don't you?" I said. "After all, isn't that why you brought us here?"

There was a cloud over his expression for a moment, and his eyes shut. Our mother, Ida, had died just after we were born. I could almost see her image painted on the back of his eyelids. Our birthday was a painful reminder.

But then his eyes opened again, as if nothing had happened. "Of course I know that, Scarlet. And you're very kind to offer to make breakfast on your birthday."

So we made breakfast while Edith just sat in her chair by the now-roaring fire and smirked. When the bacon and eggs were done, she jumped up and pushed us out of the way. "You've done enough now," she said. "Go and sit down."

Reluctantly, I let go of the frying pan and sat down at the table.

"BOYS!" Edith yelled. "BREAKFAST!"

There was a sound like a stampeding herd as our stepbrothers came pelting down the stairs and into the kitchen. All neatly dressed, I noticed, in clothes that were shiny and new, not covered in ash and cooking grease like ours.

I watched, open-mouthed, as Edith, once again, gave them the biggest helpings. She dished out plates that were nearly as full for herself and Father, and then for us...? Well, we were given the burnt scraps from the bottom of the dish. Father didn't even seem to notice.

I was hungry, and even scraps of burnt bacon and scrambled egg were better than nothing, so I ate it. But I could still feel the anger burning in my stomach.

"Good boys," Edith said, as they devoured their food. "You can go out to play now. Your sisters will wash up."

One of them, Harry – the youngest – just started laughing. And that was when I snapped.

I stood up, my chair scraping the floor loudly. "Really? Do you want us to mop the floors and make the beds, too? Happy birthday to us!"

"Don't talk to your stepmother that way," Father said, tracing his fork around his empty plate without even looking at me.

Ivy grabbed my dress and tugged me back down to my seat. I knew how much she hated conflict, but I couldn't put up with this for a moment longer. It was so unfair!

"You're making a scene again, Scarlet," Edith said, swirling the drink in her glass. She seemed to have refilled it.

"Oh, *this* isn't a scene," I muttered. I tied my dress in angry knots round my fingers. "You should see me make a scene."

Ivy decided to take that moment to make a desperate attempt at limiting the damage. "Father," she said. "Do we have any presents?"

"Oh, of course," he replied. He stood up and brushed some invisible dirt from his trousers. "I'll get them from my study while you wash up."

I sat and seethed until Ivy dragged me and an armful of plates over to the sink. I just knew that our stepmother was smiling smugly behind our heads.

"Here you go," Father said as he returned. He laid two small packages wrapped in brown paper on to the table. "Now, I'm afraid I have a lot of work that I need to be getting on with. I'll see you in a few hours." And with that, he wandered away again, whistling something that wasn't even a tune, but that sounded absent-minded and sad. I'd always thought that Father and Aunt Phoebe couldn't be more different, even though they were brother and sister, but now I was beginning to see the similarities. Neither of them seemed to be on quite the same planet as the rest of us.

"See you later, darling," Edith called after him. She stood up and went to the doorway. "I'm going for a lie-down," she said in our direction. "Sort yourselves out."

I slammed a pile of soapy plates on to the sideboard, making Ivy jump, but Edith had already gone.

"Could they be any more unwelcoming if they tried?" I asked.

Ivy didn't answer but just stared down into the dirty water. I could see a tiny tear in the corner of her eye, so I put my arm round her shoulder and led her over to the presents...

She quickly cheered up, and together we eagerly ripped off the paper. I reached into the box and... oh.

Socks.

I pulled them out. They were our school regulation ones – dark blue and made of fairly soft wool that was only slightly itchy to the touch. But still. *Socks*.

Ivy held up her pair in front of her face. "Oh. Rookwood socks," she said, echoing my thoughts.

I put them back down, curled together like little fluffy rats.

"Well, it's better than nothing," she said.

A suspicion was starting to build inside me. I went out into the hallway and down towards Father's office where I knocked on the door.

"Busy!" came the reply.

I ignored him and walked in anyway to find him sitting at his desk, scrawling on forms and doing calculations.

"Father," I said. "Thank you for the... uh... *lovely* socks. I don't suppose Aunt Phoebe gave you any presents for us from her, or from Aunt Sara, did she?" Our aunts were the best family we had, and I couldn't quite believe that they'd forget our birthday.

Father didn't look up. He shuffled a piece of paper from one pile to another, and chewed on his pipe. "Phoebe gave me something," he muttered. "A few packages in shiny paper. But as to where I put them..." He laid down his pipe and stared around the room as if it would answer his question. "Hmm. I could have sworn they were in here. Perhaps Edith tidied them away."

My fists clenched. *Of course she did.*

"Never mind, Scarlet," he said, standing up and ushering me back out into the hall. "We'll find them another time. Why don't you run along and play with your brothers?"

And with that, he shut the door in my face.

"I'd rather eat worms," I told the door.

I spun round to find Ivy standing behind me. "Did you hear that?" I asked. "She's taken them, hasn't she."

"I wouldn't be surprised," Ivy said, her eyes trailing to the floor.

The sight of her sad expression only stoked my fire even further. "Right," I said. I turned on my heels and marched up the stairs. Ivy must have quickly realised what I was up to, and started running after me.

"Scarlet, we can't..." she said.

But it was too late for that. I went straight across the landing to the master bedroom, and hammered on the door as loudly as I could. Of course, I didn't wait for an answer. I just wrenched at the handle and pushed it open.

And there was our stepmother, lounging in the four-poster bed, munching on chocolates, and surrounded by shreds of shiny wrapping paper.

## Chapter Two

### IVY

I honestly thought Scarlet was going to explode. I was just considering whether to fetch the fire brigade when Edith looked up at her.

"What are you doing in here?" our stepmother demanded. "Aren't you supposed to be cleaning up?"

Scarlet stared at her for a moment, her face as scarlet as her name, speechless with anger. And then it all came pouring out in a raging torrent. "Who do you think you are? You can't order us around like servants!

You can't treat us like dirt to be swept under the carpet! You... you can't take our only birthday presents for *yourself*!"

Edith dragged herself off the bed and stalked over to Scarlet, the familiar grimace (and a smidge of cocoa) back on her face. "I'm your mother now, and I can do what I want, you insolent little brat!"

"YOU'RE NOT OUR MOTHER AND YOU NEVER WILL BE!" Scarlet shouted.

There was a breath, an instant of heavy silence. And then Edith swung out and slapped Scarlet round the face.

I gasped, and dragged my twin backwards. There was a mark across her cheek, a ghost of our stepmother's hand.

"Girls?" Father's voice drifted up the stairs. "Keep it down, will you! I'm trying to work." There was the sound of the study door pulling shut again.

Edith just stood there, her chest heaving, her face flushed, wiry hair sticking up from its usual careful curls.

Scarlet broke away from me, tears flashing in her eyes, and ran across the landing. Even school had to be better than this.

I looked up at our stepmother, watching her

expression turn triumphant. It made me feel sick. "She's right," I said quietly. "You won't ever be our mother. Our mother was worth ten of you."

And with that, I turned and went after my twin.

I put my arm round Scarlet and comforted her until she'd calmed down just enough to simply be angry, and then we stayed in our room for most of the day. I didn't particularly want Scarlet and Edith anywhere near each other again, and Scarlet wasn't exactly keen to face up to her either.

I wasn't quite as disappointed as Scarlet about the awfulness of our birthday. It was never a particularly joyous occasion, so why would this year be any different? I thought that, deep down, Scarlet felt that the world ought to treat her better than it did. She could never understand why it didn't happen. I, however, had much lower expectations.

Of course it goes without saying that Father didn't come upstairs to see if we were all right. If our stepmother had told him anything about what had just happened, it would have been that Scarlet had attacked her for no reason. She always painted herself as the victim and Father always believed her.

As we wallowed in our misery, I finished reading

my book. Then I unpacked and repacked my bag about three times until it was neater than neat. As horrible as Rookwood School could be, I found myself wanting to go back, which was certainly a surprise. I missed our friends – Ariadne and Rose – and the other girls too. Rookwood *had* improved a lot since its former headmistress and headmaster had been taken off in a police van – even with the grey porridge, the cold and the bullies, it could still be a good place sometimes.

Around lunchtime, there was a click from the doorway. Curious, I wandered over and tried the handle, only to find I couldn't pull it open.

Scarlet sat up straight on her bed. "Did someone just lock us in?"

I nodded. "Looks like it." Scarlet had always had a habit of kicking doors (and walls, and furniture) that I had never understood, but at that moment I was tempted to try it. Instead, I bent down and peered through the keyhole. I could see right through it – so she'd taken the key away again. No chance of pushing it out to free ourselves.

My twin put her head in her hands. "Could it be any worse?" she asked.

I heard the sound of the door unlocking just before dinner time. It opened to reveal Edith with her familiar scowl.

"Your father's asking where you are," she said, in a voice that implied she couldn't be less interested and was hoping she could forget about us forever. "I said you were messing around up here. I suppose you'd better come down."

Scarlet went over to the door and stared up at her defiantly, though I could see her hands were shaking. "You locked us in," she said.

Edith put her nose in the air. "And? That's beside the point. Get down there and see your father."

I went over to stand beside Scarlet. For a moment I thought she was just going to do as she was told, but no – she was Scarlet. That wasn't how she worked.

"He's going to see through you one day," she said quietly. "He's going to realise how you treat us and –" she took a deep breath – "and *what you did*."

Edith stepped closer, looming over Scarlet. "*Did?* I don't know what you're talking about," she said, narrowing her eyes.

I knew, and I knew *she* knew. We were almost certain that Edith had accepted a bribe from the old headmistress, Miss Fox, to pretend that Scarlet was dead. Scarlet had found out Miss Fox's deepest secret, and went to terrible lengths to keep it.

Scarlet just glared at our stepmother, her arms folded tightly.

Edith glared back. "Fine. Be like that. But here's a warning for you." She leant forward, coming face to face with us. "You're going back to that school soon, and this time you're staying there for good. Your father isn't going to rescue you and neither are your crazy aunts. You're going to get an education and learn some respect, and you're not going to bother us again."

I frowned. I had to speak up. "What do you mean by 'for good'?"

"I mean," she said, holding a calloused finger up to my face, "that I don't want you back here. You think your life is a misery now? Just you wait." She straightened up and stalked back to the hallway. "Just you wait," she repeated, only now there was a flicker of glee in her mud-brown eyes. "Downstairs. NOW."

We ate dinner in silence. I watched as Scarlet stabbed every one of her scraps of meat much harder than was necessary. I knew that she wanted to shout and scream in frustration, but it wouldn't do any good. We just had to put up with the rest of this miserable day.

Father had looked at Edith with a sort of blank, distracted happiness when she'd handed him his dinner. I wondered if he even saw her at all. Sometimes I imagined that his mind had painted the memory of our mother over Edith, and he never quite noticed that it didn't fit.

As soon as dinner was over, Scarlet and I headed up the stairs, brushed our teeth and went to bed early. "This birthday can't be over soon enough," Scarlet said.

I agreed.

Tomorrow would be the first of September. A new year at Rookwood. As I lay under the dusty sheets and stared up at the dappled ceiling, I tried to forget about everything that had just happened and imagined what it would be like being a third year. New lessons, new teachers, new students to make friends with. We'd had so many new starts, but maybe this would be the one that went right...

I smiled up into the dark, and my eyes slipped shut.

We avoided saying goodbye to Edith the next morning. (She had disappeared. I didn't know where to, but Scarlet was sure she was up to something.) Father was going to be the one driving us back to Rookwood. The boys were playing football in the garden. I tried waving goodbye to them, only to be met with jeers.

"*Boys*," Scarlet said simply, rolling her eyes.

We climbed into the back of Father's motor car with our bags, breathing in that familiar smell of leather and petrol.

I watched sadly as the cottage faded from view. It had been our home once, after all. But Edith had made it very clear that we were no longer welcome there.

"Bye, house," Scarlet called out of the window. "It was nice knowing you."

"You'll be back soon enough," Father said, his hands loose on the wheel.

I shared a look with my twin. "I'm not so sure," I said warily.

He tapped his fingers. "It's only school, girls. They let you out sometimes." He sighed as he stared out at the village. "Thirteen years old, eh? Where does the time go?"

"We're fourteen, Father," Scarlet said.

He just blinked. "Fourteen, really? Hmm."

My twin rolled her eyes. I didn't blame her. Father seemed to be paying less attention to our lives than ever. We were lucky, I supposed – lucky to have Rookwood to go to; who'd have thought I'd be saying that? It wasn't as though we had a choice anyway – our stepmother didn't want us there, and she didn't want us living with our aunts either (not that they really had the room). I just had to hope that we could stay out of trouble for as long as possible. If Rookwood found any reason to expel us, well... where would we go?

The journey passed in a blur of silver skies, green leaves and grey tarmac. The route was familiar to me now, but I still remembered how strange it felt that first time, with Miss Fox and her driver. The thought made me take Scarlet's hand and squeeze it tight.

She was writing in her diary again – a new paper journal with a green jacket that she'd found at school. Her initials, SG, were written proudly on the cover. She also seemed to have acquired a new fountain pen, which was unusual since we normally used pens you had to dip in ink. I decided it was better not to ask where she had got it from.

"Don't jog me," she teased, poking me in the leg. "It's hard enough to write in this bumpy old thing as it is."

"It's always good to see you writing in there," I said.

"Well," my twin replied. "You never know when a diary might come in handy..."

## Chapter Three

### SCARLET

**F**ather's motor car pulled up on the gravel drive of Rookwood in the shadow of the enormous building, behind a queue of others and a bus. Everywhere girls were leaping out, lugging suitcases, waving to their parents. There were first years crying, clinging to mothers. But most of the older girls seemed eager to get going.

As we climbed out with our bags, I saw a familiar car arriving behind us. It came so close to ours that it almost hit the bumper, and then a familiar man who looked like a bespectacled owl got out. "Sorry!" he said.

I dropped my bag on the floor and ran over to the car, just as the door swung open and our best friend appeared behind the man. "ARIADNE!" I yelled, and jumped on her.

"Oof!" she said. "Steady on, Scarlet."

I stepped back and grinned. "Never!"

Ivy came up beside me and gave Ariadne a hug. "We missed you so much."

"Good morning, Sally and Irene," Ariadne's father said, tipping his hat at us.

"Morning, Mr Flitworth," I replied. There was no point in correcting him now. It was what he'd always called us. We'd have to be Sally and Irene forever.

We said goodbye to Father, while Ariadne said goodbye to hers. I could hear him giving her a long lecture about safety and the importance of staying away from windows and potentially poisoned food. I half wished our father cared so much. Instead he'd just said, "Off you go then, see you soon," and waved us towards the front entrance.

Ivy and I picked up some of Ariadne's suitcases (she had a little convoy of them, as usual) and together we headed inside for the first day of our new year at Rookwood.

Mrs Knight was waiting in the foyer, greeting everyone. She was the head of our house – Richmond – and as of last year had become the headmistress as well, sort of by default. She was thankfully a lot less murderous than previous occupants of the position, and had a tendency towards being annoyingly cheerful.

"Welcome, welcome!" she was saying. "Everyone head to the hall, please! Carry your bags with you!"

I looked around the foyer, taking in the faces: there were some familiar ones – Nadia and Meena standing beside their very expensive luggage, even... *ugh*, our worst enemy, Penny, was there, chatting to some of her gang. But there were plenty of unfamiliar ones too. New girls. Mostly they looked like first years, with pristine uniforms. But there were some older girls among them, as well. Mrs Knight's efforts to restore the school's reputation had clearly had an effect.

We headed for the hall where the noise was deafening. Everyone was talking at once, greeting friends who they hadn't seen all summer. We managed to find a seat, just.

"I got you these!" Ariadne said. She pulled one of her suitcases open a crack and took out two envelopes, then handed one to each of us. I tore mine open eagerly.

It was a birthday card showing a girl striding happily

along while she held hands with a cat, a dog and a bird. It said, *May you have a string of smiles for your birthday*. I laughed. "Thanks, Ariadne."

Ivy grinned, and waved hers at me. It was completely identical.

I tucked mine away in my bag. At least our stepmother couldn't take these from us.

When everyone had filtered into the hall, the sound of chatter was broken by an ear-splitting whistle from the stage. The talking died away as all of the girls stared up at the swimming instructor and games teacher, Miss Bowler. She had the loudest voice in probably the entire world; she also seemed to have been given the job of ordering everyone about. "SIT DOWN, ALL OF YOU!" she boomed.

When we had all done as she said, she stepped aside, leaving Mrs Knight in full view.

"Welcome, girls!" she said, her expression as bright and cheery as ever. "Welcome to a brand-new year at Rookwood! We will be having a completely fresh start. I'm sure if we all work together, this will be the best year yet."

She did a sort of fist-pump, clearly expecting people to cheer. Nobody did. Except Ariadne.

"First things first," she shuffled all of the papers in

front of her. "I want to announce that as I am officially the headmistress of the school, I am stepping down as the head of Richmond House. Your new house mistress will be Madame Zelda."

Well, that was an odd choice, considering that Madame Zelda hadn't been at the school very long and she wasn't exactly normal. Everyone looked around to see the silver-haired ballet teacher, who was tapping her long fingernails against her arm and smiling. She gave a small nod, and a flurry of whispers began.

"So now," Mrs Knight continued, "the first thing we need to do is get everyone lined up in alphabetical order in their house groups, then your teachers will give out room assignments and make sure that everyone knows where they're going. Then we will give out the lesson timetables, and the lists of rules and maps of the school for the new pupils." She took a deep breath, "And then—"

She was interrupted by the doors at the back of the hall flying open.

"I'm sorry I'm late," came a voice.

Everyone turned in their seats to look.

It was a girl, about our age, with incredibly long jet-black hair. She was dressed in Rookwood uniform, but instead of the regulation shoes, she was wearing a pair of black pointed boots. There was a suitcase in her hand (black too, and very battered). She stood there, chin raised, as if the fact that she had just walked in late in front of the entire school was nothing at all.

Miss Bowler strode towards her. "Who are you?" she demanded.

"I'm Ebony McCloud," said the girl. "Who are you?"

Everyone gasped and Miss Bowler spluttered. "I am your games teacher, Miss Bowler," she said, "and you are in trouble unless you sit down right this minute!"

"All right, then," said Ebony with a twitch of a smile, wandering over to a seat and sitting down.

She had a Scottish accent, and a voice that made me think of mist and mountains. There was a strange darkness to it.

"Ahem," said Mrs Knight from the stage. "Everyone! Back to me, please!"

We all turned round again, but Ebony stayed stuck in my mind. She was... interesting. She reminded me a little of Violet, my former arch-nemesis. Speaking of which, I wondered if Violet had returned. I scanned the hall, but I couldn't see her. But I did see her friend Rose – now *our* friend Rose – who had proved herself to be truly magnificent in the summer when she'd overcome her shyness to stand up to her evil relatives. I gave her an enthusiastic wave, and she grinned back at me.

"Now for a few notices," Mrs Knight was saying, "and then we'll all line up. Firstly, the library is up and running again and will be open from nine o'clock each morning for anyone who wants to read..."

I tuned out, and my mind wandered to the room assignments. Would Ivy and I get our old room back, my lucky number thirteen? I wasn't sure how it worked. First years always had bigger dorms, but everyone else was in twos. Hopefully we'd get to keep the same one. If we didn't, well... I hoped the new occupants wouldn't notice the hole in the mattress where I'd hidden my diary.

"Right then," Mrs Knight said when she'd finished reading her seemingly endless list. She waved her hands about in the air. "I repeat – line up in your houses, everyone! Richmond down the left, Mayhew in the middle, Evergreen on the right! You should have been assigned your house in your welcome letter! Alphabetical by surname, please!"

I don't think our headmistress quite anticipated the chaos that ensued. There was a huge amount of scrambling as everyone tried to pick up their luggage and head in the right direction, climbing over seats and in some cases the other students!

"Carefully!" I heard Mrs Knight call out.

"Calm down, the lot of you!" Miss Bowler yelled. "It's not a race!"

I picked up my bag (though we left Ariadne's in a heap), and tried to head for the Richmond line. It wasn't easy, given that a large amount of people were trying to head the other way.

"Watch it!" I called out to one girl who nearly swung her bag into my face. She stuck her tongue out at me as she passed.

Finally, after a lot of jostling, the three of us made it to the other side of the room and into the line. Then there was yet more jostling as we tried to figure out the order we were supposed to stand in. Ariadne's surname was Flitworth, so she had to go further up.

Ivy nudged me. "Look," she said. "Rose is near Ariadne."

I realised what she meant and smiled. Rose had had to hide her identity for a long time when she'd first arrived, but now she could tell the world that she was from the wealthy Fitzwarren family.

Ivy and I slotted in next to a first year who informed us she was named Abigail Greenwich. I peered to the front and saw that Madame Zelda was up by the stage handing out sheaves of paper and clipboards, and that she was talking to Miss Finch. It made me smile to see my favourite teacher, Miss Finch, again, and to see that she and Madame Zelda were getting on all right. Or at least, passably. That was really something, considering that Madame Zelda had admitted to pushing Miss Finch off the stage when they were at ballet school, leaving her with an injured leg for life.

I was less pleased to see Penny at the head of the line, still wearing her shiny prefect badge. Would we ever get rid of her?

The teachers started at different parts of the very long line that went all the way to the end of the hall, walking along with clipboards. It wasn't long before one of them reached us – Miss Pepper, the slightly eccentric art teacher.

"Name?" she asked.

"Ivy Grey," my twin replied.

She nodded and ticked off the name on her register. "Of course, I taught you last year. Here's your timetable and some forms to fill out for elective lessons and such." She leant forward. "I hear art is very popular," she said with a wink at the first year behind us.

Ivy took the papers and rifled through them.

"All right..." Miss Pepper ran her finger down the register. "You are assigned room thirteen on the second floor. Aaaand..."

"Scarlet Grey," I said.

"You too, Little Miss Twin!" she said. "Room thirteen. Unlucky for some." She handed me the same bits of paper she'd just handed Ivy, and then moved on to the next person.

"Phew!" Ivy said. "Same room again. And together."

"Yes!" I cheered. Everything was going to plan. "I'll just see who Ariadne got. Maybe she'll be sharing with Rose?"

I was pretty sure I wasn't supposed to leave the line, but considering I had everything I needed, I didn't think it mattered. I stepped out and wandered forward to find...

"Ariadne?"

She was leaning against the window, holding her papers. But her face was white and her hands were shaking.

"Ariadne?" I asked again, waving my hand in front of her face. "What's wrong? Who did you get?"

My friend turned to me, her eyes glazed and distant. "I can't... I can't..." she said.

And then she fainted.

## Chapter Four

### IVY

I ran over to Ariadne immediately. Her legs had gone from underneath her, and Scarlet was trying to hold her up. "What on earth happened?" I asked.

Everyone was staring now.

"SOMEONE GET THE SMELLING SALTS!" Miss Bowler boomed.

Ariadne's eyelids fluttered. "I'm f-fine," she mumbled. "Isn't it hot in here?"

It wasn't particularly hot at all, but I fanned Ariadne anyway. "Are you all right?" I took her arm.

She didn't feel that warm.

"I'm fine," she said again, standing upright and brushing herself down, but her face looked drawn and she was breathing a bit too heavily for my liking. "Perfectly fine."

Suddenly, I got the feeling that whatever the matter was, it was something she didn't want to talk about in front of the staring eyes of the whole school.

"She's all right," I called.

"Nothing to see here!" Scarlet yelled, waving people away.

"Crisis averted!" Miss Bowler shouted. Her voice drowned out everyone else's. "Carry on!"

There was the usual low mumbling of gossip, but slowly everyone went back to what they'd been doing.

Scarlet and I went into a huddle with Ariadne. "What is it?" Scarlet hissed. "What's really the matter?"

Ariadne gulped. "It's my room assignment," she said.

"Not Violet again?" Scarlet asked. I didn't think that was likely. Violet had left last term. I wasn't sure if she was ever coming back.

"Worse," Ariadne replied. "It's... it's Muriel Witherspoon."

Scarlet and I looked at each other, and then asked in

unison, "*Who?*"

"Muriel Witherspoon," she repeated.

Whoever this person was, Ariadne seemed terrified of her.

"She was the bully from my old school," Ariadne explained. "The really awful one. The one who ran the secret club in the shed that I burned down."

"Oh..." I looked around, remembering the story of Ariadne's past and how she had happened to come to Rookwood. I wondered if this girl was someone I'd already seen. "Are you sure it's the same person? Why would she be here?"

"I heard the name," Ariadne said desperately. "How many Muriel Witherspoons can there be? Oh, this is a disaster!"

"It'll be all right," I said. "We'll protect you. We won't let her pick on you again."

But Ariadne didn't look reassured. She shuffled her feet about on the hall floor. "But we're sharing a room! You won't be there at night. What if she's nasty to me then?"

"I'll give her a good punching the next morning," Scarlet offered.

I shot my twin a look. "No punching, Scarlet. We'll just... we'll tell her not to. We'll tell the teachers.

We'll do *something*."

"I'll go and look for her," my twin said suddenly.

"Scarlet, don't!" Ariadne tried to hold her back, but Scarlet was already striding down the line towards the Ws. Ariadne gave me a panicked look, and then we both set off after her.

Madame Zelda was at that part of the line, checking through the names. Scarlet lurked behind her, obviously hoping to overhear. I noticed that Josephine Wilcox didn't seem to have come back to school – which was probably no surprise, given that Miss Fox had pushed her out of a window last year.

Madame Zelda had just handed a timetable to a fourth year named Harriet Wilson, so this Muriel had to be nearby. When Ariadne froze, I knew she must have seen her. She spun round and looked the other way.

"Which one?" I whispered.

"The one with the felt cap and the blonde curls," she said out of the side of her mouth.

I tried to have a look without being too obvious, but Scarlet was already ruining that because she was standing by the line and clearly staring at everyone. I soon saw who Ariadne was talking about – near to Harriet.

I had to admit that, at first glance, this girl didn't

look like a terrible bully. She didn't have a permanent sneer like Penny's. In fact her eyes were glued to the floor, as though she was trying to make herself as small as possible.

"Muriel... Witherspoon?" Madame Zelda said, the name unfamiliar on her tongue.

The girl nodded. Ariadne squeezed my hand.

"Here you go." Madame Zelda gave her the little sheaf of papers. "Now, you'll be in room fifteen, with Ariadne Flitworth." She moved on to the next girl, revealing Muriel's stunned expression.

I turned back. "She looks almost as shocked as you did," I said. "But she didn't faint."

Ariadne gripped the back of the seat she was leaning on. "She's probably just waiting so she can humiliate me in front of everyone."

I felt a tap on my shoulder – it was Scarlet. "I don't want to worry you..." she said, "but Muriel Witherspoon's coming this way."

I turned round to see where Scarlet was pointing. I thought Ariadne was about to start hyperventilating.

"Oh no," she said quietly. "Oh no, oh no, oh—"

But she didn't get a final *oh* in because Muriel had appeared beside us. She tipped her hat back away from her face and looked down. "Ariadne?"

Ariadne appeared to be trying to sink into the floor, but eventually she looked up. "Hello, Muriel," she said softly.

There was a tense moment, like a little bubble of silence in the middle of the hall chaos, then Muriel spoke again. "It's good to see you." She paused. "Look, I'm really sorry about all that bother at our old school. I hope we can put it behind us. I've turned over a new leaf."

"Oh," Ariadne said, but I could tell by the tone of her voice that she wasn't the slightest bit convinced. "Well. That's good. Very nice."

"I'll see you in our room," Muriel said with a small smile. She nodded at Scarlet and me and then walked away.

"Well, that didn't seem *so* bad," I said.

"So bad?" Ariadne shook her head. "She's just pretending. She has to be. She was so horrible, Ivy! You wouldn't believe it."

Scarlet shrugged. "I know how horrible some people can be – we've met Penny. And Miss Fox. And—"

"All right," Ariadne replied, "I get the idea. But she's as bad as all of them. Worse!"

I wasn't sure I could believe that, especially not since the Muriel I'd seen in front of me had just been so polite. We had to reassure Ariadne somehow, or she was never going to stop worrying about it. "Don't panic," I told her. "Perhaps you just need to give her a chance? She might really have changed."

Ariadne said nothing, just bit her lip and blinked at me.

"And if she hasn't..." Scarlet said, "then she'll be sorry."

"*Scarlet...*" I warned.

"What? I didn't say I'd hit her this time..."

Finally, the time came for Mrs Knight to send us all to our rooms to get unpacked. The first lessons wouldn't be starting until after lunch, according to the timetable.

"All these maps and timetables would certainly have been useful to help me find my way around when I had to pretend to be you," I muttered to Scarlet as we climbed the stairs, lugging all the bags.

"I had mine," Ariadne said. "I think Miss Fox just didn't give them to you."

"Well, at least Mrs Knight is more organised," I said.

"And less murderous," added Scarlet.

Ariadne came to a halt at the top of the stairs, as if her feet had just stopped working. A bunch of other girls pushed round her, with a draught of angry mumbling.

"I don't want to go in there," she said, staring down the hallway.

"It'll be *fine*." Scarlet squeezed her arm. "Just leave the door open. You can come back to our room if she's awful."

"All right," Ariadne sighed. "Thank you."

Scarlet and I trudged down the corridor together and dropped Ariadne's suitcases off at her door.

"Wish me luck," she said, pulling a face.

"Luck," Scarlet said.

Ariadne took a deep breath and went inside.

When we didn't hear any shouting or screaming, we assumed things were all right. I truly hoped for Ariadne's sake that this Muriel girl really had turned over a new leaf.

We headed for room thirteen, and stopped outside the familiar door. In a strange way, it was good to see it again. Scarlet smiled up at her lucky number and then let us in. The room was just as we'd left it: the twin beds, the desk, the wardrobe, the same old threadbare carpet, the same smell of dusty air and freshly washed sheets.

I laid my bag down on my bed. "Do you think Ariadne will really be all right?" I asked, doubt beginning to creep into my mind.

"She'll be fine," Scarlet sighed. "By the end of the week Ariadne and Muriel will probably be having midnight feasts and knitting each other scarves."

I laughed. "I hope so."

Scarlet took out her timetable and squinted at it. "It's not too different from last year, although there are some new lessons on there. Some new teachers too."

"And new pupils," I said, thinking of all the girls I'd seen that I hadn't recognised. And then there was Muriel, and the mysterious Ebony...

"You've got your worried face on," Scarlet said. She had thrown her bag on the floor and was already pulling things out of it.

"It's nothing," I said with a sigh, and then remembered that we'd promised not to keep things from each other any more. "It's... it's just all this. Starting a new term again. I feel a little lost."

My twin stood up. "I was lost once. And you know what happened?"

"What?" I asked, turning to face her.

"You found me," she said with a grin.

And somehow, that was enough to make me feel better.

## Chapter Five

### SCARLET

The first class of the year was art with Miss Pepper. I'd never been very good at the subject – I preferred writing – and I didn't like not being able to do things.

We met Ariadne waiting in the hallway outside the art room, obviously trying to stand as far away from her new roommate as possible.

"Was it all right?" I asked.

Ariadne nodded. "She didn't really say very much

in the room," she whispered. "But I'm sure she's just saving up her meanness."

Muriel was leaning against the wall, her nose in a book. She didn't seem like she was about to start bullying anyone. There were a couple of other girls I didn't recognise as well in amongst the crowd of our class that was forming, two of them huddled together and whispering.

And then there was Ebony McCloud. She swanned down the hallway and suddenly everyone was silent and staring at her. She acted like she didn't even notice, and instead just walked up to the art-room door. She really was fascinating.

Dot Campbell leant forward and said, "Um, Miss said we weren't allowed in until..."

But Ebony just completely ignored her and went straight into the room.

"Well then," I shrugged. If she was going in, I was going in. And it didn't take long for everyone else to follow me.

Noisily, everyone found a seat, Muriel going right to the back as we made our way to the front. The desks were bigger and messier in art and there was no seating plan. At that moment, the bell rang, and not long after that, Miss Pepper walked in.

She pushed her red glasses down her nose and stared around at us. "I thought I'd told you not to come in before the bell, girls?"

Everyone looked at the new girl, but no one said a word. Ebony just smiled.

Miss Pepper didn't seem to know what to do. "Right then," she said. "Onwards and upwards. Art to be made. Still life!" She pulled a cloth off her desk, revealing a bowl of fruit of all shapes and sizes.

Anna Santos raised her hand. "Can we eat the fruit, Miss?"

Miss Pepper stared at her. "Where would be the art in that exactly, Miss Santos?"

Anna just blinked. She had always been a few bananas short of a fruit bowl.

"Moving swiftly on," the art teacher continued, "let's start by looking at the light and shade..."

By the end of the lesson, I had drawn something that at least vaguely resembled a bunch of fruit. I peered over at Ivy's – it was slightly better than mine, but she was left-handed and had smudged some of her pencil as she'd leant over the page. She made a face at it.

"Leave them on my desk, please, artists," Miss Pepper said.

One by one, we all left our masterpieces for her to mark. But when Ebony went up, Miss Pepper stopped bustling around and peered down at Ebony's sheet of paper through her glasses. "You, girl," she called out after her. "What's your name?"

Ebony stopped and turned back slowly. "Ebony McCloud," she answered.

Miss Pepper reached down, picked up the drawing and stared at it. "What is the meaning of this?" she asked. There was an undercurrent of something in her voice that might have been anger, or perhaps it was fear.

Ebony just stared at her. "I drew what I wanted," she said. "Isn't that okay?" And then she sat down.

I waited, holding my breath. If she had said that when Miss Fox was around, she'd have been in for a caning. Thankfully, Miss Pepper was a lot less violent, but she still didn't usually take any nonsense from her students.

*Any moment now*, I thought, *she's going to launch into her speech about how you have to follow the rules of art before you can break the rules.*

But something unexpected happened. Miss Pepper just stood there silently for a moment and then said, "Right. Well, that's enough for today, ladies. You need to head to the hall now to pick your sports." She put

Ebony's drawing back on the pile and blinked at it. "Right," she repeated. And then she left the room. The bell hadn't even rung yet.

I looked around at the class, but everyone was just sitting there. I had to see what was going on. So I got out of my seat and went over to look at Ebony's drawing.

In amongst the many drawings of the colourful bowl of fruit, there was a picture that stood out. It was black and white, and it was of a castle. There was a silhouette of a lady standing in the window, and bats flying from the tower. The lady was weeping white tears, her hair streaming out behind her. She was staring at a row of fresh graves, marked with crosses in the dirt. It was beautiful in a strange and dark way.

I picked it up and waved it at the new girl in disbelief. "I can't believe you drew this instead of the fruit!" A murmur started up around the class as everyone stood up to leave, all of them casting nervous glances at Ebony as they went.

She just smiled at me. "Why? Don't you like it?" she asked.

"It's very... artistic," Ariadne piped up.

Ivy was blinking at it, as if she were wondering whether it would transform into a fruit bowl before her eyes.

I didn't know what to say. I settled for, "You're a strange one, aren't you?"

It wasn't meant to be an insult, and Ebony didn't seem to take it that way. In fact quite the opposite. "Why, thank you," she said as she stood up. She flashed me a brilliant white smile, swung her black satchel over her shoulder and walked out like she was floating on air.

"There's something about that girl," Ivy said, once her eyes had followed Ebony out of the room. "I can't quite put my finger on it, but there's definitely something."

My mind was elsewhere. "Why did Miss Pepper act like that?" I said out loud. "Why did she just let it go? How come the new girl doesn't get a lecture? I painted a tree the wrong colour once and she said I was 'insulting Turner's legacy'!"

"It was most peculiar," Ariadne replied. "She—" Ariadne paused mid-sentence as Muriel came to stand right next to her.

"What do you do for games, Ariadne?" Muriel asked, as if they were the best of chums.

Ariadne gaped for a moment. "Um," she said, "I quite like chess."

Muriel brushed her blonde hair back from her face.

"I meant... what sport do you like?"

"Hockey," Ariadne said, when she'd recovered enough from the fact that her former bully was trying to make small talk.

"Oh, right," said Muriel. "That sounds good. See you at the next lesson, then." She smiled shyly and headed out of the art room.

Ariadne still looked horrified. I went over and shook her shoulder gently. "Come on," I said. "We'd better get going."

"Is she going to pick hockey too?" Ariadne wailed.

Ivy looked up at me. "Would that be so terrible?"

"I manage to score enough bruises on my own without her getting involved," our friend replied sadly. "She'll probably knock me into the goal on purpose. Or try to hit my legs out from under me. Or shoot the ball into my face. Or..."

"She won't," I said. "I told you that I'll see to her if she does anything like that to you."

Ariadne's head sank on to the desk, her hair narrowly missing a pot of paint. "Perhaps I should just take up swimming instead."

I think the same thoughts ran through all of our heads. *Miss Bowler. The freezing-cold swimming pool. The lake from the school trip, where Ariadne had felt something grabbing her leg...*

"Perhaps not," we all said in unison.

We made our way to the hall, where the sign-up sheets for the different sports were pinned on the boards. Of course, there was no question of what Ivy and I were going to pick. We'd loved ballet for years, even if it had got us into trouble in the past. Although that was usually more my fault than the ballet's.

Ariadne had gone from hating hockey to enjoying it. I saw her face fall as she watched Muriel sign her name on the sheet. Still, she went over and added her name below it. I gave her a reassuring pat on the back as I walked past.

"It'll be fine," I said.

"Fine for you, maybe," Ariadne grumbled.

Miss Bowler was marching around like an army sergeant, as usual. She seemed to be relishing the extra power she'd been given now that Mrs Knight was headmistress. "Girls!" she barked periodically. "Sign up and get in your groups!"

We were amongst the usual ballet crowd, minus the girls who had left the school. Madame Zelda was standing beside us, waving an incense stick (which was something she liked to do for no apparent reason).

After a lot of hustle and bustle, everyone was finally in their groups.

Everyone except Ebony.

She was standing in the middle of the hall, her boots firmly planted, her arms folded, her black hair tumbling over her sleeves.

Miss Bowler strode over to her. "What exactly do you think you're doing, Miss McCloud?"

"I won't be picking a sport," said Ebony matter-of-factly.

Miss Bowler looked flabbergasted. "Excuse me? And why ever not, missy?"

Ebony's lip curled with the ghost of a satisfied smile. "Because I don't want to."

Everyone gasped. I couldn't help but feel a little impressed. This girl had some nerve. You didn't speak to a teacher like that – and certainly not the strict games teacher – unless you wanted to receive a deafening lecture and then be forced to clean all the green gunk out of the swimming pool.

But as we all braced ourselves for the impact... nothing happened. Miss Bowler just blinked at her and then said, "Fine. But you'll be writing essays this hour every week. Understand?" Then she stormed away, muttering under her breath.

Ebony nodded, turned on her heel and left the hall. She was still smiling.

"What exactly just happened back there?" Nadia asked.

"I wouldn't get away with that," Penny grumbled.

Ivy looked at me. "You have to admit, that was strange," she said. "That's the second time today that she's just been let off the hook."

"I know." I shuffled my feet on the floor. I was itching to get back into my ballet shoes. "It's like…"

"Like she's got the teachers under *a spell*," said Nadia from behind us, her eyes wide.

## Chapter Six

## IVY

It was wonderful to be back in the ballet studio again. Madame Zelda had taken us down to where Miss Finch was waiting.

"You're older now, girls," Miss Finch said. "Things are going to get harder. We'll need you all to be on your best behaviour."

Madame Zelda nodded, tapping her long fingernails on her arm. "Discipline, discipline, discipline," she said in her unusual accent. "Work hard, and you will reap the rewards."

It *was* harder. The two teachers pushed us to do moves that were more difficult than we'd ever done before. I could feel my muscles stretching to their limits, my joints clicking as I pulled them into unfamiliar positions.

By the end of it, when we went into *reverence* and bowed and curtseyed to the teachers, I was exhausted. Scarlet and I sat down to unlace our shoes, breathless.

I stared at my face in the mirror, my hair already falling out of my tight bun. Madame Zelda walked past. "Well done, Ivy," she said, "and Scarlet. Both of you did your best today."

I smiled, but something about the sight of Madame Zelda made my thoughts return to Ebony and what Nadia had said. She did seem to have some sort of power over the teachers. But what that could be, I had no idea.

Feeling drained after the long day, we made our way to Rookwood's dining hall for supper. I hated to say it, but I was actually looking forward to the food. The air was filled with chatter, as always.

We met Ariadne in the queue. Thankfully, she didn't look any more bruised than usual so Muriel couldn't have hurt her.

"Nothing happened," she said with a shrug. "Muriel just played hockey. I couldn't believe it!"

"I told you so," Scarlet said. "I think she must have really changed. Nothing to worry about."

"Until she murders me in my sleep," said Ariadne with a theatrical shudder. But I was pretty certain she was joking.

I looked around at the rows of long tables. Both Muriel and Ebony appeared to have been placed in Mayhew House, judging by where they were sitting, and other new students were scattered about all over the place. At one end of all the tables, first years were gathering, trying their first-ever helpings of Rookwood's mystery stew, their uniforms perfect and shiny and straight.

We got our bowls and carried them on trays over to our table, where Madame Zelda was now sitting as the new head of Richmond House. I wasn't surprised to see that she appeared to have brought her own food. Whatever she was eating certainly seemed to involve far more fresh vegetables than we were ever given.

As we passed where the girls from Mayhew were sitting, I saw Ebony daintily scooping the stew with her spoon. She even managed to make eating look glamorous and faintly mysterious. I noticed that the first and second years were all staring at her, wide-eyed and whispering.

Muriel, on the other hand, was drawing no attention at all. She was sitting alone, not talking to anyone. She waved at Ariadne as we walked by, and then went back to her dinner.

"It seems so strange to think that she bullied you. What did she actually do?" Scarlet asked as we got to our table.

"Scarlet!" I said. "Ariadne probably doesn't want to talk about that."

Ariadne sighed. "No, it's all right. I haven't explained much about it, really."

Scarlet waved a fork at her. "Go on," she said. We were sitting far enough away from any of the teachers, so we could speak freely.

"She was truly horrible," Ariadne began. "Everyone at Hightower was afraid of her. Except for her gang, of course."

"Hightower?" I asked, in between mouthfuls.

"Hightower School for Girls. Where I was before." Her eyes glazed over with thoughts of the past. "I loved it there, at first. Before I met Muriel Witherspoon." She took a deep breath. "It only took her a day to give me a whole list of nasty nicknames. And then she just wouldn't stop picking on me. She would take my things and try to hurt me any time she got a chance."

"Sounds like a few people I know," Scarlet said through a mouthful of stew.

"Oh yes," said Ariadne, "but that was just the start of it. She formed this secret club called the Crow Club that met in this shed out by the playing fields. It was a bit like the Whispers, except it only existed so she could be horrible to people." The Whispers was the secret society of past pupils that our mother had belonged to. It had been quite the opposite of this Crow Club, though – they had actually tried to expose the corruption in the school and protect the other students.

Ariadne frowned at the table as she continued explaining. "They spread rumours all the time. They wouldn't let me into the club because they said I was a 'goody two-shoes'. And then they told everyone... well, I don't want to say because it was just too horrible."

"And that's when you burned down the shed?" I asked, remembering how Ariadne had been expelled.

She nodded slowly. "I was just so sick of it. They were making my life a misery!"

"You don't have to explain yourself to me," said Scarlet. "I'm not exactly the queen of self-restraint when it comes to bullies, am I?" She grinned, and we grinned back at her.

"Freaks!" I heard a quiet voice say by my ear. But... it sounded friendly. And familiar.

I turned to see Rose standing beside me, with her empty tray.

"Oh yes!" Scarlet said with a grin. "Freaks together! That's us, isn't it?"

Rose grinned. When we'd had quite the adventure in the summer, we'd reassured Rose that she wasn't alone in being an outsider. She may have been locked in an asylum and plagued by nasty relatives, but we knew all about that too.

"Nice to see you again, Rose," I said.

She nodded. She didn't talk a lot and she chose her words carefully.

"Everything all right?" Scarlet asked. "No more rogue relatives bothering you?" I shuddered. Rose's cousin had nearly got us killed in the process of trying to steal her inheritance.

Rose nodded again. "I got a lawyer," she said in her voice that was barely above a whisper. There was a mischievous sparkle in her eyes.

At that point, Mrs Knight appeared and began hovering around our table. "Good evening, girls," she said. "Is all well over here in Richmond?"

"Wonderful, thank you," said Madame Zelda, twirling a lettuce leaf with her fork. And it *was* true – everyone did seem to be behaving so far, which was quite unusual for our table. Madame Zelda was certainly a bit more intimidating than Mrs Knight, which helped. I got the impression she wanted the headmistress to go away.

"Oh good, good," Mrs Knight said. She walked over to where we were sitting. "Staying out of trouble, girls?"

"Of course," said Scarlet, batting her eyelashes comically. I nearly snorted my drink out of my nose. Rose laughed and walked away to join the back of the dinner queue.

"Ah," said the headmistress. "I hope you will continue to keep an eye on Rose."

"Is she allowed to stay now, Miss?" Ariadne asked. After all, Rose hadn't always been a pupil at Rookwood.

Mrs Knight smiled and rubbed her sleeves. "Oh yes. We were able to secure some of Rose's inheritance to pay for her to be here full time. She'll be joining some lessons as well. Not all of them straight away, mind. That might be too much. She's had a tough time."

"That's so kind of you, Miss," I said, and I meant it. I couldn't imagine our former headteachers showing any sort of compassion for a student.

Mrs Knight blushed. "Oh, it's nothing. Right, girls, I mean it – you'll stay out of trouble this term, won't you?"

"Yes, Miss," we chorused. I *hoped* we meant that.

When we'd finished (and Ariadne had gone back for a second helping of tinned peaches in custard, which was admittedly unusually nice for Rookwood), we picked up our trays to take them away.

We passed Ariadne's former roommates, who were from the year below us, and were all sitting together.

They all waved. "Hello, Ariadne!" they called out in unison.

I recognised the girl who had become the unofficial leader of the group; she was Agatha, who had a bird's nest of frizzy brown hair and loved to be in charge. "Psst," she hissed, leaning forward. "Have you seen that new girl, Ebony McCloud?"

"Oh yes," Scarlet replied.

"She's certainly... interesting," Ariadne said politely.

Agatha's eyes slid across the room, as if she were checking for spies. Then she leant across the table again. "We heard she's a *witch*!"

The other girls all nodded, wide-eyed and serious.

Ariadne paused. "Really?"

Scarlet looked at them incredulously. "A witch? As in... pointy hats and broomsticks and cauldrons?"

"Oh yes," said Evelyn, the red-haired one. "All of that. And she can do *spells*."

"Isn't it *exciting*?" said another of them, Bonnie, her bright eyes sparkling. "Do you think she'll teach us?"

"She can probably teach you how to be even more weird than you lot already are," Scarlet said, but they didn't seem to notice. The rumour mill was in full flow.

"Do you think she can make potions? Maybe she'd make a love potion for me..."

"I bet she can see the future!"

"If we look in her window at night we can see if she transforms into a bat!"

Wordlessly, we backed away. Ariadne's old roommates were a little intense once they got an idea in their heads.

"Ebony's certainly strange," I said, as I scraped my bowl clean. "But where can they have got this idea from?"

Ariadne wrinkled her nose, though whether it was at the food slops or at her friends' gossip I wasn't sure. "Who knows?" she said.

Scarlet frowned. "I think they believe anything

anyone tells them. I think she's just eccentric, that's all."

I nodded in agreement. It wasn't surprising that Ebony was a little strange — who wasn't, at Rookwood?

But as I walked past her, with her hair the colour of the night sky and her eyes grey as storm clouds, I began to wonder if perhaps there was more to her than met the eye.

## Chapter Seven

## SCARLET

It was our first night back at Rookwood, and it didn't take long for trouble to find us.

We'd unpacked and were heading to the bathrooms to get ready for bed. An hour or so earlier, Ariadne had sloped off to her dorm with Muriel.

The lavatories were packed, filled with girls jostling to get to the mirrors and brush their teeth. As we waited at the back, Matron came in and whistled. "One at a time, you lot! The sinks aren't going anywhere!"

She left again, but the chaos didn't improve by much. Some sort of queue began to form behind each sink, but it was messy.

We waved to Ariadne, who was on the other side of the crush. Muriel was there too, her beanpole legs making her stand head and shoulders above most of the other girls. She was staring at her Rookwood regulation toothbrush, looking unimpressed.

But everything changed when Ebony walked in.

The crowds parted like she was Moses. She had that enigmatic smile on her face as she glided along. She walked straight up to where Muriel was standing and said, "I'm going to use this mirror."

Muriel stopped, the toothbrush still in her mouth, and turned to look down at Ebony. Despite being smaller than Muriel, Ebony gave the impression she was eight feet tall.

"Mmscuse me?" Muriel said around the toothbrush.

"I said I'm going to use this one." Ebony didn't raise her voice. She didn't need to. Everyone had gone silent and was staring at her. "Or..."

Muriel spat a foamy mouthful into the sink. "Or what?"

"Or you'll regret getting in my way," said Ebony. She tipped her head on one side. That smile wasn't going anywhere. "The world has a way of punishing people who don't do what I want."

Now, having heard about the fearsome Muriel from Ariadne, I assumed we were about to witness something dramatic. So of course I stood on tiptoe to get a better look.

But to my surprise, Muriel just looked *hurt*. "Why?" she said. "I waited my turn. I'll be done in a moment."

And then, as I watched, she turned, slipped on something and fell backwards into a heap on the floor. There were gasps. But no one moved.

Ebony looked down at her. "I told you so," she said. She stepped over Muriel and began brushing her silky hair in the mirror and humming something. It was a tune I didn't recognise. It sounded almost like a nursery rhyme.

I didn't like what I had seen one bit.

*How did that happen?* I wondered. There was a moment when there was no sound in the bathroom but the strange humming. And then a second later, Muriel sat up and choked back a sob. It was as if there had been a spell that had just been broken, and everyone started talking again.

I frowned and began shoving my way over to the sinks. "Come on," I said "Are none of you going to help her up?" I reached down. Muriel reluctantly took my hand and climbed up unsteadily. She rubbed her bruised legs and glared at Ebony. And without a word, she ran into the corridor.

I didn't know what Ebony was playing at, but she was reminding me uncomfortably of our old enemy Violet – or at least, how vile Violet had been in our first year. The sort of person who thought they were better than everyone else and ordered them around. And people were just letting her get away with it!

I stood beside her, hands on my hips, while she preened. "What did you do that for, Ebony?" I asked.

She just blinked at me, and then she leant forward and whispered one word: "Power."

"What?" I looked around at the other girls to see if they were listening, but everyone had moved on to something else. It was as though the events of the past few minutes had evaporated from their minds.

"Power," she repeated. "Some of us have it..." She looked towards the door. "Some of us don't." And then she turned back to the mirror and carried on humming that same song.

"Right, well," I muttered. "Perhaps you could use some of that power to stop being a nasty piece of work."

She ignored me.

Ariadne pushed through and stood next to me. "I should... I should go and see if Muriel's all right," she said.

I was a little surprised, but not completely. No matter what Muriel had done to Ariadne in the past, they'd been getting on better and Ariadne was very forgiving – a good person at heart.

I didn't think I'd be able to say the same about Ebony.

Ivy and I eventually managed to reach the sinks and get ourselves ready for bed, and then we headed back to room thirteen. I had to admit I was a little relieved not to run into Ebony again. Something about her just wasn't quite right.

Getting under the sheets was the strangest feeling after being away from Rookwood for so long. Our beds had been made with hospital corners as usual, meaning I had to untuck the whole thing before I could actually climb into it. But once I was lying down, I had to admit... it almost felt like home. More than anywhere else did, anyway.

I thought briefly about hiding my new diary in the mattress, but that wouldn't be much of a hiding place, since everyone knew about it now. *Do I need to hide it?* I thought. I didn't have so many secrets these days.

But then I thought of what had just happened in the lavatories. I was no longer faced with Miss Fox or Violet, and Penny seemed to have mellowed a little, but then there were people like Ebony.

I decided to put the diary inside my pillow, just for now. I'd have to find a better place, though, or it could get tossed into the laundry.

Ivy yawned in the bed across the room. "Back at Rookwood," she sighed.

"Everything's different, but..." I took a deep breath. "There's more of the same. Bullies and secrets and—"

"Stew," Ivy finished for me. "Lots and lots of stew."

We smiled at each other in the darkness.

"Night, Scarlet," she said.

"Night, Ivy."

It was chilly and the sheets were a little scratchy against my skin. But only a few moments passed before I slipped into a deep and dreamless sleep.

I woke to a loud clanging, and almost panicked before I realised it was Rookwood's regular morning bell.

I sat up, stretched and looked around to find Ivy already sitting at the desk, brushing her hair with our mother's brush.

"How are you awake already?" I asked.

She shrugged happily. "I slept well."

"Me too," I said. I unfolded myself from the covers and got up. A glance out of our window with its threadbare curtains revealed a bright day outside. The leaves were rustling in the trees, waving gently like green fingers.

"I wonder how Ariadne got on," Ivy said. "With her first night sharing with Muriel, I mean."

Once we were dressed and ready, we went to investigate. We knocked on their door and Ariadne's mousy face peered out. "Morning," she whispered, slipping into the corridor.

"So... did you survive?" Ivy asked, even though it was plainly obvious that she had.

Ariadne's brow wrinkled. "Nothing happened. She seemed upset after that incident with Ebony, and I asked if she was all right. That cheered her up a little. Then she just said she was going to read a book and didn't speak another word."

"See?" I poked her gently. "I told you it would be fine."

"Scarlet, stop poking people," Ivy said.

I poked her in the arm, just to prove a point.

Ariadne still didn't look very reassured. I noticed

there were bags under her eyes, and her hair was a bit of a tangle. "So you didn't sleep as well as we did?"

She shuffled her feet. "Well, I know it's silly, but I couldn't relax knowing *she* was in the room. It was like... being *haunted* or something. I can't forget what she was like before."

As if on cue, the door opened and Muriel appeared. We all looked up – and Ariadne went a bit white. But she didn't seem to have heard what we'd been saying. She just smiled at us. "Morning," she said. "What do they do for breakfast around here?"

"Porridge," I said.

"Oh." She didn't seem too disappointed. For someone who had apparently been the worst bully since Penny, she appeared to be quite cheerful. "Well, see you down there." She strode away towards the stairs.

We both looked at Ariadne without saying anything. I raised my eyebrows, as if to say: *A bully? Really?*

"I'm serious!" she squeaked. "She *was* awful!"

"It's all right," said Ivy. "We believe you. It's just that... she seems different now."

I nodded in agreement. "I think it's Ebony we need to worry about."

In the dining hall, the familiar thick smell of porridge greeted us, but I could see something was different straight away.

Ebony had gained a following.

It was only a small one, but it was still a following. She was up at the serving hatch and there was a little group of girls trailing her like kittens round their mother.

As we got closer, I realised that the group mostly consisted of Ariadne's old roommates, as well as some of the other younger girls.

"What's that about?" I hissed, gesturing over to them as we joined the back of the queue.

Ariadne's eyes were wide. "I think she has a fan club."

We watched as two of the girls fought over who was going to carry Ebony's tray for her, which was eventually solved by Ebony handing one of them her mug of tea. They went over to one of the tables and all gathered round her. She was talking. I had no idea what she was saying, since it just faded into all the surrounding noise, but they were all leaning in and hanging on her every word. She waved a hand at one point and all their eyes followed it, as if she were drawing something in the air.

"Now that's just odd," I said. "She can't be *that* interesting, surely?"

One of the new teachers went over – by the looks of it, she was telling some of them off for not sitting at their house table. But they didn't pay her any attention, and she walked off looking red-faced and flustered.

When we'd picked up our helpings of porridge, we headed for our table. I couldn't help taking a sneaky detour past where they were sitting. Pieces of their conversation floated to my ears.

"Is it true?" I heard one of the younger girls say.

"Teach me, Ebony, please!"

"Show us what you can do!"

I rolled my eyes. They were so unbelievably desperate for her attention.

But the last exchange I caught as I walked past them was more interesting.

"Can you *really* do magic?" I heard Agatha say, her voice glittering with awe.

For a moment, Ebony said nothing. I stopped in my tracks. She was looking straight at me, and her stormy eyes seemed to crackle with lightning.

"Yes," said Ebony. "Yes, I can."

## Chapter Eight

### IVY

We managed to finish breakfast without incident, but the first lesson of the day was to be a different matter altogether.

I'd studied the new timetable carefully. It was a relief to actually have been given one, and not just to have to trail after Ariadne like I'd done when I'd started at Rookwood, pretending that I knew what was happening. The first lesson was history, with Madame Lovelace – a teacher so old that she appeared to have acquired cobwebs.

"Anywhere you like, girls," she was saying in her creaky voice as we filed into the room. "It's a new year, after all."

Scarlet and I darted to get desks side by side. I only realised once I'd got there that it meant Ariadne would have to go behind us. "Sorry," I whispered.

"It's all right," she said, finding a desk a few rows back.

Madame Lovelace sat down at her desk. "Right then, everyone," she said. "Open your books at page one hundred and fifty-three. And make sure you memorise those dates." She waggled her finger at us all.

And while we were pulling out the books and finding the pages, she bowed her head and began to snore.

"Did she just fall asleep?" I heard Muriel say.

"That's normal," Scarlet remarked. We didn't even need to whisper. Madame Lovelace was rather deaf at the best of times. I didn't think even a speeding train could wake her up once she'd nodded off.

"So what do we do now, then?" another new girl asked.

"*I* have an idea." A voice came from behind me.

I gulped. That Scottish accent was becoming familiar to me now. The way Ebony spoke... it was like she was inviting you into a dream.

Or a nightmare.

"Why don't I demonstrate something for you?" she said. Before anyone could say a word, she was striding to the front of the class. She turned to face us. There was a strange, far-off look in her stormy eyes.

"Just ignore her," Scarlet muttered, looking for the page in her textbook. "Then maybe she'll go away."

"I'll need a volunteer," said Ebony, raising her voice. Madame Lovelace continued to snore in the chair.

Ebony looked around the room slowly, her eyes falling on each of us in turn, holding our gaze for just a little too long.

"You!" she said suddenly, pointing a long, white finger at Muriel Witherspoon.

Muriel pointed at herself. "Me? What do you want with me?"

"I want you to come up to the front," said Ebony in a singsong voice.

Muriel sat back and folded her arms. "Why should I get involved with this, exactly?"

There was a hush, broken only by Madame Lovelace, who occasionally snorted in her sleep.

Ebony was staring at Muriel, giving nothing away. "We wouldn't want you to have another accident, now, would we?"

Muriel's face paled. She seemed to be trying to hide the fact that Ebony scared her, but she was no longer doing a very good job of it. She stood up slowly and then rolled her eyes, bringing down the curtain of false bravado again. "*Right*," she said. "If you insist."

She approached the desk and Ebony waved her hands over it. And then suddenly, as if from nowhere, a deck of cards appeared in her palm.

Muriel blinked down at it. "I... what?"

Ebony held up the deck in her long, thin fingers and displayed it to all of us. The back of each card was black, with an intricate pattern etched into it. Then she flipped it to show us the front, and I saw that each suit was decorated with skulls, and the Kings and Queens and Jacks were all skeletons. How cheerful.

"Pick a card," Ebony ordered.

Muriel reached down gingerly, as if she thought the cards might singe her fingers. The look on Ebony's face was expectant, almost hungry.

Muriel's hand came to rest on one of the cards. She didn't meet Ebony's eye.

"Show the class," said Ebony, with a flicker of her eyelashes.

Muriel slipped the card from the pack and then held it out to all of us, so that only we could see. The three of Hearts. I shared a look with Scarlet. What was this about?

"Now, return the card." Ebony watched as Muriel turned the card face down and put it back.

In the corner, Madame Lovelace snorted in her sleep and a cloud of chalk dust floated up from her dress.

A slow smile crept across Ebony's face. She shuffled the cards, her hands moving in a blur. "Open your palms," she instructed.

"I really don't see why—" Muriel started, but faltered under Ebony's gaze. She sighed and did as she was told.

The entire class seemed to be holding their breath. Everyone had leant forward in their seats. I expected Scarlet to tell them to sit down and shut up, but even she appeared to be fascinated.

With a strange grace, Ebony started moving her hands over the deck of cards, her fingers curling. She kept doing it, over and over, in a circular motion.

"*Nothing's happening*," someone whispered, but everyone shushed her. Because just then, the cards began to move – at a snail's pace, but moving nonetheless. The deck began to slice in two, the two halves shifting apart, leaving a card in the middle.

And then... the card shot out of the deck.

Everyone gasped. I blinked. Had that really just happened?

Muriel was clutching her arm. "Ow!" she said. "You cut me!" She pulled her hand away and there was indeed a small flash of blood on her skin – a paper cut.

Ebony just laughed, and her laugh was like a misty mountain stream. "Never mind that," she said. "Pick up the card. Show them."

Scowling, Muriel bent down and picked up the card from the floor. I watched as she cautiously turned it over and then picked it up. She held it out to the class.

The three of Hearts.

There was a hush, followed by a ripple of hesitant applause. But Madame Lovelace chose that moment to wake up, and the spell was broken.

"Hmm?" she said loudly, one rheumy eye shooting open before the other. She looked around and wrenched herself up straight. "You two! What are you up to? Back to your seats, this instant!" She picked a ruler up off her desk and waved it at them threateningly.

Muriel dashed back to her seat, still frowning and clutching her arm. Ebony just swept up her cards and sauntered back, as if she didn't have a care in the world.

Madame Lovelace coughed and then fixed us with a steely gaze. "Have you even got your books out? Anyone would think you didn't have a teacher! Get on with it!"

It was lunchtime before we finally got a chance to talk about what had happened. I knew, as soon as I stepped into the dining hall, that everyone was talking about it. *The new girl did magic in class. She made cards move all by themselves. How did she do it?*

The whispers rushed past us like the wind. And the moment Ebony entered the hall, all eyes were on her. She smiled. I knew then that it was exactly what she'd wanted. She was relishing the attention.

"That was quite a trick," said Ariadne as we sat at the table.

"You think it was a trick?" Scarlet asked. She hadn't even bothered to touch her food. This was too exciting.

"As opposed to what?" I turned to my twin.

"Real magic," Scarlet said. "I mean, did you see her

touch those cards? I didn't."

Ariadne put her thinking face on, the one where you could almost see the cogs turning. "She probably had the cards up her sleeve to start with," she said.

"But after that?" Scarlet shook her head. I had to admit, I hadn't seen her touch the cards either, and I'd been concentrating hard. "It was too weird. And did you see the way everyone just stared?"

"It was creepy," I admitted. It wasn't the Rookwood I knew, where show-offs were usually quickly dispatched by bullies. People had just sat and watched. Ebony was like a ticking time bomb, it seemed, and you felt like you had to keep an eye on her in case she went off.

And why had she involved Muriel in her prank? She seemed determined to single her out. "Where's Muriel?" I wondered aloud.

"She ran off." Someone from further down the table spoke. I looked up to see Penny, who looked distinctly fed up. She was poking her sandwiches – Mrs Knight had altered the menu somewhat, and we had cheese and ham sandwiches instead of the usual stew. "I saw her," she said in a flat tone. "She got her food, took one look at Miss Mystic over there and headed outside."

"Is something wrong, Penny?" Scarlet asked,

although there was no real concern in her voice. Penny had always been the school's worst bully. "Are you not getting all the attention for once?"

"Ha!" Penny laughed drily. "That's rich coming from you." I could tell her heart wasn't in the insult, though. "I'm just... tired, that's all." She smiled a weak smile. "Tired of all this."

Although talking to Penny was usually the last thing I wanted to do, I felt a little intrigued – she wasn't being actively horrible. "What do you mean?" I asked.

Penny hesitated for a moment, as if she wasn't sure whether to set the words free. She ran a hand through her copper hair and sighed. "Violet's gone. Josie's gone. I don't think Nadia likes me. And my parents, well..."

"I'm sorry," I said. And I meant it. It must be tough for her, not having her friends around.

Penny just shrugged.

But Scarlet wasn't going to be as soft on her. "Thinking of giving up the bullying business, then?" she asked.

I expected Penny to get angry at that, but there was no explosion – just a quiet resignation. "Maybe I just can't count on things being the same any more," she said as she picked up her sandwich and began to chew thoughtfully.

I hated to admit it, but I thought I knew how she felt. I turned to my twin. "Things are certainly changing around here," I said.

"But we'll always have each other." She grinned.

Ariadne was silent for a moment, her cogs still spinning. Then she stood up. "I... I'm going to see if Muriel is all right," she said, "...again." She took her plate and wandered off outside.

I watched her go. "Do you think Ariadne's starting to forgive Muriel?"

"It's Rookwood School," said Scarlet. "Anything could happen."

## Chapter Nine

## SCARLET

The rumours about Ebony were flying around the school faster than I could follow them. I heard someone swearing that they'd seen a black cat coming out of her dorm room, followed by someone else insisting they'd seen her *turn into* a black cat.

It was ridiculous. Her magic had been convincing, and maybe, *maybe* I'd been fooled for a little while. But the more I thought about it, the less I believed it. She was an ordinary girl. She just had to be.

Whether or not she was up to no good, though... that was another matter.

That afternoon we had English with Miss Charlett. It was the first lesson that Rose joined us for. She smiled as she found a desk close to Ivy, Ariadne and me. *It must be exciting for her*, I thought. I didn't know how much she'd learnt before she was locked away by her family, but I did know that she loved to read. Especially books that featured ponies.

I didn't know how Ariadne had got on with talking to Muriel, but I did notice that Muriel was sitting very close to her, and that Ariadne didn't look quite as terrified about it as she had before. Maybe, just maybe, they were becoming friends.

As the bell rang for the start of class, Miss Charlett rapped on her desk to get us to keep quiet. "Right!" she called out. "This term, we'll be reading one of my favourites – Shakespeare's *Macbeth*."

There were a few groans. One of them might have been mine.

"Oh, none of that," she said. "I think you'll find this play is full of excitement." Miss Charlett seemed even more excited by reading than Ariadne and Rose put together. "It has murder, betrayal and..." She waved the playbook with a little flourish. "...of course, *witches*."

That got the class's attention. You could almost see the ears pricking up.

"You should all have a book on your desk. We're going to read Act One, Scene One, together. But first, we're going to need three witches."

A hush descended. Nobody raised their hand. But Miss Charlett looked around and said, "Ah, how about you, Miss McCloud?"

Ebony stood up with a smirk that implied it was exactly what she'd intended. *Of course* she should play the first witch.

Well, I was fed up with her being so smug. I put my hand up. "I'll be the second witch, Miss," I said.

Miss Charlett nodded. "Come up, then. Now, just one more..." She looked around at the class. "How about you, Miss Fitzwarren?"

For a moment, Rose didn't react. I didn't think she was used to hearing her name. But then she looked up and her face had gone white.

"Um, Miss," I whispered as I got to the front of the class. "I don't think Rose is a fan of talking in front of people."

"Oh, right." Miss Charlett turned.

"We should have another new pupil, shouldn't we?" Ebony suggested. She looked a little devious.

Miss Charlett nodded at the suggestion. "Let's have another new pupil for the third witch, then. What's your name?" She pointed at Muriel.

"Muriel Witherspoon," said Muriel. She stood up reluctantly and came to the front to stand beside us.

Our English teacher handed us all a playbook. She sat on her desk and grinned as she began reading. "*Macbeth, Act One, Scene One. A desert place. Thunder and lightning. Enter three witches.*"

Ebony's expression turned dark and twisted, her voice high-pitched and threatening. "When shall we three meet again? In thunder, lightning, or in rain?"

I glanced down at my page and tried to put on my best crackly crone voice. "When the hurlyburly's done, when the battle's lost and won."

Muriel didn't say anything for a moment, until Ebony elbowed her sharply in the ribs. A glare fell over her features. "That will be ere the set of sun," she read.

"Where the place?" Ebony turned her head between us both.

"Upon the heath," I replied.

"There to meet with Macbeth," Muriel said, not looking happy about it.

Ebony took hold of her skirt and swished it sideways, as if it were a vast black cloak. "I come, graymalkin!"

"Paddock calls," I said, half wondering if I was supposed to be looking for a horse.

"Anon!" read Muriel.

Now we all chanted together, *"Fair is foul, and foul is fair: hover through the fog and filthy air."*

Miss Charlett clapped enthusiastically and the rest of the class soon followed suit.

I blushed a bit. I had to admit, Ebony was the most witchy of all of us. She not only looked the part, but she sounded it too. She read those lines as if it was the sort of thing she went about saying all the time. Muriel, however, was tall and blonde and just sounded uncomfortable. And as for me, well... I should probably just stick to ballet.

"Well done, girls," Miss Charlett called. "Head back to your seats now, please. We're going to be taking a look at the beginning of the play and thinking about how this scene... sets the scene, as it were."

As we wandered back to our seats, I saw Rose give me a relieved smile. Muriel, on the other hand, was glaring daggers at Ebony.

"Let's get started, then," the English teacher said. She rubbed her hands together with glee. *"Something wicked this way comes..."*

At half past three the bell rang, signalling that our first full day of lessons was over. Nobody seemed more relieved by this than Muriel. She practically ran back to her room, leaving Ariadne shuffling along beside us.

"I feel sorry for her," Ariadne said. Then she stopped suddenly in the middle of the corridor. "Oh gosh, I can't believe I just said that. Me! Sorry for *her*!"

"She doesn't seem to be getting on very well, does she?" Ivy said, taking Ariadne's hand and pulling her along with us.

"And Ebony's got it in for her already. Not a good start." I hated bullies.

Ivy's expression fell into a frown. "We should do something," she said. "Otherwise Ebony's going to turn into the new Penny, and one Penny was enough."

We waved goodbye to Ariadne at the top of the stairs and headed for room thirteen. I pulled my tie from round my neck and threw it at the desk, where I had an already mounting pile of prep work from just two days of school. My stomach rumbled. I wondered why I was starving, until I realised that we'd barely eaten because we'd been too busy talking about Ebony's... trick. Her cards spun through my head. It was all so strange.

And of course, it was about to get stranger.

We were first in line at dinner time, which was definitely a rare occurrence. Usually we arrived fashionably late and ended up at the back of the queue. In fact, we were so early that the cook hadn't even opened the serving hatch yet. When she did, she gave me a very suspicious look.

"You up to something?" she said.

"Why would I be?" I asked innocently.

Her squint narrowed even further. "Nobody's that keen for stew," she said.

"If you know that," I said, holding out my plate, "why do you keep making it?"

The cook said nothing and just stared at me in a thoroughly unimpressed fashion as she ladled a steaming pile of the stuff on to my plate, where some of it promptly slipped off the sides.

Ivy wisely kept quiet and got a much neater helping than me. We headed for our table, where Madame Zelda had just arrived with a plate of food that looked much nicer than anything we'd been given.

"You are keen, girls," she said with a smile.

"Hungry," was all I could say before shovelling the stew into my mouth. "Ow. Hot." Ivy laughed at me.

We'd almost finished by the time Ariadne appeared, the hall now filled with bustling bodies. We waved to her as she walked in, but instead of going to queue up as I thought she would, she made a beeline for us.

"You came down early?" she asked, twiddling her thumbs nervously. "I knocked on your door, but there was no answer."

"Sorry," said Ivy. "I was afraid Scarlet was going to eat her pillow if I didn't get her to the dining hall."

I whacked her on the arm and she laughed.

Ariadne gave a weak smile. "All right," she said, before heading to get her dinner.

The Rookwood School dining hall was always noisy, no matter what the teachers tried to do about it. But just as I ate the final mouthful of my stew, I noticed the noise starting to get louder. Something was happening.

I turned round to see Ebony standing on the table over Muriel.

I jumped up and ran across, hearing the teachers start to shout, which wouldn't do any good.

"You won't tell anyone," Ebony said, her eyes burning, her body coiled like a spring.

Muriel was trying to protest, but the words weren't really getting out.

"You won't tell anyone!" Ebony repeated.

In seconds, Madame Zelda was beside me. She pointed at Ebony. "Get down, this instant!"

Slowly, Ebony turned her head and just smiled. She didn't move.

Madame Zelda gaped at her and then walked away, muttering to herself.

I couldn't believe it – was Madame Zelda afraid of Ebony?

## Chapter Ten

### IVY

After dinner, no one could forget the incident that had taken place. Ebony may have eventually climbed off the table, but the image of her facing down Madame Zelda had stuck in everyone's minds. And she hadn't even been given a detention! I knew Rookwood was a little different now, but I was sure shouting at people from the dining-room tables was still against the rules.

Not long after everyone had been ejected from the

hall, we went to knock on Ariadne's door. "Come in!" she called.

She was sitting on her bed, talking to Muriel.

"What happened?" Scarlet asked. She was always direct.

Ariadne looked up at us. "Muriel saw something in Ebony's room."

Muriel nodded. "She has a *cat*!"

"What?" I said.

"Really?" Scarlet said. "I thought that was just another stupid rumour."

Muriel's expression turned a little sour. "I'm not lying," she said. "She has a cat. A black one. Her door was ajar and I saw it walking in. I was just telling someone about it at dinner and I suppose she must have heard me. And the next thing I knew, she was screaming in my face."

I wrinkled my nose. Ebony hadn't exactly been screaming, but it wasn't really a gentle whisper either.

"Well," Scarlet said, "there's a rule about pets. We're not allowed them."

Ariadne sighed. "There are rules about *everything*."

"It's more than that," Muriel insisted. "You saw the way she stood over me. She wanted to silence me. Can't you see it yet?" Muriel got to her feet, an imposing sight given how tall she was. "What she really is?"

Scarlet and I shared a glance. "We heard the rumours..." I started.

"But Rookwood and rumours go together like Rookwood and stew," Scarlet finished. "You should hear the rumours about *me*."

"I did," Muriel blinked. "Apparently you smashed a piano and got locked in a loony bin."

"Now listen here," Scarlet said, holding a finger up to Muriel.

I batted her hand down again. "Scarlet, calm down."

She glared at me. "Right, well, the point has been made."

"They're right, Muriel," Ariadne said from her bed. "People say a lot of silly things at this school. Just because they say Ebony is a wi—"

"Ssh!" Muriel waved her hands to silence her. "Don't say it!"

Ariadne floundered uselessly for a moment. "Well... well just because they say that about her, it doesn't mean it's true."

"And you believe that?" asked Muriel, folding her arms. She was looking at us as if we were slow.

I went and sat down beside Ariadne, my muscles

still aching from the previous day's ballet. "If she really is –" Muriel shot me a look – "what people say she is, then shouldn't she be making potions and casting spells, and things like that?"

Scarlet nodded in agreement. "Exactly. All she's done so far is been a bit of a scary bully and done a card trick. And possibly owned a cat."

Ariadne started picking at her blankets thoughtfully. "It *was* an impressive trick, though. And there is something spooky about her. That performance in English was certainly strange."

"But she's just a person, isn't she?" I began. "There's nothing—"

I was going to continue, but I was interrupted by Muriel sobbing.

We all looked at each other, unsure how to react. It was strange to see this tall girl crying, especially knowing her past.

"Muriel?" Ariadne asked. "What is it?"

Muriel sniffed and wiped her eyes. "I just – I just wanted a fresh start! And she's ruining it!" She sat down heavily on her bed again, the slats creaking beneath her. "She won't stop picking on me. It's not fair – I don't even know her! I've never done anything to her!" Her sobs echoed around the small room.

"Well..." Ariadne said quietly, "that was how you made me feel."

Muriel choked back her final sob and looked up at Ariadne. "And I'm so sorry," she said. "I was beastly. I truly was. I know that now and hope you can forgive me, even though I don't deserve it." There was something hopeful in her eyes.

My friend bit her lip. She clearly hadn't been expecting that, I could tell. And neither had I, to be honest. After a long pause, she said, "All right. I can forgive you, Muriel. If you're really sorry and you've changed."

Muriel nodded gratefully and wiped away another tear. "Everything's changed."

A small smile shimmered on Ariadne's face. She'd clearly dreamt of this moment for a long time. A stain on her past had been wiped away.

"I meant what I said," Muriel sniffed. "There's something *really wrong* with Ebony. And I'm scared she won't stop torturing me."

Scarlet folded her arms. "We'll stop her."

Ariadne nodded. She looked a little more fierce than usual. "We'll stand up to her."

I said nothing. We'd tried standing up to bullies in the past. Sometimes it had worked, but sometimes it had just made things worse. I didn't know if Ebony really had magic powers, or if she was just another bully – but who was to say what would happen if we got in her way?

That night, I thought that I would never go to sleep for the thoughts racing around my head. But it wasn't long before the curtain of darkness fell over my eyes and I slipped into a dream.

*I was in a forest, the wind whipping around me. Everything seemed grey, as though the colour had seeped out of the world. But I could see something up ahead: a fire. It was burning brightly. I couldn't feel the heat, but I knew in my mind that it was there, that I could feel it brushing my skin as I moved closer.*

*When I set foot in the clearing, I realised that it wasn't just a fire. It was hundreds, maybe thousands of candles, burning all around me. There was someone standing among them. I saw the shadow of a tall hat, a long black dress, sinister sharp fingernails. She was chanting words in a language I couldn't understand.*

*She turned to me and her face was a blur. But it was Ebony. It felt like Ebony. The figure wore Ebony's boots and had her black and battered suitcase at* her feet. The girl's features shifted like someone was crafting them out of clay, and soon the face was Ebony's too.

She smiled her unnerving smile at me. "Ivy," she said. "You're just in time." The flames roared behind her.

"What are you doing?" I asked.

She didn't reply, but reached down towards the suitcase and flicked the catches open.

I had no idea what was inside it, but I felt instant dread filling my entire body. I didn't want to look. I couldn't.

"You really should look more closely," her voice insisted, singsong and seductive.

"Why?" I asked, my feet carrying me nearer, even though I urged them to turn and run.

The smile remained. "Because I'm going to do a trick."

And as she said that, black plumes of smoke began rising from the suitcase, until they were enveloping me, filling my lungs, and I was pulled down inside...

And I was falling...

And falling...

And I woke up.

I sat bolt upright and started coughing, feeling like

the smoke was still in my lungs. I fumbled for the mug of water I'd left next to the bed and gulped it down eagerly. The smoke cleared away and I blinked in the darkness.

I wasn't in a forest. I was in bed. At Rookwood.

"She doesn't scare me," I whispered in the darkness.

But I wasn't entirely sure who I was trying to convince.

## Chapter Eleven

### SCARLET

As the sun streamed in on another day at Rookwood, Ivy told me about the nightmare she'd had featuring Ebony. I didn't know what to make of it, and it seemed that she didn't either.

"I was really frightened," she said. "But it didn't feel real. Certainly not after I'd woken up."

"It's that nonsense Muriel was spouting," I reassured her. "Don't let it get into your head."

I said it was nonsense, but, well... Did I really believe that? I wasn't sure.

I was getting fed up with Ebony. Who did she think she was? Swanning about with her gaggle of little followers, picking on people, and now she was scaring my sister in her sleep as well. She needed to be taken down a peg or two.

While Ivy was getting dressed, I decided to investigate Muriel's theory that Ebony had a secret black cat by using my great detective skills – well, all right, I knocked on her door and then opened it when no one answered. I didn't know who Ebony shared a room with – presumably another new girl – but as I peered in, you could easily see whose side was whose. Ebony had some sort of black embroidered throw on her bed that was definitely not Rookwood regulation. She had a stack of books piled on her suitcase, some of them with mysterious engravings on the top. The other side of the room was plain, except for a teddy bear wearing a pink and frilly dress.

But there was no cat.

I tried cooing through the doorway and saying, "Here, Puss!" but absolutely nothing happened. If she really did have a cat, it was either hiding, or it was off stalking around the school. *Hmm*. I would have to keep an eye out.

At breakfast, Ebony was already surrounded by the younger girls. She wasn't even talking this time, just eating, but all of them were watching her as if flames were about to shoot out of her ears. I rolled my eyes at them, but I noticed Ivy took an unusually long route to our table to avoid Ebony. The nightmare was obviously staying with her.

According to our timetable, we had a chemistry lesson first, with a new teacher – whose name was Mrs Ember, apparently. I wasn't a fan of the chemistry lab. It always smelt like burning and formaldehyde in there, and it made my eyes sting.

Ivy, Ariadne and I sat together on one of the long benches, all of which were covered with various items of scientific equipment, along with an occasional tap and gas pipe. These were accompanied by tall wooden stools, most of which wobbled; some girls couldn't even touch the ground when they sat on them.

The seats all filled and I thought everyone had arrived and that we were just waiting for the new teacher, but of course there was someone missing. Ebony floated in, not a hair out of place, and walked straight up to Muriel, who was in front of us.

"I want to sit here," she said, all matter-of-fact.

Muriel had a look on her face that said, *Oh no, not this again.* "There're no other seats," she said quietly. I watched as the girls either side of her shuffled away, as if being targeted by Ebony was contagious.

Ebony said nothing. She put her hands on her hips and just stood there, waiting expectantly.

I had to say something. "Oh, come off it, Ebony! Go and find your own seat!"

Her gaze snapped on to me. "Are you sure you want that?"

I stood up. "Why? What are you going to do to me?"

For a few moments, we had a staring match, but I held on. Her storm-cloud eyes did nothing to me.

We were interrupted by the new teacher walking in. "Something the matter, girls?" she asked in clipped tones.

"No, Miss," I said, sitting back down.

Ebony, for once, seemed a bit uncertain what to do. Her eyes flashed quickly across the room.

Mrs Ember chalked her name on the board in big letters. She had tanned skin, greying dark brown hair and crows' feet round her eyes. There was something sharp about her, I could tell. She didn't look the sort to be pushed around by the likes of Ebony.

"Sit," she instructed.

"I..." Ebony paused. "I don't have a seat."

"Get one from the next classroom, then. There's no time for messing around. Come along, girls!" Mrs Ember began assembling tubes and vials on her desk, while Ebony headed out of the door, looking (or so I thought) a bit sheepish.

*Ha!* I'd showed her. I smiled at Muriel, expecting a thankful smile in return, but Muriel was just staring straight at the board. Not a flicker. It seemed a bit strange.

The class got off to an all right start – Mrs Ember took the register and then began demonstrating a reaction with some of her chemicals. Ebony seemed to recover quickly and I saw her staring in fascination at what was going on.

*"Probably reminds her of brewing magic potions,"* I whispered to Ivy, who shushed me.

Everyone *oohed* and *aahed* as the chemicals turned an unusual shade of green and bubbled.

"Now it's your turn," said Mrs Ember. "I want you in pairs."

I grabbed Ivy's hand. Of course we were a pair! But I turned to see Ariadne's face fall, just a little. "Oh," she muttered. "Hmm." She leant forward across her bench. "Muriel, do you want to be in a pair?"

Muriel nodded and smiled. I felt a warm feeling in my heart at seeing the two of them becoming friendly. Or possibly it was the fact that Ivy had just turned the Bunsen burner on.

Everyone began carrying out the experiment, pouring the liquids together, putting them on the heat, writing down what we observed.

Admittedly, Ivy was doing most of the work in our pair. I was chewing on my hair and keeping an eye on Ebony. She was looking quite at home, pouring out her chemicals and watching them bubble. She had teamed up with Anna Santos, and wisely wasn't letting Anna touch the vials (Anna would have won the trophy for World's Clumsiest Person, and then she probably would have dropped it).

But then I noticed a dark expression come across Ebony's face. She was looking at Muriel the way a wolf looks at a sheep. Then I saw her looking down at the frothing green liquid in the vial.

*No*, I thought. *She wouldn't.*

Anna had turned her back and was talking to someone else, and it seemed Ebony was really going to do it. I watched as she turned off the gas and went to pick up a pair of tongs.

Well, I wasn't about to let her do something so

terrible. Not on my watch.

I looked down at the desk in front of me and an idea sprang into my mind.

*Perfect.*

I picked up a spare piece of rubber tubing, the kind we used on the Bunsen burners, and attached it to the tap.

"What are you doing?" Ivy hissed.

Ebony had picked up her bubbling beaker with the tongs and was heading towards Muriel. And that meant she had to pass right in front of us.

I had to act fast. So when Ebony was right in front of me, I turned on the tap – and sprayed her right in the face with a jet of water.

Ebony screamed.

Spluttering and dripping wet, she lowered the beaker to the table.

"Drop that tube right now!" Mrs Ember shouted.

I did as she said, but honestly, that just made things worse. The thing curled back and forth, hissing like a snake, and sprayed water in all directions. Ariadne and Muriel both screeched and dived out of the way. Ivy ducked behind the desk, to a chorus of shrieks from everyone around us.

"TURN THAT TAP OFF!" Mrs Ember cried.

I reached for the tap, but it was a little difficult, given that the hose-tube was flipping around it and soaking the front of my dress.

"Ivy, help!" I called out in the general direction of the floor.

Reluctantly, Ivy bobbed up again and slammed her hand down on the tube, momentarily blocking the water. The thing started to expand and I quickly twisted off the tap before it could burst like a balloon.

There was a moment of silence that was quickly broken by the class falling about laughing.

Ebony's white cheeks were flaming red, though whether she was angry or embarrassed (or both) I couldn't tell. She looked like a drowned rat.

*Serves you right*, I mouthed at her.

She looked at me and there was something dark in her eyes that I didn't quite recognise. But it definitely wasn't happiness.

Mrs Ember marched towards us, having carefully kept away when the tap was soaking everyone. "Young lady," she said quietly, an angry wobble to her voice. "What do you think you were doing? What is your reason for disturbing my entire class?"

I pointed an accusatory finger at Ebony. "*She* was about to tip chemicals on Muriel!"

Ebony blinked, damp hair hanging over her eyes. "No, I wasn't!"

*The lying toerag.* "I saw her," I insisted.

"Young lady," the teacher repeated. "Have you forgotten all of the safety procedures since your previous year? Have you forgotten the *school rules*?"

I stared at her. "Is there a rule about not spraying people with water when they're about to horribly injure someone with boiling chemicals?"

Mrs Ember just stood there, hands on her hips, and seethed at me.

Ivy raised a finger. "To be fair, Miss, I don't think there is—"

The rubber tube fell off the desk, taking the opportunity to shake the final drops of water on to her shoes.

"HEADMISTRESS! BOTH OF YOU!" she said. "NOW!"

## Chapter Twelve

## IVY

"I don't see why I have to go with you," I said to Scarlet, as we walked through the echoing corridors. "I didn't do anything!"

Scarlet squeezed my arm. "As my twin, you're my partner in crime, regardless."

I sighed. Perhaps I shouldn't have spoken up for her. Now we were both in trouble. "Are you *sure* she was about to attack Muriel?"

"Certain!" My sister dragged her feet a little. "Well, pretty certain. She was looking at her threateningly.

And then she was heading over in Muriel's direction with her beaker. She didn't have any other reason to take it there, did she?"

"Well, I suppose not."

"And that stuff is dangerous! It could have hurt Muriel. It could have hurt *Ariadne*. They were working together."

I nodded slowly. If that really was Ebony's plan, then she was more dangerous than we'd imagined. "Maybe she was just going to tip it on their work or something."

Scarlet wrinkled her nose. "I suppose, but that's still awful. She needed someone to show her up. She's getting too big for her witchy boots."

I had to stifle a giggle at that. Seeing Ebony get completely drenched had been a little bit funny.

We reached the headmistress's office. "At least it's Mrs Knight now," I said. She was always so cheerful. If it had been Miss Fox or Mr Bartholomew we'd been sent to, we would have been in for a really nasty punishment. It didn't bear thinking about. But whatever Mrs Knight could do to us... it wouldn't be that bad.

Scarlet knocked on the door.

There was no response. I leant my ear to the wood and could hear Mrs Knight talking, but it was muffled.

"Yes, yes... I see. No, it won't be a problem. Thank you."

"Sounds like she's on the telephone," I whispered to Scarlet.

We waited a short while longer and then the door opened. Mrs Knight looked a little tired and she exhaled heavily at the sight of us. "What is it now?" she asked.

By the time we'd sat down in the office and Scarlet had given a dramatic re-enactment of foiling Ebony's plot, Mrs Knight looked even more exasperated than she had to begin with. "It's all very well that you thought Ebony *might* do something dangerous, Scarlet, but why didn't you tell the teacher?"

"There was no time!" Scarlet protested. "I had to stop her."

She turned to me. "And Ivy? What did you do?"

I stared down at my damp dress. "Um... I hid under the desk." Mrs Knight blinked at me and then I realised that wasn't exactly what she'd meant. She wanted to know why I was there, in trouble too. "I said it wasn't against the rules to spray everyone with water."

Mrs Knight frowned and wrote something down on a piece of paper beside her – presumably making a note to add this to the list of rules in future.

"Girls," she said, taking off her glasses and

beginning to polish them. "You really need to pull your socks up." She pretended not to notice Scarlet reaching down towards her shoes. "You need to *do better*," she emphasised. "Rookwood School is under pressure. We have people that are helping us to improve, but..." Her words came to a halt, as if she wasn't sure how much to say. She put the glasses back on. "We need to have everyone on their best behaviour. I know you girls have shown great initiative in the past—"

"We have!" Scarlet said with a grin.

Mrs Knight waved a pen at her. "But now you need to be settling down and following the school rules. If you have a problem with another student, you should not be fighting them or spraying them with water or anything of the sort; understand?"

"But, Miss," I ventured, about to protest my innocence. I realised I was starting to sound like Scarlet.

"No, girls, this is serious." Mrs Knight put her best serious expression on. "There will be no more trouble. I'm afraid, if there is –" She took a deep breath – "both of you will be expelled. For good."

We left Mrs Knight's office in shock. Or at least, *I* did. Scarlet didn't seem particularly perturbed by what had just happened. But I was worried. If we were expelled, we would be sent straight back to our stepmother, wouldn't we?

"I'll just have to stay out of trouble," Scarlet said.

"Scarlet, this is *you* we're talking about." I waved my hands in frustration. "Trouble would need a six-foot barbed-wire fence to keep you out!"

Scarlet leant against the wall and rolled her eyes. "All right. I suppose. But what's new? They threaten me with these things all the time."

I folded my arms and fixed her with an intense stare. "Firstly, I think Mrs Knight was serious. In fact I've never seen her look more serious. And secondly, she said she'd expel *both of us—*"

"For good, I know. Would that be so bad, really? Or are you in love with Rookwood now?" She made a face at me.

"No," I said. "We've talked about this before! Rookwood is horrible, but all our friends are here. And don't you remember what Edith said? She said she'd make our lives miserable if we got sent home!"

Scarlet didn't say anything for a moment. Then she kicked her shoe against the skirting board and started marching away down the corridor.

"Where are you going?" I called after her. "We can't

go back to chemistry!"

"Going back to our room until next lesson," she yelled over her shoulder. "Maybe I can manage to stay out of trouble there!"

I followed Scarlet, but I took my time. I felt a little numb and I was trying to reassure myself.

It felt strange wandering the empty corridors while everyone was in class. It reminded me of the first time I'd walked through them, when everything had seemed so dark and quiet. Now that Miss Fox had gone and some of Rookwood's hidden secrets had come to light like a breath of fresh air, the atmosphere had changed. It wasn't exactly noisy during lesson time, but peering through the windows in the classroom doors I could see girls talking, getting involved. Everything felt lighter now that no one was fearing the cane – or worse.

Possibilities ran through my head. *We might not get expelled. We might manage to stay on the straight and narrow.*

But what if we couldn't? What if we really were kicked out? How would we see Ariadne and Rose again? And where would we live?

There had barely been room for me at Aunt Phoebe's, let alone both of us, and she was getting more scatterbrained by the day. Where else could we go? There was Aunt Sara, who I loved, but we barely knew her. She lived above a shop and I didn't think there would be room for us there either.

So if we got expelled, that meant... *home*. A home that wasn't really a home in the first place. Home with a father who forgot to care about us and a stepmother who would rather see us dead than cluttering up her cottage.

There was only one thing for it: I would have to stop Scarlet from getting into any more trouble. Whatever it took.

## Chapter Thirteen

## SCARLET

I thought Ivy was worrying over nothing. Of course, it would be terrible if we got expelled. Of course, there couldn't possibly be anything worse than getting sent back to our stepmother. I imagined Mrs Knight pinning a note to our clothes that read *Twins: no longer wanted.*

But we weren't going to be expelled! I felt certain of it. The only person I knew who'd actually been expelled from Rookwood was Ariadne, and that was because they'd thought she'd burned down the library (and I wasn't planning on committing arson any time soon). Usually Rookwood just went in for punishment, not prevention.

Mrs Knight could threaten us as much as she liked, but I didn't believe she'd have the heart to go through with it. And besides, I wasn't intending to go around just picking fights with people.

*The real threat*, I thought as I slammed the door to our dorm, *is Ebony*. I wasn't convinced that she had powers, but I *was* convinced that she was bad news. What would have happened if I hadn't stopped her in time? Ebony had it in for Muriel and I was the only one standing in her way. It had been practically *essential* to spray her with that water.

I kicked my shoes off and lay down on my bed, wondering where Ivy had got to.

Had I done enough in chemistry to stop Ebony causing Muriel trouble? Ebony was a little humiliated, but would she stop all of this? I had a suspicion that the answer was no.

Just how far was she likely to go?

Ivy eventually arrived, and later we reluctantly went back to lessons. At lunchtime, I wasn't the least bit surprised to see that Ebony was back with her gaggle of girls. She had completely dried off as well.

Someone touched my arm in the lunch queue. "I can't believe you did that." It was Muriel, standing beside me.

"She was going to throw—" I started.

"I know, I know." Muriel smiled. "I told you what she's like. Thank you. For saving me."

"Oh," I shrugged. "It was nothing."

When we reached our table, Ariadne looked concerned for us. "So what happened?" she asked. We hadn't had a chance to talk about it in lessons – I was trying my hardest to listen and work hard, which was not as easy as I'd thought it would be. "Do you have detention?"

Ivy put her tray down a little more heavily than necessary. Her glass of water wobbled and threatened to cause another water incident, before I grabbed and righted it. "No," she said. "We just got told off. I'm worried we might get expelled, though."

Ariadne gaped at us. "But... but... they can't! They can't make you leave! Did she say you would be expelled?"

"Not exactly," I said. "But I still think we need to be careful. I think we'll be all right, as long as we behave," I grumbled in the direction of my sandwich.

"Oh," said Ariadne. She didn't look very convinced that we could manage that. "Well, that explains why you seemed rather keen to give answers to all the arithmetic questions. Though I'm not sure they were the right ones."

I stuck my tongue out at her. "*Ha ha.*" We had a new teacher now for arithmetic, since Mrs Knight was too busy running the school. I was hoping I could make a good impression.

"I can't believe Ebony," Ariadne said. I looked round, half expecting Ebony to be fixing me with a deadly glare, but she wasn't even looking my way. That was almost worse, somehow. "I wish she would just leave Muriel alone."

Penny approached the table and sat down, closer to us than I would have liked.

"Funny, isn't it?"

I resisted the urge to ask her if she was talking about her face. I was being *good*.

"What is?"

"That you always called me a witch, and now a real one has turned up." She gestured in the direction of Ebony.

"You think she's a real witch too?" Ariadne asked, wide-eyed.

Penny seemed a little more upbeat than she had before. I wondered if it was the joy of throwing petrol on the rumour fire. "Haven't you heard what everyone's saying?"

"People say a lot of things." I sipped my drink.

"Well, perhaps you should listen to them sometimes," Penny said, raising her eyebrows at me. "Because Ebony's got something planned for Muriel, and it's not nice. And after this morning, you're probably next on her list."

"And why should I listen to you?" I asked.

Penny just shrugged. "Fine. Don't. But don't come crying to me when she turns you into a frog."

We carried on with lessons for the rest of the day after that. Ebony was there, but she didn't say a word to me. Instead, she whispered to the girls around her. I wondered if Penny was right – it did seem like she was plotting something.

At one point I saw her passing notes to Ethel Hadlow. That wasn't a good sign. She didn't even try to hide it either, and the teacher said nothing.

I was trying my hardest to be on my best behaviour. I wrote things down. I *listened*. It didn't come naturally to me, that much was certain. Of course, I loved writing in my diary, but that was different. That was for me, not for some stuffy old teacher who wanted me to memorise pointless facts that I would never need to know, ever.

We headed back to our room after dinner, tired and full. We were walking with Ariadne and Muriel, when Ebony came along in the other direction. Her eyes slipped across Muriel, and then narrowed and darkened. Muriel shivered, as if a cold breeze had just whipped round us. Then Ebony was gone, drifting away without a sound.

"Are you sure you didn't... do something to get on the wrong side of Ebony?" Ivy asked. I was a little surprised that she asked. It was the sort of question that I would usually bring up. "It's a bit strange how she only seems to have it in for you."

"I didn't do anything!" Muriel snapped. Then her voice lowered and took on a sadder tone. "She just hates me and I don't know why."

We neared Ebony's room and that was when it happened.

A cat, small, thin and black as night, was standing in the middle of the corridor.

It looked at us, unimpressed, arched its back and then slunk in through Ebony's door, which was slightly ajar.

"Well, I never," said Ariadne.

"Did that just happen?" I asked.

"This," said Muriel darkly, "is a very bad omen."

## Chapter Fourteen

## IVY

Of course, the first thing Scarlet did was go and put her head round the door of Muriel's room, to try to spot the cat.

"I can't see anything," she said. "It must be hiding."

"It's her *familiar*," Muriel hissed. "We shouldn't go near it!"

"I thought it was rather sweet," said Ariadne, blushing.

Scarlet spun round. "She's breaking the rules, though. She has a pet in her dorm room and that's definitely not allowed!"

I raised an eyebrow. "Since when did you care about rules?"

"As soon as Ebony started breaking them," Scarlet said. "Come on. Let's tell Matron. Ebony deserves some trouble!"

We all followed Scarlet down the corridor, and found that Matron's door was wide open – she was about to begin her evening rounds. She shuffled out of the apartment in her housecoat.

"Evening, girls," she said, taking a pin from her mouth and pinning her hair back. "Something the matter?"

I opened my mouth, about to explain the situation delicately, but Scarlet beat me to it. "Ebony is keeping a cat in her room, Miss!"

We all nodded.

Matron squinted at the four of us, as if she could tell we were making things up just by staring hard enough. "I *think* I would have noticed if one of my girls had a cat in her room."

"It hides, Miss," Muriel protested. "And it's black, so it's hard to see. But honestly, it was just in the corridor, I saw it go into her room—"

But Muriel didn't get any further with her sentence

because that was when Ebony appeared from a door beside us. From her expression, I could tell she'd been listening the whole time. Her eyebrows knitted as her gaze swept across all of us. She mouthed something at Muriel and then strode away. Matron didn't even try to stop her.

"You're probably just seeing things," Matron said. "Miss McCloud is a good girl."

Scarlet looked at her. "Are you sure you aren't the one who's seeing things?"

Luckily for Scarlet, Matron didn't seem to have heard what she'd said. She was still looking down the corridor. "If there's a cat in here, I'll find it," she said. "Go and get ready for bed, the lot of you."

I looked at the others and shrugged. What else could we do?

We headed back, but Ebony was waiting for us outside Ariadne and Muriel's room. She was leaning against the door, her arms folded.

We surrounded her. "What are you doing?" Scarlet asked.

Ebony ignored my sister and just stared straight at Muriel. "You shouldn't meddle with things that you don't understand," she said. She didn't raise her voice, but she didn't have to. Her tone was laced with quiet threat. "Especially you."

I looked up at Muriel, who had gone pale and tight-lipped. "Please. Just leave me alone."

Ebony stood up straight. She was like a vacuum – pulling in all of our attention. "After midnight," she said. "You'll know that I'm serious."

Scarlet tried to step in front of her, but I instinctively pulled my twin back. "No trouble!" I whispered in her ear. We watched in silence as Ebony strode away, her black boots scuffing the floor.

Hurriedly, Muriel opened their dorm-room door and ducked inside without saying another word.

Ariadne bit her lip. "What did she mean by that?"

Scarlet's fists were shaking by her sides. "She's planning something at midnight, isn't she?"

"And we have to find out what," I said.

My twin looked at me. "*Without* getting into trouble!"

We agreed that Ariadne would keep an eye out for Muriel in their dorm room and make sure no one came in. Scarlet and I would hide out near Ebony's room at midnight and watch for her.

I'd argued a fair bit because I still wasn't convinced that we could do it without being seen. But as Scarlet pointed out, we'd had many night-time excursions through the halls of Rookwood without running into a single teacher. Any who stayed at the school were usually fast asleep by that time, and Matron didn't tend to come out of her bedroom for anything less than the school catching fire (which had only happened the once).

"All right," I conceded as I lay under the covers, still wearing all my clothes. "If she really does go anywhere, and isn't just making idle threats, we can trail her. But no confrontations. We can't risk another telling-off after what Mrs Knight said. We have to stay out of sight!"

Scarlet sighed. "Yes, of course." She was doing the same as me. Neither of us fancied the idea of running around in our nightgowns again. This time, we were going to be prepared. And less freezing, hopefully.

Our lights were out, so with any luck Matron wouldn't suspect anything. But there was a full moon in the sky and it was bathing our room in ghostly light. It was enough to see by, so I picked up my copy of *Jane Eyre* and began to read. From the other side of the room, I could hear the unmistakable sound of Scarlet writing in her diary. It made me smile. It wasn't so long ago that I had only heard that sound in my dreams.

I was so caught up in the book, it only seemed like minutes later that Scarlet whispered urgently, "Ivy! It's midnight!"

Sure enough, there was the distant chiming of a grandfather clock. I thought I would feel tired, but I was surprisingly awake. I realised that there was a small buzz of excitement in my stomach. I wanted to know what Ebony was up to.

As soon as I felt that, it became tinged with guilt and with worry. What if she did something really bad? How would we stop her?

Before I had time to ask Scarlet, she was out of her bed and slipping through the door. Quickly, and trying to be as light on my feet as possible, I followed her.

Scarlet stopped suddenly and flattened herself against the wall, and I did the same. My heartbeat raced. We were just in time to see Ebony sneaking out of her room. And she wasn't alone.

There were six other girls with her. I recognised a couple of them as Ariadne's former roommates. They were all carrying candles. We watched as they tiptoed from the dorm and headed for the stairs.

Scarlet looked back at me and tilted her head in their direction. I nodded silently. We had to follow. *At least they don't seem to be going after Muriel*, I thought.

We waited, hopefully just long enough for the others to get some way down. And then we went after them, our footsteps light on the moonlit stairs.

When we reached the bottom, the last of the girls was disappearing from sight – I recognised her as Agatha with the frizzy brown hair. Her head turned for a second, and my breath caught in my throat, but we were in shadow and she didn't seem to have seen us.

Scarlet put her hand out in front of me and we stopped again. "Are they going outside?" she whispered.

"I thought the doors were always locked at night now," I said. But as we waited and listened, we heard the unmistakable sound of the front door swinging shut.

"She must have pinched the key!" Scarlet hissed.

We ran to the door and I knelt down and peered through the large keyhole. The girls were all standing in a circle round Ebony at the bottom of the front steps. I watched as Ebony pulled out a book of matches, and one by one she lit each of their candles.

Scarlet shoved me aside with her shoulder. "Oof!" I fell out of the way and glared at my twin.

"What are they doing?" she whispered.

"I don't know! I can't see any more!" I stood up

and brushed myself off. Considering that the foyer always smelt strongly of floor polish, it was rather unexpectedly dusty.

"They're off somewhere with those candles." Scarlet frowned into the keyhole, then got to her feet beside me. "Well, the joke's on them. We can follow them easily now!"

"But we still need to stay back," I cautioned. I wasn't as worried about the group seeing us as I was about potential conflict. I was a *little* afraid of Ebony, but not as afraid as I was of being sent back to our stepmother.

Scarlet made a face at me and then pulled the door open. Together we slipped out into the night.

The air was brisk and chilly as we followed the trail of bobbing amber lights in the distance. Soon it became clear where they were heading.

"They're going to the chapel?" Scarlet whispered.

Rookwood's chapel was a relic from the days when the school was a grand old house. It was fairly large, large enough to squeeze all of us in on a Sunday morning, as it had originally served the local village as well. It was encircled by a graveyard, bearing battered and worn old stones that jutted from the ground like teeth. For most of the week, nobody went near it.

In the moonlight, the chapel was a looming shadow

on the landscape. We headed towards it, but that meant crossing the gravel. It was incredibly difficult to be quiet on the small stones, and I felt as though we sounded like a herd of elephants. But the other girls' footsteps masked ours, and they were all looking straight ahead to their destination, anyway. We darted on to the grass as they reached the gate to the graveyard. I could see Ebony leading them all inside.

"What has this got to do with Muriel?" I whispered to Scarlet, who just shook her head in response. I could tell she had no idea either.

We sneaked over to the graveyard and crouched down behind the dry-stone wall. The grass was wet and cold to the touch, and I shivered. Even in my uniform, the night was still chilly.

Scarlet waved her hand and I looked to where she was gesturing, and realised there was a gap in the wall. We both scuttled over to it and peered through.

Ebony had found a space between the gravestones, and she was directing the other girls into a circle round her. I could hear her from where we sat – she was making no effort to lower her voice.

"You, there," she was saying. "Not there! We need to make the four corners."

"But there are six of us," Agatha pointed out.

"It doesn't matter," Ebony snapped. "As long as four of you are in the right place. The rest can make up the circle."

I could see red-haired Evelyn staring in awe at Ebony. I was surprised that Ariadne's old roommates had got so caught up in all this, but they had always been a little fascinated by anything dramatic.

When they'd finished assembling, they all sat down on the grass while Ebony stood in the centre. She took a deep breath and a wind whipped up, blowing her black hair out behind her.

She smiled, and it sent shivers down my spine.

"Now," she said, "let the curse begin."

## Chapter Fifteen

### SCARLET

"*C*urse?" I hissed, but Ivy shushed me. I didn't think Ebony would be able to hear anyway, not with the wind whistling through the graveyard. So that's what they were up to! Ebony was going to put a curse on Muriel!

Ebony spread her arms wide and began talking to the sky in a language I didn't understand. It sounded cold and ancient, but there was almost a tune to it.

The eyes of the girls surrounding her went glassy. They couldn't stop looking at her, and neither could we. She was mesmerising.

Her voice got louder and louder, until she threw her head back and shouted into the wind. The girls tipped their heads up.

And then Ebony clapped her hands together and the wind swept over them, and the candles went out.

And everyone screamed.

"*Honestly*," I heard Agatha say. "What did you lot have to go and scream for? You've probably ruined it now!"

*Little toad*, I thought. She'd screamed as loud as the rest!

Ebony looked at them, and it was as if she was coming back down to earth from somewhere up high. "No," she said, "it's done."

"You did it?" asked one of the girls I didn't know. "You put the curse on Muriel?"

Ebony nodded as Ivy tried to stifle her gasp.

"You'll see tomorrow. These darker magics... sometimes they take a little time." She smiled her bewitching smile. I wanted to slap her.

"Ebony," Evelyn said, whispering just loudly enough for us to hear. "Are you sure about this? What if she gets really hurt?"

"She will get exactly what she deserves and no

more. That's how this works." Ebony shrugged off the younger girl and began striding out of the cemetery. I grabbed Ivy's arm and pulled her round the corner of the wall. I tried not to breathe too loudly, but my heart was racing.

After a few moments, I peered back round and watched as they all trouped out through the old iron gate. Half of them were shivering. Ebony didn't seem to have noticed the cold one bit. She lit one of the candles, which was probably quite unnecessary given the white ghostly light that was bathing the school, and led them away.

"What she deserves?" Ivy whispered to me.

I frowned. "Muriel hasn't done a thing to Ebony, has she?"

"Maybe it's because of what Muriel did in the past? She was a bully herself, after all. What if Ebony's found that out and is punishing her?"

Having made sure that they had gone and weren't looking back, Ivy stood up and brushed the damp grass from her skirt.

But Ivy's theory didn't make sense either. "She picked on Ariadne, of course," I went on. "None of that lot were there, though, were they?" I got to my feet and perched on the graveyard wall.

The stone was rough and cold to the touch.

"If anything," Ivy said, "it should be you she has a problem with. You're the one who's been standing in her way."

I shuddered in the cold breeze. Whatever had just happened, it was beyond creepy. Perhaps it wasn't real magic, but there was no denying Ebony's dark intentions. Ivy was right. Maybe I was next.

We made it back to our room (thankfully Ebony hadn't thought to lock the school door behind them). For the first time ever I was questioning my choice of favourite numbers. I didn't believe in bad luck or superstitions, but now that there was a girl with a black cat down the corridor, putting curses on people, and we were in room thirteen, it began to worry to me.

"We'll have to tell Ariadne and Muriel about this tomorrow," I said, although some of it got lost in a yawn. I started to get changed into my nightgown, which did nothing to warm me up, but it at least felt soft against the goosebumps on my skin.

"Do you really think that was a curse? Will anything happen?" Ivy asked from the other side of the room. She sounded unconvinced, but there was a slight tremor in her voice.

I wrinkled my nose as I thought about it. "I think Penny was on to something. I think Ebony's a witch in the same way Penny was plain nasty, but as for having magical powers, I'm just not sure." I took a shaky breath of chilly air. "But that was certainly very strange. She's not your typical bully, that's for sure." But even as I spoke the words, there was doubt in my mind.

I climbed into bed and shut my eyes, but images of the curse in the candlelight kept flashing behind them. It felt like I'd seen something unearthly that I wasn't meant to see. That language Ebony spoke...

"Goodnight, Scarlet," Ivy whispered.

"Night," I said back.

I took a deep breath and went to roll over on my side...

Which was when something jumped on to the bed, and I screamed.

"Aaargh!"

"What? Scarlet, what is it?"

I sat bolt upright, and saw what it was.

"Cat!"

The black cat. *Ebony's* black cat.

It was standing on my bed, blinking yellow eyes

at me with indignation, as if I was the one who had intruded into its sleeping place.

I could hear Ivy sink back into her bed with relief. "That's not so bad," she yawned.

"It must have sneaked in when we came through the door," I said, wriggling about under the covers. The cat didn't move, just continued to stare at me.

"Shoo," I said.

It had no effect. The cat flicked its tail and curled up in a ball.

"Are you spying on us?" I asked, but I wasn't really expecting a response to that one. Reluctantly, I climbed out of bed, dislodging the cat, and opened the door. It ran out, but not before looking up at me angrily and hissing.

"Well, sorry!" I whispered. I didn't want a teacher walking into our room in the morning and thinking we were the ones with the secret pet.

I heard Ivy start to snore. She had obviously been exhausted. I knew how she felt. I climbed back into the catless bed and pulled the covers up over myself.

This time there were no interruptions and I began to slip into sleep. But not before candles flickered in front of my eyes and somewhere on the edge of hearing, a cat meowed.

The sun rose the next day, but clouds came with it. I could hear the rain drumming against the windows, and it almost washed away the memories of the midnight curse.

Almost, that is, until breakfast.

The first thing that happened was that Mrs Knight came over to our table looking concerned. She took Madame Zelda aside and I heard her muttering something. The words "front door" and "unlocked" reached my ears.

I bit my lip. So they had noticed. But if they didn't know who had done it, that meant we hadn't been seen. There was no way they could know who had been outside – or at least, that's what I tried to tell myself.

The next thing was that Ebony walked in, looking surprisingly bright-eyed for someone who had been conjuring black magic in a cemetery the night before. She almost seemed... *excited*. And so did her little group of girls, who were all whispering to each other. I watched them with narrowed eyes. How was Ebony managing to string them all along?

But the final thing, and the thing that mattered most, was that Ariadne came running into the hall. Her mousy hair was springing around her ears and her blazer was done up wrong. She ran straight for our table.

"Slow down a little, Miss Flitworth—" Mrs Knight began.

"It's Muriel!" Ariadne cried. "She's disappeared!"

## Chapter Sixteen

## IVY

I looked at Ariadne in shock. In my mind, she and Muriel had been about to wander in together, and we would all have laughed over breakfast about Ebony's strange theatrics in the middle of the night. I didn't know what to say. Scarlet appeared to be speechless as well. Was this what the curse had done?

Most of our table had stopped eating and were now staring at Ariadne, who was breathless and flustered.

"What do you mean?" Mrs Knight asked.

"I woke up and she was just gone," Ariadne said. She gave me a fleeting worried glance. "I've looked everywhere. She wasn't anywhere on our floor, not in the lavatories or the bathrooms! And –" She looked around desperately, just in case Muriel was hiding somewhere in the dining hall – "she's not here either!"

Mrs Knight walked over and put a gentle hand on Ariadne's shoulder. "Don't fret yourself, dear. I expect she'll be around somewhere. Have some breakfast. If she doesn't arrive at her lessons, we'll look for her."

Ariadne bit her lip and stared at the floor. "All right. Thank you, Miss."

Mrs Knight gestured to Madame Zelda and they walked off together.

Our friend sat down beside us and brushed her hair back from her face where it had fallen.

"Stop staring!" Scarlet hissed at the rest of the table. Penny laughed, while the others went back to their porridge and tried to pretend they hadn't been looking.

"She's gone," Ariadne said. "I don't know how, but she's completely gone."

"Maybe she just went to lessons extra early," I suggested limply. "Or to the library."

Ariadne's face crumpled. "I didn't try the library! But she isn't really much of a fan of reading. Oh gosh..."

She looked as though she was about to faint. Scarlet slid her a bowl of almost untouched porridge and she began to tuck in gratefully.

My twin watched her for a few moments before putting her foot in it, as usual.

"Why are you so worried? You don't even like her that much."

Ariadne's eyes rose and glinted with tears. "It's my fault," she whispered.

*Oh no.* I reached out and took her hand. "No, it's not! How could it be your fault?"

"I was supposed to keep an eye on her, in case anything happened!" Ariadne sobbed.

"Well, yes," Scarlet agreed, "but not for the entire night! You couldn't stay awake that whole time. And who knows, maybe Muriel's just wandered off somewhere. Perhaps she fancied having a look around Rookwood. Perhaps she heard about what happened last night and—"

I gave her a warning look, but it was too late. The words were already out.

"What happened last night?" Ariadne asked, her voice shaking.

Scarlet put her hands on the table and had a quick glance around, I guessed to make sure Ebony was nowhere nearby. "We followed Ebony and her cronies at midnight. They went to the graveyard by the chapel. And they... well, they tried to put a *curse* on Muriel."

Ariadne gasped and dropped her spoon with a clang. "A *curse*? What sort of curse?"

The strange scene replayed in my mind, the unknown language spilling from Ebony's lips. "I don't know," I said. "We couldn't understand what she was saying."

"It didn't look good," Scarlet said, subtle as usual. "They all lit candles and they said it was dark magic."

"You don't think..." Ariadne started. Her lips were nearly white.

I kicked Scarlet gently under the table. Ariadne didn't need to be any more upset than she already was. "I'm sure it's all right. I expect Ebony was just messing around. We'll find Muriel, I promise."

As soon as we'd finished breakfast, we headed for the library. The rain was still pouring down and I thought it was very unlikely that Muriel was outside in it. The library was one of the few places, besides the dining hall, where Rookwood pupils gathered outside of lessons, so it seemed the most likely option.

Despite the fire that had ravaged the library last year, it was looking more or less back to normal. There were lots of new shelves and most of the books had been replaced – although it was still looking a little bare in places. All of the fire damage had been fixed and repainted.

The librarian, Miss Jones, looked as good as new as well. She was smiling and humming happily to herself at the desk as we walked in.

"Morning, girls," she called. "Have you met my new assistant?"

A girl popped up from behind the desk, looking surprisingly like a miniature version of Miss Jones, with dark hair and dark eyes. "Hello," she smiled. She had a neat little badge that read LIBRARY ASSISTANT. "Nice to meet you."

"This is my little cousin, Jing." Miss Jones smiled down at her and ruffled her hair. "She's just started at Rookwood, in the first year."

"Nice to meet you," we chorused.

Jing looked like she was enjoying herself. "Where shall I put these, Auntie?" She held up a stack of heavy-looking books.

"In the history section, please," Miss Jones said, watching proudly as her niece headed off to the stacks with them. "She's wonderful!" Then she leant forward and whispered, "So much better than Anna. She used to get lost in Reference all the time."

Scarlet laughed, but I could feel Ariadne fidgeting beside me. We couldn't forget the pressing issue.

"Miss," Ariadne started. "Have you seen Muriel Witherspoon today?"

"Great name," said Miss Jones. "Almost as good as mine." (Miss Jones's real name was Catastrophe Jones, as we'd discovered last year.) "I'm afraid I haven't yet made her acquaintance. What does she look like?"

"She's very tall," said Scarlet helpfully.

I thought the librarian might need a little more information than that. "She's in our year, but she's new. She has blonde curly hair and she sometimes wears a felt cap."

Miss Jones tapped her nails on her desk while she thought about it. "I don't think so. We've only had a few girls in so far this morning, and none of them fitted that description."

Ariadne's face fell. "Oh gosh. That's not good."

Miss Jones leant forward again and lowered her voice. "Is something the matter?"

"We're just looking for her, that's all," Scarlet said. It was probably best not to mention the curse –

Miss Jones was easily frightened.

"I haven't seen her since last night," said Ariadne weakly. "I've looked everywhere."

Miss Jones gave us a gentle smile. "I expect she'll turn up soon. I'll keep an eye out for her. Have you told Mrs Knight?"

We all nodded.

"Perhaps she's outside—" Miss Jones started, but she was interrupted by a roll of thunder and a brilliant white flash illuminating the library. "Perhaps not," she finished. "Sorry I couldn't be of more assistance."

"Thank you anyway, Miss," I said.

"She'll turn up," Miss Jones insisted, giving us a friendly wave as we turned to leave.

But Muriel hadn't turned up by lunchtime.

Nor by dinner time.

She didn't attend a single lesson, and by the evening, you could tell the teachers were beginning to panic, as much as they didn't want to show it. We'd overheard Mrs Knight muttering about having to telephone her parents if she couldn't be found soon. Of course students skipping a lesson or two was fairly common (Scarlet had managed it quite a few times in the past), but not even appearing for meal times was practically unheard of.

As we ate dinner, Ariadne barely touching hers because she was so worried, we watched the teachers talk to each other in hurried, hushed voices. The torrent outside had eased, but it was still raining and everyone was fairly certain that Muriel wouldn't be out in it. Even so, there weren't many more places to look.

"We could send Eunice," I heard Mrs Knight say to Madame Zelda as she passed our table.

Scarlet snickered. "She won't like that." They were talking about Miss Bowler, who had already been sent out into a storm once this year, on the school trip.

"Scarlet," Ariadne moaned. "It's not a laughing matter."

"Sorry, sorry. I know you're worried." Scarlet had another mouthful of her stew. "But I'm sure she's fine. I do wonder, though..." She glanced over in the direction of where Ebony sat. "Miss McCloud has been looking smug all day. I mean, the curse—"

Ariadne squeezed her eyes shut. "Don't say it! I don't even want to *think* about it."

"No," said Scarlet, "I mean we can't say whether it was real or not. If it *was* real, we don't know what sort of awful thing might have happened."

Our friend put her hands over her ears. "La la la! I can't hear you!"

Scarlet swatted her arms back down. "BUT! What if Ebony was just pretending? Then she would still want everyone to believe that she had done it, wouldn't she?"

I thought about it as I chewed a lacklustre piece of carrot. "Are you saying she's trapped Muriel somewhere?"

Ariadne's face relaxed a little. "Ooh. Good point."

"Exactly!" My twin leant in closer to make sure no one else could hear. "What if she's been locked in Ebony's room or something, to make it look like the curse worked?"

Ariadne nodded. "Oh, Scarlet, you might be right. We have to look!"

That worried me a little. We were supposed to be avoiding trouble, but every step closer to Ebony felt like a step too deep. Before we knew it, we would be up to our necks. "What if she finds out?"

Scarlet stood up, craned her neck, then returned to her seat, gulped down the remains of her dinner and slammed the plate down on the table.

"Careful with the crockery, Miss Grey," Madame Zelda said as she went back to her seat.

Scarlet leant in again. "Ebony's too busy eating and

bathing in admiration right now. She'll never know if we peek into her room. I'm pretty certain she's been leaving the door ajar for that cat!"

I thought about it, and it was the hopeful light in Ariadne's eyes that convinced me. "All right. Just a quick look."

We finished our dinner in a hurry and raced back upstairs. There were still some other girls bustling around the corridor, who had either finished dinner already or not yet been down, so we didn't look too out of place.

We reached Ebony's room and, sure enough, the door was open – just a crack. Scarlet and I leant against the wall and tried to look completely uninvolved in what was occurring, while Ariadne pushed the door a little wider and craned her neck round to peer in.

She reappeared with a sigh, her shoulders sagging. "Nothing. No Muriel, not even the cat. Just Ebony's things and... well, whoever the other side of the room belongs to."

Scarlet screwed her face up. "Really? I was so sure." She scuffed her foot on the carpet, then raised her eyes towards us. "What if she's in the wardrobe or something?"

"Scarlet," I said, "Muriel's very tall and our

wardrobes aren't that big. Besides, she would be shouting or banging, wouldn't she?"

"I suppose," my twin replied begrudgingly. "But I just ought to check." She tipped her head towards the opening in the door. "Muriel! If you're in there, make a noise!"

We all stood silently and listened, but there was no sound other than the footsteps and chatter of the girls walking around us in the corridor, and the rain lashing at the windows.

"Looking for something?"

We whirled round. And there behind us, tapping her boot and wearing a cruel smile, was Ebony.

## Chapter Seventeen

## SCARLET

I folded my arms and squared up to her. "Good evening, Ebony," I said, not bothering to hide the anger in my voice. "I don't suppose you've seen *Muriel* anywhere?"

She just smirked at me. "Oh yes. I did hear she'd gone. Perhaps she's run off home. She didn't really belong here, did she?"

"Oh, what is your problem?" I snapped. She didn't seem to have any good reason to dislike Muriel so much. "Cut the nonsense. What have you done with her?"

155

Ebony laughed. Or maybe it was a cackle.

"Scarlet..." Ivy warned from behind me.

I turned round. "Calm down, Ivy, I'm not starting a fight, I'm just asking a question!"

Ebony tapped one of her nails against her pale face. I noticed she had painted it black. That was *definitely* breaking a rule. How did she get away with all this? "I'm not sure what you're talking about. Why would I have done anything with Muriel?" She was no longer laughing out loud, but her eyes were doing it for her.

"Oh come off it! We saw you—"

But I was interrupted by the arrival of Matron, striding down the corridor. "You girls! Stop dithering about in the hallway. If you've finished dinner, you should be getting ready for bed now, shouldn't you?"

"But Matron—" I began.

"No buts!" She waggled a finger at me. "There's a missing student, so I need to make sure everyone is in their rightful place. And I've been told you're on thin ice anyway, young lady. No trouble from you, please." She slid her gaze across the rest of us, but it stopped short at Ebony. It was as if she were invisible or something. "Or you, Ivy and Ariadne. Go and get your things." And with that, she walked away.

"How are you doing this?" I hissed at Ebony. "Why

don't they tell you off?"

Ivy was tugging on my arm at this point. The warning was really getting to her.

Ebony just shrugged, and ignored the question. "Excuse me," she said, "but you're in the way." She pushed past and slid through the door into her room, before closing it behind her with a click.

Ariadne looked distraught as we hurried back towards our dorms. "It's getting dark!" she whispered. "And we still have no idea where Muriel is!"

I patted her on the arm. "The teachers will find her, I'm sure of it."

Ariadne's forehead crinkled with lines of concern. "I think we should look for her!"

I could tell from Ivy's expression that she was very much against the idea, and I could immediately understand why. Matron was going to be making extra sure that we were all brushing our teeth and then getting tucked up in our beds this evening. And she clearly knew about Mrs Knight's decision to expel us if we caused any more trouble.

Several realities immediately flashed through my head: one where we found Muriel and she'd just been hiding somewhere, staying away from the bullies. She would probably be grumpy and ungrateful, and we'd have risked getting kicked out of school for nothing. Another where there actually was some sort of curse, and we found her lying in a ditch somewhere, rain-soaked and black with mud, her eyes rolled back into her head. And another where we got caught before we could find her. Where the teachers found us sneaking out, ignored our pleas and sent us packing to our stepmother. And what she would do to us, well... I couldn't imagine, and that somehow made it much worse than the awful images that had gone before.

"Sorry, Ariadne," I said with a heavy shrug of my shoulders. "It's just not worth it."

"Not worth helping to find her?" Ariadne gaped at me and then turned to Ivy. But I already knew Ivy wasn't going to agree to help look either. "I... I think Scarlet's right," she said. "Unless we have some real proof that anything bad has happened to Muriel, I don't think we can risk it."

"But the curse..." Ariadne pleaded.

"...might just be made up," Ivy finished. "And as for the other idea – that she's trapped somewhere – well, if it's somewhere in Rookwood, she'll probably be all right and the teachers will find her soon enough."

"How could it be anywhere else, really?" I pointed out. There was nowhere particularly near Rookwood, unless you walked all the way to the village or managed to catch the rare bus. I didn't think Ebony was strong enough, nor that dedicated, to drag Muriel all that way.

Ariadne still didn't look happy. "If it were me, then you'd look, wouldn't you?" she said quietly.

"Of course!" we both replied.

"You know we would," Ivy reassured her.

"And we chased a crazed man into a thunderstorm for Rose," I pointed out. "But we knew something was wrong then. And besides, we're friends. We don't really know a jot about Muriel, except for the fact that she bullied you horribly."

Ariadne's voice had started to get quieter, and now she sounded all mousy again. "But she's not so bad any more – she doesn't deserve this."

I couldn't bear our friend looking so upset, so I pulled her and my sister into a hug. "Buck up, you lot! It'll be fine! The teachers will find Muriel and Ebony will get what's coming to her."

"Promise?" There was hope in Ariadne's eyes.

I swallowed. I didn't know if that was something I could really promise. But if it would make her feel better...

"Promise," I said firmly.

*

I lay in bed later that night, listening to the last of the torrential rain dying down outside and telling myself that we had done the right thing. It would have been stupid to go racing off looking for Muriel.

So why did I have this feeling that something was terribly wrong?

I couldn't stop seeing Ebony that night in the cemetery, reliving the look on her face. Not to mention how she'd nearly thrown those chemicals on Muriel before I'd bravely thwarted her. She was *cruel*.

Curse or no curse, I couldn't shake off the idea that Ebony could have done something awful, and that I was just letting her get away with it.

I clenched my fists tightly round my bedsheets.

"Scarlet?" I heard Ivy's voice whisper. "Do you really think..."

"...that they'll find her?" My twin didn't have to finish her sentence for me to know what she was asking.

"Yes," I said firmly. "Yes, I do."

They didn't find her.

Morning came. The clanging bell, the frantic pulling-on of uniforms, tugging the brush through our hair. We raced down to breakfast only to find Ariadne alone, staring into her bowl with a face the colour of the porridge she was eating. We asked her about Muriel and she just shook her head sadly.

Well, I couldn't just leave it at that. I marched up to the nearest teacher, who happened to be Madame Zelda. She was at the side of the dining hall, near our table, attempting to tie her silver hair into a bun and poking her incense sticks through it.

"Miss? Is there any word about Muriel Witherspoon?" I asked.

She looked up at me and I thought she seemed faintly embarrassed. She dropped the incense stick and stood up straight. Everything about Madame Zelda was long and slender. "I'm afraid not, Miss Scarlet. We are still hard at work trying to find her."

I bit my tongue. "Are you sure you've looked everywhere?"

Madame Zelda folded her arms. "We have turned Rookwood inside out, but that is not for you to be worrying about, hmm?"

I didn't understand what she meant. "What should I be worrying about then, Miss?"

She reached out and spun me round, pointing me in the direction of the Richmond table. "Your breakfast. Go along now. We will continue searching for your friend."

"Hmmph." I marched back to our table. When I glanced over my shoulder, Madame Zelda was fiddling with her hair again.

"Does she know anything?" Ariadne asked hopefully.

"As much as us," I said. "Which is to say, not a bit."

As the day passed, I kept thinking about Muriel. I looked everywhere for a glimpse of her blonde hair, or for that silly hat she sometimes wore. I wondered if Mrs Knight had told her parents yet.

After lunch, I was walking towards our next lesson when I saw a hint of blonde hair as someone went through a classroom door. I ran after the girl and grabbed her by the arm, and she whirled round...

It was Rose.

"Oh! Rose! I'm so sorry, I thought you were... someone else," I panted.

Rose looked a little horrified, but her expression soon melted into a relieved smile.

"We're looking for the new girl, Muriel Witherspoon. Have you seen her?"

Rose just stared at me a little blankly. "She's blonde like you, but, um..." I sized Rose up and realised how stupid I'd been. "A lot taller."

Ivy finally appeared in the doorway. "What are you playing at?"

"Sorry, sorry," I said. "I've got Muriel on the brain. Anyway, Rose?"

Rose shook her head. "I haven't seen her," she said quietly. "Not even in the stables." She said it as though you might expect everyone to hang around in the stables.

"That's all right," I said, leaning on the teacher's desk. "We'll just keep looking."

And I did keep looking. I looked for Muriel, but I also kept an eye on Ebony. I hoped she would betray herself somehow. But all she did was wear this smug smile that I just wished I could wipe off her face. She glided around the school as if she owned the place. And every time she passed me, I could swear I felt the air get colder.

By the evening, Ariadne was in even more of a state than she had been before.

"It's my fault," she kept saying as she peered under the door of each lavatory cubicle, just in case.

A group of other girls were in there, jostling for the sinks as usual. Several of them were staring at Ariadne, as if she'd just grown antlers.

"How can it possibly be your fault?" I replied.

Ariadne dodged an angry-looking girl who had just exited a cubicle. "I should have looked harder for her. I should have gone out in the rain. What if she's unconscious in a ditch somewhere? I should have—" She stopped, gulping down her words.

"Whatever happens," Ivy said, putting her hand on our friend's shoulder, "it isn't your fault."

"But it's almost certainly Ebony's fault," I growled. "That smug *witch*."

At the mention of her name, a hush rippled out through the crowd, until everyone was silent and staring at me.

I looked around. "What?" My voice echoed off the bathroom tiles.

A first year looked up at me with wide eyes. "You shouldn't talk about her like that. She might hear you."

"Yes," said another, a dark-haired girl who was nervously tugging on her tie. "Didn't you hear? She put a curse on that girl. I heard she ripped her soul from her body and sent her to he—"

"THAT'S QUITE ENOUGH, THANK YOU!" I said, clapping my hands over Ariadne's ears. "Come on, let's go to bed."

\*

Saturday came and I dragged myself out of bed reluctantly. It would be nice to sleep in, but then you'd miss breakfast. I yawned and stretched, and only then did the problem of Missing Muriel flash into my mind.

Ivy was standing at the window, staring outside.

"What is it?" I asked. All I could see from where I was standing were grey skies and the leaves of the trees that were turning a crisp orange at the edges.

"Look," she said.

I went over and squeezed in beside her to get a better look. I could see Rookwood's long drive snaking away from us.

"Down there!" Ivy pointed.

There was a group of teachers and pupils standing at the front of the school, leaning over something. There seemed to be quite a commotion going on. "What the—"

"We need to go and see what's going on." There was fear in my twin's eyes. And I didn't blame her. The cold feeling that spread through my bones whenever Ebony passed had returned, like icicles melting under my skin. Something was wrong.

We dressed as quickly as we could and then raced down the stairs, heading for the foyer. The enormous front doors of Rookwood were wide open, a crowd had gathered at the bottom of the steps. As I reached the doors, I saw Ariadne there, trying to push her way in. She was standing on tiptoes and craning her neck. The desperation was pouring off her.

"Ariadne!" I called. "What's happening?"

She turned, her face panicked and pale. "They've found Muriel!"

## Chapter Eighteen

## IVY

When Ariadne spoke those words, I felt the hairs on the back of my neck stand up. Scarlet and I ran down the school steps, and each one sent a shock through me. I imagined the worst outcomes in my head, over and over again. The seconds felt like hours.

"Hold on," Scarlet said. She grabbed my arm, and Ariadne's too, and began doing what she did best – pushing her way through the crowd.

We made it a good way through before encountering

a significant roadblock, in the form of Miss Bowler.

"STAND BACK!" she roared. "EVERYBODY STAND BACK!"

The blast of her voice nearly knocked me over, but Scarlet pulled us sideways and suddenly we had a clear view of what was going on.

There was Muriel, lying at the bottom of the steps. Her eyes were closed. Her hair was tangled and snagged, her clothes torn as if by claws.

And that wasn't the worst of it.

There was a wound on her head, bright red and ugly.

I couldn't breathe. I pressed my hand to my chest. *I couldn't breathe...*

"Is she dead?" I heard Penny ask, somewhere to the left of us.

"I SAID, STAND BACK!" Miss Bowler repeated, waving her arms, pushing people away. "GIVE THE GIRL SOME AIR!"

I was in such a state of shock that I thought for a moment that Miss Bowler was talking about me.

But then Muriel's eyelids fluttered, and she moaned and curled up on her side.

We all exhaled in relief. Ariadne collapsed against me.

"Miss Winchester!" Miss Bowler boomed in the

direction of Penny. "You can make yourself useful and fetch the nurse, quick sharp!"

Penny wrinkled her freckled nose, but she did as she was told and disappeared from the throng.

Mrs Knight was kneeling over Muriel. "Are you all right, Miss Witherspoon?" she asked.

"Quite a question, given the circumstances," Scarlet whispered. I elbowed her. This was no time for jokes.

Muriel blinked slowly and then sat up in a painful, jerky manner, as if she were a puppet and someone had just tugged on her strings. Her blank eyes gazed at nothing. "Miss Witherspoon?" she repeated in a low voice.

"That's you, gal," Miss Bowler said, prodding her in the shoulder.

The puzzled expression didn't leave Muriel's face. "I don't... Where am I?"

There were gasps from the crowd. "Oh gosh, oh no," I heard Ariadne say under her breath beside me. Had Muriel lost her memory?

"We're at Rookwood School, my dear." Mrs Knight pushed her glasses higher up her nose. "Do you remember what happened? Are you hurt?"

Still Muriel's eyes didn't focus. "Hurt...?" She reached a hand up to her temple and brought it back down again. There was blood on her fingers. "Oh my..." she wobbled perilously, and would have collapsed on to the ground if Miss Bowler hadn't caught her.

"That's it!" Miss Bowler snapped. "I'm taking her to Gladys myself!"

We watched as the large teacher picked up the tall girl to take her to the school nurse. It was certainly a sight to behold.

"OUT OF THE WAY! DON'T YOU ALL HAVE SOMEWHERE TO BE?" Miss Bowler boomed as she shouldered her way through the crowd and pounded up the steps.

"I have to go with her!" Ariadne said. And before we could stop her, she was running back into the school.

Eventually, the crowd outside the front doors was persuaded to head in for breakfast. The dining hall was always a hive of gossip, but that morning the buzzing was even louder than usual. And Ebony sat in the middle of it, like the queen bee.

"Are you happy with yourself now?" Scarlet asked her as we passed.

Her gang of girls all stood up quickly, surrounding her. Ebony didn't so much as move a muscle. "Very happy, thank you," she said. "Why?"

"You know what you've done," my twin said. If she hadn't been holding a tray full of breakfast, I probably would have tried to hold her back. "I don't know how you've done it, but you have. Somehow. This ends now, you hear?"

Ebony leant forward slightly, a twinkle in her eye. "I don't know what it is you believe I've done. But what makes you think I won't do it again?"

We reached our seats in a daze. Scarlet wouldn't stop glaring at Ebony. I wasn't sure that was helpful. And anyway, was Ebony *really* responsible for what had happened to Muriel? Even Muriel hadn't been able to give an explanation. We didn't know yet that she hadn't just gone for a walk and hit her head somehow.

Ariadne appeared just as we were finishing our porridge. I wasn't surprised to hear that she hadn't been allowed into the nurse's office with Muriel.

"They said she's too fragile," Ariadne sighed. "I had to wait outside the door for ages. But they told me a little bit, although I think they were just trying to make me go away. They said that she remembers who she is now, but that she doesn't remember what's happened to her at all. And, well..."

Ariadne's lips pursed and she didn't look as though she wanted to continue.

"What?" Scarlet asked.

Our friend paused for a few more moments before the words eventually spilt out all in one go. "They said that they found her in the graveyard. And that she doesn't remember anything since around *Wednesday at midnight*."

Scarlet clapped her hands over her mouth.

I nearly choked on my breakfast. "Are you *sure*?"

"That's what they said." Ariadne bit her lip.

I couldn't believe it. Surely Ebony's curse couldn't really have done anything to Muriel?

My twin's face went white as milk, and as her mirror image, I was fairly sure mine was doing the same. Suddenly I couldn't face eating another mouthful.

Scarlet slammed her hands on the table and leant forward. "Do you know what this means? Maybe the curse was *real*!" she hissed.

Ariadne gulped. But I was determined to use logic. We had to keep our heads. Whenever things seemed supernatural, there was usually a rational explanation. But whatever that explanation was, I felt certain that Ebony was at the heart of it. "Or maybe Ebony wants everyone to *think* it's real. So she somehow hurt Muriel to convince us."

Ariadne summoned the strength to speak again. "Either way, we need to stop Ebony!"

This time, I had to agree. "You're right."

"I think we really need to investigate what she's up to," Scarlet said, with another choice glare in Ebony's direction.

Ariadne nodded quickly, desperately. "We need to—"

She was interrupted by Mrs Knight striding into the room, looking unusually authoritarian.

She clapped her hands. "Girls! Quiet!"

It was very rare that everyone had to be silent in the dining hall, so the silence took some time to grow. It spread over the room until eventually the final dregs of gossip were squashed and everyone was staring over at the doors.

"Right," she said, raising her voice as loud as it would go. "I'm sorry to report there has been an incident with one of our students, which I'm sure many of you have heard about already. Please be reassured that she will be fine."

There was a small flurry of quiet muttering, and I thought that at least some of the other girls looked disappointed. Rookwood loved nothing more than a good drama.

"But I have been informed that *bullying* has been taking place, and that this incident may be linked." She said "bullying" as if it were a dirty word.

"Snitches," I heard Penny whisper. Scarlet rolled her eyes.

"Girls, we will not tolerate bullying in this school!" Mrs Knight hit her fist into her palm. "We cannot have anyone else getting hurt!" Her voice seemed strong, but I detected an air of desperation. The events of last year flashed through my mind, when Mrs Knight had tried so hard to deny what was going on, and to salvage Rookwood's reputation. If news of what had happened to Muriel got out among the parents, then all of her work would be undone.

As I sat there listening to Mrs Knight while she made her thoughts on bullying very clear – "Does she just have her eyes shut when you're around?" Scarlet whispered to Penny – and told us all to be kind and positive and to dare to dream of a brighter day, I nodded along. But it was her final words that really made me sit up and listen.

She took a deep breath. "So, girls, if this continues, I will have no choice. If I see anyone involved in a confrontation. They will be expelled. I am serious! No more trouble!"

And I swear, her gaze landed right on us.

I looked at Ariadne across the table. And I thought for a second that I could read her mind.

*Please. We have to stop Ebony. Whatever it takes.*

## Chapter Nineteen

## SCARLET

Personally, I thought it was a bit late for Mrs Knight to take a stand against bullying. You couldn't stop bullying at Rookwood any more than you could stop a steam train with missing brakes on a downhill track. There was *always* bullying.

But I believed her when she said that she was going to start expelling people. I hardly dared to hope that Ebony would be the one to be caught in the act (or Penny, even if she seemed to be keeping herself to herself these days). Knowing our luck, it would be us three that got the blame for anything that happened.

Ebony, though, needed to be stopped more than ever. She'd threatened to hurt Muriel, and now she actually had. Whether Muriel had been a bully herself or not didn't matter. If we didn't do something about Ebony, the steam train was going to have a fiery crash and there were going to be casualties.

Since it was the weekend, we were able to go back to our room after breakfast, while Ariadne returned to the sick bay to see if there was any update on Muriel. Ivy was strangely quiet, but my mind was whirring and I assumed it was because hers was too.

I had a quick glance out of the window before I lay back on my bed. The sun was out again, though the sky was still grey and a mist was hanging over the grounds. I couldn't see the chapel or the graveyard.

The inside of my brain felt the same way, like a fog had descended over it, but there was an idea in there that I was slowly pulling out. Eventually, enough of it had formed that I had to say something.

"Ivy?"

My twin looked up from the book she was reading.

"I have an idea. But I don't think you'll like it."

She squinted at me dubiously. "Oh, really?"

"I think we should—" I started.

"If it's going to get us into trouble, then the answer's no."

"Just shut up and listen for a moment!" I sat up and swung my legs over the side of the bed. "It'll be the opposite, hopefully. Right. So, we could confront Ebony. We could try and get in her way. But it'll probably end in a fight and all of us will be expelled."

"That was my worry," Ivy said with a sigh.

"So we need a different approach. What if... we got closer to her?" I winced a little at the thought. "What if we get to know our enemy a little better?"

Ivy closed the book and looked over at me. "Are you suggesting that we join her? That... doesn't seem like a good idea. Won't that just lead us into trouble?"

"Ah, but it won't!" I jumped up. "You've *seen* how the teachers treat her. They don't pay the slightest bit of attention to what she gets up to."

"Hmm." Ivy tapped the book against her chin. "Perhaps you're right."

"I am," I said, pacing up and down between our beds. "We can just observe, without getting too involved if she does anything awful. But we need to —" I searched for the right word — "*align* ourselves with her. And not with Muriel. We need to gain her trust, just enough of it that she doesn't mind us hanging around."

Ivy was silent for a bit. I thought for a moment she was just going to tell me to forget about it, that it was all too ridiculous. But instead, the words that came out of her mouth were, "Okay. We'll try."

I wrung my hands. "Let's get started today. We'll tell Ariadne when she comes back. This is the best plan *ever*!"

"That is the worst plan *ever*!" Ariadne's jaw hung open.

She had just returned from the nurse's office and was standing in the middle of the room. I had just filled her in on my genius idea.

"It's foolproof!" I insisted.

"But Ebony's no fool, Scarlet! She'll see right through you!" Ariadne waved her hands. "And she's *dangerous*. They finally let me in to see Muriel, and gosh, she's in a bad way. She looks terrible, poor thing. I talked to her a little, but she just seemed so confused and upset. And Ebony did that to her!"

"Well, we *think* she did," said Ivy gently. "That's the point. We need to find out more."

"But we shouldn't join her," Ariadne said. Her voice quavered with desperation. "We should just... spy on her or something!"

"That's the thing." I couldn't quite meet her eye. I knew she wouldn't like this part, but it had become clear to me while we were waiting for her. "It would just be us. You can't join in on this."

"But why?" Ariadne's face filled up with a mixture of puzzlement and hurt. And it felt awful, even as I was talking myself into it.

"It's too suspicious," I explained. "You're Muriel's roommate! They know you like her. It has to be just us two."

"Oh. Right." Ariadne stared at the carpet. "I suppose I can see what you mean."

"That's not so bad, is it?" I stood up beside her. "I mean, you think it's a terrible plan and here's me telling you that you don't have to get involved!"

She gave me a weak smile in response. "I suppose that's true. But what if you get hurt? What if you lose your memories too?"

I glanced back at Ivy, who was starting to look worried. I had to convince both of them that this plan would work. "We'll be together, we can look out for each other. She won't hurt us." I gulped, suddenly picturing the wound on Muriel's head. *No, don't think about that.* "And besides, she'll just think we've come to join her scary gang!

"Or at least that we're interested," Ivy said. "Have you noticed how spellbound all the girls around her look? If we act like that, she'll definitely fall for it."

"Don't fret, Ariadne," I said. "Ebony's no Miss Fox. We're going to get to the bottom of this before she even knows what's going on."

"All right," Ariadne sighed. "I suppose I shall go back to my room, then. Perhaps I can do Muriel's prep work for her. Just promise me you'll be safe!"

I gave her a hug. "It'll be easy," I told her. "You'll see."

Our first task was to track Ebony down, which wasn't easy on a Saturday. Many people trekked to the nearby village, to buy sweets or post letters. But it was a chilly day and you couldn't see very far in front of your face in the fog. Besides, Ebony didn't seem the type.

"Unless she's gone to buy frogs' legs and bat wings," I joked, as Ivy jabbed me in the ribs.

We eventually spotted her and her gang, hidden in a far corner of the library. As soon as I saw them, I grabbed Ivy and pulled her back round the bookcase so that we were out of their view.

"Okay," I said. "We need to look starstruck, remember?"

"She's going to see right through this," Ivy hissed, her brow furrowed with worry.

"She is if you don't believe in it! Now come on – summon your inner actress." I had always rather fancied being on the stage. I was even convinced Ivy and I would make it on to the silver screen one day, as famous ballet-dancing twins. But we had no chance if we couldn't even fool a few teenage girls.

We rounded the corner again. Ebony was sitting in the centre of the group and their heads were all bent together, their hair hanging forward and mixing. Blonde, black, brown, red. I wandered nearer, hands in my pockets, as if I were just looking for a book.

They must have heard me because one of them suddenly looked up and jumped to her feet. I recognised the frizzy brown hair.

"Sit down, Clarissa," Ebony said, sounding a little weary. I could see her now. She had a book spread open at her feet, filled with strange drawings.

*Clarissa?* I knew the girl's name was Agatha, but this wasn't the time to mention it.

"What are you reading there?" I asked, gesturing at the strange book. "Looks interesting."

"Ah," said Ebony. Her stormy eyes stared up at me and I had the uncomfortable feeling that she was looking right into my soul. "Are you interested in forbidden knowledge now, Scarlet?"

I shrugged. Couldn't look too enthusiastic.

Ivy knelt down beside the group. "Can you read all that?" The book was full of odd symbols and a language I couldn't understand.

From the look on Ebony's face, her desire to tell us to go away was conflicting with her desire to show off. "Oh yes," she said. Her wry smile was back. "It's easy, if you know how. But that doesn't mean you *should*."

"Why not?" I asked, kneeling down beside them. I nudged my way into a space beside Clarissa/Agatha.

"*It's dark magic*," one of the girls hissed, so quietly that I wasn't sure if I'd even really heard it.

Ebony waved a hand and the group's eyes followed it the way they did her every movement. "It's complex," she started. "Deep. Only those who truly understand the darkness can even comprehend it. These girls have merely stepped up to the edge."

"And us?" Ivy asked.

Ebony went silent for a second as a third former walked past us, only to grab a book and hurry away. "You are on the outside. It isn't real to you yet. But it will be."

"And what about you?" I asked. The metaphor was

swirling in my brain. It sounded like nonsense, but it was oddly mesmerising.

She smiled and slammed the book shut. Clouds of dust puffed outwards from its pages. "I am the darkness," she said.

## Chapter Twenty

### IVY

We sat with Ebony and her crowd of admirers for some time. To my surprise, she wasn't talking about cursing people or turning anyone into frogs, but was instead telling stories of her life back in Scotland. She spoke about living by a lake that she swore contained kelpies – grey ponies with manes that dripped with green water, who would entice you to ride on their backs, before pulling you down into the deep. The girls were hanging on her every word. It was almost a kind of magic in itself.

She spoke about how they celebrated All Hallows' Eve with carved turnip lanterns grinning fiendishly in the night, going from door to door with painted faces and tattered clothes, listening for spirits in the wind. "It's my favourite time of year," she said with a sigh. Her eyes had a faraway glitter to them. She obviously missed Scotland.

"Perhaps we could bring some of your traditions here," I suggested. It was the first time anyone had spoken in a long while, and her eyes snapped over to me in surprise.

I thought for a moment that she might shout at me, but instead she just said "That's an idea," and smiled.

The dinner bell rang and Scarlet gazed up at the ceiling – her turn to look surprised. I realised she'd been caught up in Ebony's words as well, and the time had flown.

My thoughts went to Ariadne. We'd left her for so long. Would she be all right? Would she go to see Muriel again? The sudden guilt rose hotly inside me. At least we could go and find her at dinner.

We stood up and I shook out my legs, which ached from sitting on the library floor.

"WHEN SHALL WE MEET AGAIN?" Agatha asked in a shrill voice.

Ebony gave her a look.

"Sorry," Agatha whispered.

"Soon," Ebony said finally. "Later. I have more to teach you."

Scarlet still seemed a little hypnotised as we walked to dinner. "She has quite a way with words, doesn't she?" she said.

I nodded. Some of them were still echoing in my head. I looked out of the tall windows at the fog outside that seemed to be eating the world. I imagined the Rookwood lake, with its grasping skeleton trees, filled with misty horses just waiting to drag you down. I couldn't help but shudder.

"So what do you think?" my twin asked after a quick glance over her shoulder. "Do we keep following her around?"

"I think we have to, if we want to find out more."

No one had said a word about Muriel, nor about curses. Whether that was just because we'd been present, I didn't know.

"What a strange afternoon," Scarlet said.

We found Ariadne standing with Rose in the dinner queue. I was pleased to see that she wasn't alone.

"I was just telling Rose about the plan!" she whispered. "Did you find anything out?"

"Not really," Scarlet said as she picked up her tray. "We wormed our way in, but she just talked a lot about Scotland."

Ariadne wrinkled her nose, looking a little confused while Rose just shrugged.

"We have to go back tonight," I said. "She invited us. I think."

"Well, be careful," Ariadne replied. "You never know what she might be up to."

That was true, for certain. Ebony was unpredictable.

"How are you getting on, Rose?"

Rose smiled. She reached the hatch and held her tray up while one of the dinner ladies ladled out a big helping of stew. "Well, I like the food at least," she said quietly.

"Really? This slop?" Scarlet asked. The dinner lady glared at her.

"It's better than nothing," Rose replied. I supposed it was. Rose had lived on asylum food, and then on the scraps that Violet could scrounge for her. Before that... I had no idea. I suddenly felt a little more grateful as I was handed my dinner.

We walked past Ebony and her group, and for a

moment I wondered if we ought to go and sit down with them. Weren't we trying to convince her that we were as enamoured with her as all the other girls were?

But I saw the look on Ariadne's face and immediately realised it was a bad idea.

She was afraid of Ebony. She was angry too. I knew that because I felt the same way, but I was trying to convince myself to keep going with the plan anyway.

As we approached our seats, my hand brushed my pocket and I realised there was something in there. *That's odd*, I thought. I put my tray down on the table and fished about for whatever it was, pulling out a folded piece of paper. When I opened it, it read:

> *TOP SECRET MEETING*
> *MIDNIGHT*
> *IN THE ENGLISH CLASSROOM*

I looked back at the group surrounding Ebony. This had to be from one of them, but none of them was looking up or meeting my eye. Still, if it was, it meant we'd been accepted into their circle.

I tapped Scarlet on the shoulder and held the note in front of her eyes. She blinked at it and then snatched it from me. "We have to go!"

"What if it's a trap?" I hissed.

"Then at least that proves something! We'll have caught Ebony in the evil act!"

"What if *we* get caught?"

"We never do! Sneaking around at night is our forté, remember?" She winked.

Scarlet sat down then and I hastily tucked the note away again. She was right. We had to investigate. It was a risk I was willing to take, especially since we'd never been caught out of our rooms at night before. At least, not by teachers.

Ariadne hadn't noticed what was going on. She was chatting away to Rose and smiling. It was nice to see her looking happy again. I didn't want to bring up the note and spoil it.

That night, Scarlet and I pretended to get ready for bed. We showed Matron our freshly brushed teeth and waved her goodnight as she made sure our lights were out for the third time. We didn't show her that we were wearing dresses underneath our bedsheets.

Scarlet had insisted that we had to dress for the occasion, whatever the occasion was, so we were both wearing simple black dresses that were one of the few such things we owned. I supposed she was right –

Ebony liked to look the part, so perhaps we should be trying to fit in with her.

No matter how I tried, though, I couldn't shake off my guilty feeling about not telling Ariadne what was going on. Especially since she had gone back to her room alone, with Muriel still in the sick bay.

I had to admit, I was just a tiny bit excited to be going. I'd had a glimpse of how Ebony was entrancing all the younger students and I wanted to know more.

When midnight struck, we slipped out of our room and into the corridor. We saw a few other girls disappearing down the stairwell ahead of us. I looked at Scarlet and took a deep breath.

"Are we really doing this?" I whispered.

She nodded at me and grinned in the moonlight. Scarlet believed more in Ebony's magic than I did, and whether it frightened her I didn't know, but she certainly seemed keen to get up close to it.

We sneaked downstairs and along the darkened hallway until we found the door to the English classroom. I knew some of the classroom doors were locked at night, like those to the science labs where there were dangerous chemicals and strange things in jars. But this one was wide open – I wondered if it was kept open because it didn't contain anything more valuable or dangerous than pencils and books, or whether Ebony had somehow stolen a key.

Scarlet and I peered in, and the sight that met our eyes was a strange one. The desks had all been pushed to the side, with the exception of the teacher's long one, which had been moved to the middle. There was a wide circle of candles round it, burning brightly, dripping wax on to the floor.

Ebony and most of her followers were standing in a group near the blackboard. I looked up at it and gasped. It was covered in strange diagrams and drawings, similar to those that Ebony had been looking at in the old book. They were all written up in white chalk, a stark contrast to the black surround. I assumed Ebony must have been responsible for those too, but her hands were clean and her dress was immaculately black. So much so that she almost blended into the night.

When she caught sight of us, she smiled, but said nothing. She was always smiling and it was hard to read – though I had to say, this one seemed triumphant. As if she had been convinced she would draw us into her world and now she had done it.

I hovered anxiously by the doorway while Scarlet walked towards the group. They were all whispering amongst themselves, but they looked up when she appeared beside them.

"Welcome," Ebony said finally.

Agatha (or was it Clarissa?) was the last to slip in through the door. She pulled it shut behind her and grinned excitedly. "Are we going to do more magic?"

"Wait and see," Ebony said. I stepped closer. Her eyes sparkled in the candlelight. "First, we need a volunteer."

I grabbed my twin's hand to stop her raising it. We needed to observe what was going on, not become the victim if this was some sort of trap.

Several of the other girls raised their hands, while others just looked around, biting their lips.

Ebony scanned the room before pointing to a smaller girl who I had barely noticed. I realised that it was another of Ariadne's old roommates – Mary. Mary was shy with bottle-thick glasses and a perpetually frightened expression. She almost faded into the background, but this time, somehow, she had stood out.

And as I thought that, I realised it had been me who had always faded into the background in the past. I didn't feel that way any more, though, which surprised me.

Mary pointed at herself and mouthed *Me?* Ebony nodded.

"Are you ready?" Ebony asked.

"For... for what?" Mary stuttered.

Ebony walked into the centre of the candles and spread her arms wide. "Are you ready..." she whispered. "...to take a trip to the Other Side?"

## Chapter Twenty-one

## SCARLET

I had to admit it, Ebony had caught me in her spell. I was becoming fascinated. After what I had seen her do with the card trick, and the curse in the cemetery... anything seemed possible.

We watched as Ebony lightly took Mary's hand and led her into the candlelit circle. "You must lie down first." Ebony used the same commanding, eerie tone of voice that she'd used when reading lines from *Macbeth*.

Mary was shaking a little, but she did as she was

told and lay down on the classroom floor.

Ebony put a finger to her lips and then began to whisper in that strange language. Mary was blinking up at her, wide-eyed, until Ebony reached down and took off her glasses, putting them aside. Now Mary squeezed her eyes tightly shut.

At this point, I couldn't guess what was about to happen. I hoped this wasn't a curse – I didn't want anything to happen to Mary, the way it had happened to Muriel. If it was, I'd have to stop Ebony. And I didn't think she'd take kindly to me getting in her way a second time.

"All of you," Ebony said, suddenly speaking English again. "Come round, in a circle. Kneel down."

With a wary glance at Ivy, I stepped forward and so did the rest of the girls. We knelt all round Mary, the floor cold beneath our knees, backs warm from the heat of the candles.

"Now," said Ebony. "We are going to send her soul to the Other Side."

Everyone gasped.

"Only briefly," Ebony reassured them, though a reassurance from someone dressed like the inside of Dracula's coffin was hardly reassuring at all. "This is not a curse. It's a ritual. Or perhaps it is more of a journey. Now first we will try to lift her, using only our fingertips."

She placed her fingertips under Mary and looked at the rest of us until we did the same. Then she nodded slowly, three times, and everyone tried to lift Mary up. Nothing happened.

I raised my eyebrows at my twin. What was this supposed to achieve, exactly? Of course we couldn't lift her with our fingertips. And what did that have to do with magic?

But what came next was when things *really* started to get strange.

"I'm going to say the phrases," Ebony said, her voice quiet so that we had to strain to listen. "And then we will all chant them. Three times. That's important. And..." She took a deep breath. "Whatever you do, don't look down."

"What...?" I started, but she silenced me with a look. I turned my eyes to the ceiling, alongside everyone else. Then she raised a hand, apparently signalling that she was about to start.

"She's looking ill," Ebony whispered.

I wondered for a second if that was just an observation, since Mary had gone rather pale when I'd last been looking at her. But I knew Ebony was staring upwards, just as the rest of us were. It was the start of the chant.

"*She's looking ill,*" we chanted. "*She's looking ill. She's looking ill.*"

"She's looking worse," Ebony said this time.

"*She's looking worse. She's looking worse. She's looking worse.*" The chant grew. Our voices shook.

"She is dying."

There was hardly room for shock or worry at this point. I felt swept away by the tide of the chant. "*She is dying. She is dying. She is dying.*"

There was a pause and then Ebony spoke again, more slowly this time. "She is dead."

I gulped. "*She is dead. She is dead. She is dead.*"

*Don't look down*, I kept telling myself. Suddenly, just the thought of looking down became frightening. Our fingertips were still under Mary's body... under Mary. Could I hear her breathing? I wasn't sure, not with the frightened breaths of the others mixed in.

"Her spirit has gone," Ebony recited. "But soon she will return. For now, she is light. Repeat after me again: light as a feather, stiff as a board."

"*Light as a feather, stiff as a board. Light as a feather, stiff as a board. Light as a feather, stiff as a board.*"

I could have sworn that I felt Mary go stiff, that perhaps she felt a little lighter, but it was hard to say.

All I could feel for certain was the cotton of her dress on my fingertips and the weight of her lying on the floor. I kept my eyes up and hoped Ivy was doing the same.

"Now we may lift her," said Ebony. "On three. One. Two. Three."

And suddenly, we were lifting Mary. Like she weighed nothing. Just our fingertips, lifting her high in the air, almost up to our heads.

*Light as a feather. Stiff as a board.*

It *felt* like magic.

Ebony's voice rang out again, a little louder this time. "Her spirit will return. We must lower her. Don't look down."

So with great care, we lowered her back to the floor. A shooting pain went down my neck, but I ignored it. I didn't want to look down.

Once Mary was back on the ground, there were a few moments of silence, of waiting. I almost wanted to scream.

"She's coming back to us," Ebony whispered. "She is here. Mary, open your eyes. Now we may look."

We all looked down and I was strangely relieved to see that Mary was there, alive and well, blinking in the candlelight.

"I can't believe that just happened," one of the other

girls whispered. I knew how she felt. Things were getting curiouser and curiouser.

"You have been to the Other Side, Mary," Ebony said simply. "It's an important magical journey. May it bring you great wisdom."

Mary shuddered a little before stretching out her arms and sitting up. She groped around for her glasses and Ebony placed them back on her face.

"What did you see?" Agatha asked, breathless.

"I saw... *darkness*," Mary said.

And then she fainted.

A few moments later, Mary had been revived by being non-magically (but gently) slapped round the face by Agatha.

"Are you all right?" Ivy asked her as she lay there, looking dazed.

"I... yes... I'm fine..." Mary sat up again, spinning a little. "It was just a little scary, that's all."

"Did you feel anything?" One of the other girls asked.

Mary shook her head.

"See anything?"

Mary's face was white and drawn. "I think I'd like to go to bed now," she said.

I noticed that Ebony was beginning to look a bit

unhappy, presumably because things were no longer as mystical as they had been. "No more questions, Xenia," she said.

Even with the strange atmosphere, I had to stifle a laugh at that. I didn't know the girl, who had freckles and pigtails, but I was fairly certain that no one at Rookwood was called "Xenia".

Ebony took charge again as Mary got to her feet. "It is done. Now we must move on to the next stage."

*Next stage?* I had no idea what she was talking about.

"It worked," I heard Agatha whispering beside me. "We lifted her. And the curse worked too... It's *real...*"

"Will there be more curses?" the girl who was definitely not named Xenia asked. She seemed oddly excited about the idea.

"Perhaps," said Ebony. "But we cannot curse the same person twice. Though perhaps –" and she looked directly at me and Ivy as she said this – "you can curse someone close to them."

A shiver went down my spine. If she moved on from Muriel... then who was next? Ariadne? Us? Where would it end?

"But that's for another time," Ebony continued, and I wondered if I was right to read into it that she was planning something for when we weren't around. Suddenly, the spell that surrounded Ebony and made her so enchanting seemed to slip. *Magic isn't magic if you use it to hurt people*, I thought. *Then it's just malice*. Now I was wishing I was back in bed and away from all of this as well.

"We have to go," I said, forcing a yawn. "It's really late."

Ivy nodded in agreement.

Mary was leaning on Agatha, looking wobbly and exhausted.

Ebony folded her arms and then she nodded too. "You'll all be told the time of the next meeting. You may go."

The rebellious spark that had been kindled again in my chest made me want to challenge her then, to ask who made her the boss of everybody, but I thought I already knew the answer.

She did.

Everyone began to filter out of the classroom, slowly and silently. I grabbed Ivy's arm as we left, wanting to wait a moment, to see what Ebony did next. But all that happened was that she blew out the candles one by one, and then stood there alone in the sliver of moonlight that remained. She was just staring out of the windows.

I couldn't read her expression.

"Come on," Ivy whispered. "We need to get back."

The other girls had all gone on ahead, and for the moment we were alone in the hallway when a sudden movement and a dark shape crossed our path. Ivy gasped, but as the thing moved again, I realised it was the flicking of a tail. It was the black cat! It slunk away into the shadows.

I didn't know where it came from, but there in the darkness, I had a flash of my old self. That horrible feeling of being trapped, of walls pushing in on me. Of asylum whispers and clacking heels. My breathing sped up and my heart pounded.

Ivy sensed something was wrong and she took my hand. "Together," she said.

I squeezed her hand back, tighter. No matter what was in those corridors, whether it was dark magic or ghosts or worse – Miss Fox – we were together. I told myself that over and over again as we walked. Whatever happened, we could face it.

But then we climbed the stairs and walked back to our room...

Only to find Matron standing right outside.

## Chapter Twenty-two

## IVY

I felt my heart skip a beat. Matron was standing right outside *our* door. Matron who slept like a log, who never left her room past ten o'clock. Matron who had told us we were on thin ice.

And she had seen us.

There was no use in running away now. There was nowhere to hide. In fact, I knew running away would just make things worse. Then we would definitely look as if we were up to something.

Matron held out her torch and we both shielded

our eyes from the beam.

"Matron?" Scarlet asked, her voice laced with innocence.

"Girls?" she answered, pointing the torch back down and keeping her voice low. "What are you doing out of your room?"

I fumbled for an explanation. I was about to say that we were going to the lavatories, which would be the easiest excuse, but then I looked down at myself and realised that both of us were wearing dresses and not nightgowns.

Scarlet was faster than me. "We saw the cat again, Miss!"

"What?" Matron screwed up her face, her eyes wrinkling at the corners.

"You know, the cat? That we told you about?" Scarlet gestured at her. "We saw it. It's running around the school. We thought we'd try and catch it."

"Because... because cats aren't allowed," I added, silently thinking that this was the worst excuse we had ever come up with.

"And that's why you're dressed?" Matron asked. "Girls, honestly, I—"

"It's true," Scarlet said. "I swear." I was fairly certain she had crossed her fingers behind her back.

"Well," said Matron, putting her hands on her hips. "I think that excuse is rather stretching it. Now, are you going to tell me why you're *really—*"

She didn't get to finish that sentence because something slipped out of the darkness and began curling its tail round her leg.

A look of horror descended over Matron's face and her eyes went slowly downwards until they came to rest, finally, on the black cat.

"Oh," she said.

"See," said Scarlet, who I thought was about to burst with self-righteousness. "I told you so."

The cat gave a dissatisfied meow, obviously realising we weren't about to feed it, and trotted away in the direction of Ebony's room.

Scarlet said nothing this time and just raised her arms in a gesture that expressed rather a lot.

Matron gaped after the cat. "Just go to bed, girls," she said.

We shut our bedroom door behind us.

"Ha!" Scarlet laughed as she pulled her dress over her head and changed back into her nightgown. "Matron has to believe us now! We have a smoking cat!"

I gave her a look and then began getting changed myself. "True," I said with a yawn. "But weren't we trying to stay on Ebony's good side? If she gets into trouble over the cat, then..."

"Then how will she know it was us?" Scarlet asked. She threw herself on to her bed with a thud. "Nobody saw anything. She'll just think Matron spotted the cat herself."

I didn't feel quite so sure. Ebony always seemed as though she was watching everything, all the time. I knew it was ridiculous, but I couldn't get the idea out of my head that she was one step ahead of us. Especially after what we had just witnessed in the classroom.

*It had to be a trick.*

Didn't it?

I climbed into bed and shut my eyes, exhausted. But all I could see on the back of my eyelids was Mary, blank-faced like a death mask, being lifted into oblivion.

I jumped awake as the morning bell rang, throwing back the covers. I couldn't get them off fast enough. I'd been dreaming that it was a sea of black spiders.

As I got my breath back, the real world seeped in. Scarlet was looking at me strangely. "Nightmare?"

I nodded. I hadn't had nightmares in quite a long time, until Ebony had come to the school. I shuddered at the thought.

We hurried down to breakfast. We left the queue with our trays of porridge and milky tea. Something felt a little off, but I wasn't sure what. I wondered if I was still simply feeling strange after the night before.

We headed off to meet Ariadne. I wanted to talk about what we'd seen the previous night, but... it didn't seem right. Especially not when I saw her sitting next to a bandaged Muriel, the two of them chatting away happily.

I swallowed my guilt and smiled at the two of them. "Good morning," I said as I sat down with my tray.

"Morning!" Ariadne said cheerfully. "Muriel's been allowed to come and sit with me. I'm to be her chaperone while she's recovering."

"Do you get a badge?" Scarlet teased, sitting down beside me. "I'm glad you're feeling better, Muriel."

Ariadne grinned at her. Muriel, on the other hand, had a somewhat glazed expression.

"Thank you S... S..." she tried.

"Scarlet," Scarlet said.

"Sorry," Muriel said. She gave Ariadne a desperate glance.

Ariadne put her hand on the tall girl's shoulder. "It's okay, Muriel." She turned to us. "She's not feeling quite right yet. I think some of her memory is still jumbled."

Muriel smiled then, but that blank look didn't leave her eyes. She swayed a little in her seat.

I had to admit, the sight of her made me feel a little queasy. It wasn't just that I remembered what her wound had looked like under the bandage, or that I kept thinking Ebony might have been the one to do this to her. It was the faraway gaze she had in her eyes now. That was somehow the worst part.

*I don't believe in curses*, I told myself.

But I didn't like having to tell myself that. It was what Ebony wanted, surely? She wanted us to believe that she had the power to curse people. But why?

"Did you have a good night?" Ariadne asked.

I gulped my mouthful of porridge. What did she mean? Did she know about us meeting Ebony in the classroom?

"Without any nightmares, I mean," Ariadne said. "Ghastly things. I had one. I dreamt that Father had bought me a new pony, but it was bad-tempered and kept throwing me off. And then it turned into a bat and flew away." She stuck her tongue out in disgust.

I breathed a quiet sigh of relief. "Actually I did

have one." I glanced at Muriel, who wasn't looking at anything. "But it was a bit horrible. I won't talk about it over food." Hopefully that would prevent any further questioning.

When we'd finished our breakfast, the Sunday teachers began ushering everyone out in the direction of the chapel for the day's service.

"Come on," Ariadne said gently to Muriel. "Time for chapel."

A strange expression crossed Muriel's face. "I can't," she said. "I have to..." Her eyes darted back and forth across the hall, as if she were surrounded by people. Suddenly, and with surprising speed, she jumped up and ran out of the hall.

"Well, that was odd," Scarlet said. "She looks like she could do with a priest, to be quite honest."

Ariadne picked nervously at the sleeve of her uniform. "She'll be all right, won't she?"

I took my friend's hand. "I'm sure she will. We'll find her afterwards." Those were the words I spoke aloud, but inside my head, the word CURSED was echoing. But Ariadne didn't need to be any more worried than she already was, so I kept quiet.

*

At the end of the service, we shuffled out of our seats. I couldn't help the smile twitching on my face as my knee brushed the kneeling mats, remembering how Scarlet had hidden a clue inside one of them not so long ago.

The inside of Rookwood's chapel was fairly plain, but there were a few elements that stood out amid all the bare stone and wood. The kneeling mats were one such thing, having been sewn by students over the years, many of them bearing brightly coloured scenes. Another was the gold of the candlesticks and the altar, and the stained-glass windows that spilt amber light over the rows of pews.

And in the far corner, behind a carved wooden screen with a door that was always locked, there was a tomb. We'd peeked in once, one Sunday, and saw it was protecting a stone effigy of some great Lord of the Manor. He was lying at rest in a cavity in the wall, his arms crossed neatly and his head lying on a stone pillow, which didn't seem the most comfortable thing to lie on for eternity.

But what stood out to me that morning in the chapel was none of those things. It was the fact that Ebony wasn't there.

As we stood in a huddle among the gaggle of girls

waiting to leave the church, and with Ariadne chatting to Dot Campbell, I nudged Scarlet. "Have you seen Ebony today?"

"No," Scarlet said, frowning.

It probably wouldn't usually be noticeable in a school full of girls if just one were missing. But Ebony was such a big presence that her absence left a hole in the world. I realised that was why something had felt strange at breakfast. There had been no Ebony, no group of girls crowded round her and hanging on her every word.

"Do you think it's because of the cat?" Scarlet whispered as we moved forward slowly, everyone trying to filter out through the chapel door all at once, causing a jam.

"Maybe." If Matron had followed the cat to Ebony's room and realised that what we'd told her was the truth, then Ebony would be in *big* trouble. And I didn't think I wanted to be present when that happened.

Once we'd got inside the school and the crowd was somewhat dispersed, I finally spotted Ebony standing outside Mrs Knight's office with a group of her friends. As we got nearer, Ebony's eyes flashed over to us. I felt my palms begin to sweat. Was she in trouble? Did she know that we'd told on her?

She was explaining something to the other girls. "...said I can keep him in my room for now, but that he has to go back in the holidays."

Scarlet, apparently, decided to brave the question. "What happened?"

The whole group turned round, almost at the same time. It made my skin prickle, and I realised it was reminiscent of how the ballet girls had looked at me on the first day of school. As though I was an outsider.

But after a few seconds, the strange tension melted away and Ebony began to speak again. "Matron discovered my cat. I think someone must have told her."

I bit my cheek on the inside, hoping no one would notice.

"Are you sure the cat didn't just go wandering around the school of its own accord?" Scarlet suggested. She had a point.

"I don't know," said Ebony, waving her arm as if wiping the suggestion away. "But he's important. I need him."

Agatha leant over to us. "Midnight is Ebony's *familiar*," she hissed. Mary stood beside her, pale and silent.

"I..." I started. "Midnight? Is that the cat's name?"

Ebony nodded slowly. "He's important," she repeated. "And someone is responsible for trying to get me into trouble." She folded her arms and her stormy eyes stared down the hallway without blinking.

I followed her gaze and saw where she was looking. Ariadne was standing there, talking to Muriel. She must have tracked her down again.

Ebony didn't move a muscle and her voice came out low and quiet. "People who stand in my way soon find themselves on an uneven footing. And who knows where they might fall."

With that, she turned and swooped away, her skirt sweeping out behind her.

## Chapter Twenty-three

## SCARLET

"If she touches a hair on Ariadne's head, I'll make her wish she'd never been born," I hissed, my nails digging into my palms.

"Shush," Ivy silenced me. "Wait until we're back in our room. Then it'll be safe to talk."

My feet hammered on the stairs as I ran up. I should have listened to Ivy, I knew, but the words just kept on coming out. "Who does she think she is? It doesn't sound like she even got into trouble over the cat. A cat! In her room! That's against all the rules and yet they've said she can keep it till the holidays!"

"I know, I know," Ivy panted as she caught up with me. "Well, it's Mrs Knight. She's not really very strict, is she?"

"I thought she was strict *now*. She said she'd kick us out!" I threw my hands up in disgust. "No, it's Ebony. She's doing something. She's got this... this *thing* over people."

"Even us," Ivy said quietly.

I opened my mouth to protest, but she was right. As much as I despised Ebony and what she was doing, I was fascinated by it. With everything that I'd witnessed, I felt sure she had some sort of control. But how was that even possible? In the end, I said nothing.

Which was probably a good thing because there was a ton of girls at the top of the stairs, all milling around their rooms, as often happened on a Sunday. Any one of them could have been a friend of Ebony's. Ivy was right *again* (and it pained me to admit that). I needed to shut up.

But as soon as we'd shoved through the crowd and made it to our room, I started again. "I'm serious; if she does anything to Ariadne..." I trailed off, letting my silence speak volumes.

"Of course," Ivy said suddenly. I looked up at her in surprise. "You think I wouldn't defend Ariadne too?" She asked. "Of course I would!"

"Probably not in quite the same way I'm thinking," I said, kicking at my bed frame, making the whole thing shudder.

"Well, no," she admitted. "And you shouldn't be thinking that either. You're going to get us all thrown out, for one thing."

I screwed up my face. "All right, no more fighting. I promise."

She put her hands on her hips and gave me an expression that said she didn't believe me.

"I promise!" I said again. "And I promised about promises, remember? I'm not crossing my fingers behind my back either!" I waved my hands at her.

"Perhaps rather than revenge, we ought to try and prevent her from doing anything to Ariadne in the first place," she suggested.

"We can try," I said, rubbing my hand through my hair. The mist outside had turned it frizzy. "But we can't follow her at all times. And who knows what she can do. She could be watching us right now—"

I was interrupted by a knock at the door, which made both of us jump.

With a glance back at me, Ivy cautiously went to open it.

But it was only Ariadne and Muriel, who were laughing about something together.

I felt an uncertain knot of jealousy in my stomach at the sight.

"Yes?" I said, perhaps a bit more snappily than I meant it.

Ariadne grinned at me and then pointed at Muriel. "I found her!"

"I can see that," I said. "How come you ran away earlier?" I asked Muriel, having to tip my neck up a little to direct the question at her face.

"Sorry." She stared down at her feet for a moment. "It's just that I'm not feeling myself at the moment. I thought it would be crowded in the chapel, and loud with all the singing." She winced and put her hand to her ear, which was half covered by the bandages that were wrapped round her head.

I sighed, and felt the knot inside me loosen a little as I began to feel sorry for her again. She'd been badly hurt and had lost her memory. I had to remember that.

"Can we come in?" Ariadne asked, and I realised then that I was blocking the doorway.

"Oh, right, yes!" I moved out of the way and the two

of them came in and sat on my bed.

Ariadne looked over at me once I'd shut the door. "Anything to report? About you-know-who?"

Ivy's eyes had gone wide. She wasn't quite shaking her head, but I could see the suggestion there.

I sighed, perhaps a bit too loudly. "Not really."

I had to admit, it wasn't just Ivy's reluctance to talk about all this in front of Ariadne and Muriel that was making me keep quiet. What we'd witnessed the night before had been so strange, so out of this world, that it felt like some sort of bad dream. The words just wouldn't form properly in my brain.

"Oh," said Ariadne. "I thought she'd be up to *all* sorts. I can't have been worrying myself silly about you spying on her for nothing."

"Well..." There was something I wanted to say, despite Ivy's face silently protesting. I couldn't let it go unsaid, and I was sure I could do it while leaving out the gory details. "Earlier, we overhead Ebony talking outside Mrs Knight's office. You know how we tried to tell Matron about her cat before?"

Ariadne and Muriel nodded, Muriel's brow furrowing slightly.

"Well, it seems that someone finally saw the cat and tried to get Ebony into hot water. But unfortunately

Mrs Knight went soft on her, as usual."

Ariadne's jaw dropped open. "She got away with keeping a cat in her room?"

"Indeed." Ivy's expression relaxed a little, now that she realised I wasn't about to terrify them both to death. "She just has to take it home at the end of term."

The other girls muttered in disbelief. People didn't often get off lightly at Rookwood.

"*But where does it go to the lavatory?*" Ariadne whispered.

"Outside, hopefully," said Ivy.

I knew I had to steer us to the point eventually, but I was approaching it carefully, like a mouse sneaking up to a crocodile. "That's not the end of it, though. She started talking about her cat being 'important' and wanting to pin the blame on whoever spilt the beans. And... I think she thinks that's you."

"Me?" both of them said at the same time.

Ivy winced. "Both of you, we think. That's what it looked like, anyway."

Ariadne gasped and her eyes darted around as if Ebony were about to burst in through the door at any moment. Muriel was gripping handfuls of my bedsheets.

"But it wasn't us!" Ariadne protested.

"I know," I said, though I wasn't going to say how I knew. "But we have to stop her from targeting you." I looked at Muriel's frantic expression, at her lopsided bandages. "Again, in your case."

"She can't keep up this horrible vendetta." Ivy got to her feet. "Can she?"

"At the moment," I muttered darkly, "it seems like she can do whatever she pleases."

I couldn't help but notice Ebony's eyes following Ariadne and Muriel round the room at breakfast on Monday. She was planning something, that much was clear.

Muriel seemed to be clinging to Ariadne like a limpet now. I didn't know if it was as a result of her head injury, or whatever *curse* had led to it... or perhaps even just that she was nervous of what Ebony might do next. But now they were going everywhere together. Where they'd both been apprehensive before, it was like the gates had been opened and they were talking like old friends. It made me feel strange, and a little envious.

Ariadne yawned as she talked and there were shadows under her eyes, but she seemed contented.

"Aren't you bothered about what Ebony might do to you?" I whispered to her when Muriel had gone up to clean her plate. "She's been staring at you all morning. Something's up."

Ariadne bit her lip. "A little," she whispered back. "But I have to keep up appearances for Muriel. I don't want her to get too upset about it all. It's probably nothing." She winced. "Isn't it?"

Part of me wanted to tell her exactly what we'd witnessed Ebony doing, with her bizarre candlelit ritual in the dark classroom. But just as Ariadne didn't want to upset Muriel, I didn't want to upset her.

Instead, I'd written an account of the whole thing in my diary the night before. Pouring things on to the pages had a funny effect – they went from being something that haunted your mind to just being words on paper. You could crumple them up and throw them away if you wanted to (which I sometimes, but rarely, did). It made them less pressing, somehow.

I realised, as I was thinking all this, that I hadn't said a word in response to Ariadne's question. I was just staring blankly at her.

"Oh," she said in a very small voice, and looked away.

*Oops.*

*

The first lesson on a Monday morning was Latin, which I thought should be some sort of crime.

Miss Simons, the teacher with unusually long red hair, had apparently been persuaded to return after having a very public confrontation with Miss Danver the year before. She was still twitchy and nervous, and flinched whenever you handed her a piece of paper.

We were halfway through the lesson. I was sitting next to Ivy on my left and Rose on my right, who I was surprised to see had been asked to do Latin.

"Can you manage it?" I'd asked.

She wrote something down on a note in tiny handwriting, almost a whisper, and passed it across to me.

I read it and screwed up my face. "What?"

She gestured to me to hand the note back, scribbled another line below it, and then returned it.

*It means 'I am good at writing Latin'. I had a governess when I was young. I quite like it.*

I giggled and wrote back to her.

*Ergo... I am rubbish at reading Latin!*

Miss Simons looked up from her desk, then shot to her feet, pointing a quivering arm at us. "No notes! I will not have anyone passing notes in my class! Ever!"

Rose went wide-eyed and held on to her desk, as if it were about to float away. I supposed she'd never been in trouble before. I tried not to laugh.

"Well, at least they're awake, Miss," Penny called out.

"What?" Miss Simons snapped her head back and forth like an owl. I turned too, trying to see what Penny was talking about.

And I noticed then that Ariadne was fast asleep on her desk – and not only that, but the contents of her inkwell were rapidly spreading in a deep blue stain all over the classroom floor.

## Chapter Twenty-four

### IVY

M iss Simons made Ariadne stay behind after
the lesson to clean everything up, and she
wouldn't even let Scarlet and me stay to
help. Ariadne then missed the next lesson
and we were only able to meet up with her
at break time.

"What happened?" I asked. We were sitting outside
the school on the grass, since the sun had come out
enough to make it bearable, though there was a chill
in the air. Muriel sat beside Ariadne, tying plaits in

her own blonde hair.

"I fell asleep," Ariadne said sheepishly. "That's all." Her cheeks were red (and slightly blue).

"We know that," Scarlet said. "But why? That's not like you."

She yawned and rubbed at her skin in a futile attempt to get the ink off. "We were up rather late talking. We had some fascinating conversations."

Muriel smiled at her. "We did!"

I was surprised, but I didn't say so. I imagined they were both surprised about it too.

"Were sweets involved?" Scarlet teased.

"Naturally!" Ariadne laughed.

I was glad she was happy with her new roommate, and especially so that Muriel didn't seem to have any plans to bully her, but still... We'd kept Ariadne up late before with some of our night-time adventures and she'd always been wide awake for class the next day. She almost seemed to be fuelled by learning, no matter what the subject. Scarlet was right – it was unlike our friend not to be paying attention, let alone to fall asleep on the desk and spill her ink everywhere.

It wouldn't have been that strange on its own, but Ariadne managed to get in trouble twice more that day. In art class, she and Muriel got into trouble for passing notes. And when we met her after lessons had ended, she said she'd been sent off the hockey field for hitting someone on the leg with her stick.

"Did someone swap Ariadne with me this morning?" Scarlet asked as we went back to our room to get ready for dinner after ballet. "Suddenly she's getting in a lot of trouble."

It was only then that an odd little seed of an idea started to sprout in my mind.

*Ebony blamed Ariadne and Muriel for telling on her about the cat. She's got it in for them... So could she have put a spell on them both?*

But that was a foolish thought. I knew it as soon as the seed sprang up. Ebony couldn't make other people get into trouble when she wasn't even there! I did my best to squash it down again. Still, I felt a vague sense of unease.

A sense that wasn't improved by finding Ebony standing right outside our door.

For once, she was alone. She had her arms folded and her feet were tapping impatiently in her black boots. She was watching the other girls pass through the corridor, her eyes dragging over them.

I considered for a moment that we could just run away, but it was too late. She had spotted us.

"Ah. Just the mirror twins I was looking for," she said as we got closer. "And alone. Good."

"What's that supposed to mean?" Scarlet asked, though she kept the edge off her tone. We were still supposed to be keeping an eye on Ebony's activities.

"You keep bad company. You should be careful." She didn't say it as though it were a warning – more as fact.

Scarlet shrugged. I didn't know what to say.

"Anyway," Ebony continued, "we meet again, Saturday night. In my room, this time. Are you in?"

"At midnight?" I asked.

That gave her a momentary pause. "No, just after lights-out this time." She stared blankly away from us for a moment. "This ritual doesn't require it to be midnight. Only moonlight."

I looked at Scarlet. Her face didn't give anything away. "All right," she said finally, without much conviction.

Ebony nodded, content with the answer. "I'll be seeing you," she said.

*That* sounded more like a threat to me.

For the rest of the week, I began to notice Ariadne's strange behaviour more and more.

For one, she had forgotten to do her prep work for

English. Then, in French, she couldn't remember any of the verbs. In chemistry, she and Muriel once again got into trouble for talking over the teacher. In arithmetic, she added up all of her numbers backwards and got the wrong answers. Even Scarlet, who hated arithmetic, had got the sums right.

On Wednesday morning, she fell asleep again. On Friday, she got detention.

Twice.

Ariadne had once been expelled, through no fault of her own. She'd occasionally been in trouble for being part of whatever Scarlet and I were up to. But other than that, she was usually a model student. It was bizarre to watch this happen to her, like she was sliding down a slope and I couldn't pull her back.

I felt strangely distant from her, watching from behind glass. I only caught snippets of what she and Muriel talked about, which seemed to be a lot relating to their old school, or just what was going on around them. When we were all together, I didn't feel I could talk freely with Muriel sitting right beside us. And I hadn't told either of them anything of what we'd observed of Ebony. Whenever Ariadne asked, I just told her we hadn't learnt anything.

Which was partly true, I supposed. Ebony remained

as mysterious as ever. We were no closer to finding out where her true power lay. That was why it was all the more important that we attended whatever she was planning on Saturday.

On Friday afternoon we had ballet, as usual. It was always reassuring to descend those chilly steps into the basement studio.

Ballet practice was where I felt most at home. No matter what else changed, Scarlet and I dancing side by side always felt right. We greeted Miss Finch and Madame Zelda cheerily.

"Warm up, then, girls," Madame Zelda called, clapping her hands sharply. She pulled out an incense stick and waved it around the room, filling the air with strange smoke that tasted of spice on my tongue. It was a habit she had, although no one was quite sure why. "You may talk during this, but then you will be silent afterwards." Miss Finch sat at the piano, playing soft music that gently stirred the air.

Scarlet and I began warming up together at the *barre*.

My twin laughed at her reflection and then turned to me. "It's funny. Sometimes, when we do this, I think there are four of us."

I saw that Penny was smirking. She turned and whispered something to Nadia, although I noticed Nadia didn't reply.

"What are you looking at?" Scarlet snapped at her.

"You're going to need your reflections for friends at this rate," Penny said. "Because you won't have any others left."

I think Scarlet would have thumped her, were it not for the fact that Madame Zelda swept past at that exact second. That meant I got a chance to say something, though I kept my voice low. "What do you mean?"

"Flitworth has a new friend. Maybe she won't need you any more."

Scarlet glared at her. "You're not exactly doing brilliantly in the friendship stakes yourself, Penny, are you?"

Penny shrugged, put her leg up on the *barre* and stretched it out. "I've decided I no longer care. I like myself. I don't need to bother with the rest of you."

Scarlet made a disgruntled sound and then, to my amazement, carried on warming up. She didn't say another word to Penny.

And well, for Penny, it was a fairly mild comment. She had certainly eased up on her bullying. Normally Scarlet would have jumped at the chance to fight back over the smallest insult, whether the teachers were watching or not.

But then I realised why, because as I watched Scarlet's eyes in the mirror, I saw a reflection of myself. Penny's comments had touched a nerve. We were worried about Ariadne.

Penny leant over again, after a quick glance to check that Madame Zelda was nowhere nearby. "You ought to keep an eye on Ariadne," she said quietly, just to me. Her tone of voice had completely changed. Become more serious.

"Why?" I whispered back.

"She's got herself on the wrong side of a venomous snake. Trust me, it takes one to know one." Penny straightened and stretched her arms up to the stone ceiling. Her voice stayed quiet, and with the girls all around us and the flickering gas lamps, it almost seemed unreal, as if I wasn't really hearing her. "She's going to get hurt. And the Wonder Twins won't be able to save her this time."

Penny turned away and her words melted from my ears, but they played on over and over in my mind.

## Chapter Twenty-five

### SCARLET

Saturday came and flew by and soon I saw the sun begin to set on the horizon. That meant there were only a few more hours before we met with Ebony to find out what her next move would be.

We were sitting at dinner with Ariadne. Muriel wasn't present this time, since she'd gone to get her bandages taken off.

"She's feeling much better now," Ariadne said happily.

"I think she's still not quite right," I said. "She forgot my name again the other day." Muriel still seemed a little zombie-like to me, though she came to life more when Ariadne was around.

Ariadne shrugged and took a cautious bite of broccoli. "I think she's doing jolly well. No thanks to you-know-who. But, you know, I don't think she's done anything to us! Perhaps we're off the hook," she said hopefully.

I frowned. I had seen Ebony that morning in the corridor, holding her cat in her arms and glaring in Muriel's direction. She didn't look like someone who had let them off the hook.

And what about all the trouble that Ariadne was getting into? She'd been given a *detention* that day. Me, I'd been given a gold star for getting all my spellings right. And Miss Finch had said I'd done "excellent work" in ballet. Ariadne, on the other hand, had apparently spent her entire hockey lesson chasing the ball and not once getting it, only to finish off by whacking it up into a tree, where it balanced for a few seconds before falling on to a first year's head.

"Has Muriel been getting into trouble in class?" I blurted out, which must have seemed to come from nowhere.

Ivy looked up and blinked at me, but Ariadne didn't seem fazed by it. "A little," she admitted, poking the broccoli round her plate. "Just here and there. She forgets things." She punctuated her sentence with a yawn.

It was strange. Both Muriel and Ariadne seemed exhausted. Muriel had had a head injury, I suppose, but Ariadne hadn't. Yet this... whatever *this* might be... was happening to both of them. Both of whom were now enemies of Ebony McCloud.

But there wasn't time to ponder further. At that moment, a rumble shook the dining hall and everyone gasped. Moments later, a flash of white lightning splashed against the windows, lighting up the world. The conversation surged.

"Thunderstorm!" I said, my eyes going wide. "Nearby!"

"Calm down, girls," I heard one of the teachers call out from the other end of the hall. "It's just a storm."

I turned and looked around. The hall was filled with faces, some excited, some afraid. Outside there were grey clouds boiling and that strange electrical crackle in the air.

There was another crash and girls screamed, but one face stood out.

Ebony stood and her face lit up white, the storm clouds dancing in her eyes as she stared out of the windows. The rain began to pour. And Ebony laughed and laughed.

When everyone had finished dinner, we were ordered to return to our rooms and absolutely not to go outside for any reason. Well, they didn't have to tell me twice. The storm was so close that the windows were rattling in their frames.

I couldn't shake Ebony's laughter from my mind. As we headed for our room, the corridors ran with girls streaming for the safety of their beds. But while I could hear plenty of people muttering about the storm, just as many were saying the word "witch".

Everyone had seen her. Her reputation was spreading. But she couldn't create storm clouds, could she?

It had set my teeth on edge and raised the hairs on the back of my neck.

*You need to stay away from her*, I told myself.

But since when had Scarlet Grey ever shied away from trouble? No, we were going to her room after lights-out and that was that.

Ivy didn't exactly agree.

"I think we've done enough," she said as we got to our room. She rubbed her arms where her skin had risen into goosebumps. It had been warm earlier in the day, but the rain had brought a chill with it. "All we've done by watching her is scared ourselves silly. We're still no closer to finding out what she's really up to. Or if she's really a wi—"

There was a BANG and our window flew open, sending a gust of rain spilling into our room. I ran over and leant out, stretching for the handle with the rain splashing against my sleeve. I could see the trees swaying in the breeze and the ground far below me, and tried to push back the memories of the time when I'd been held over the rooftops, nearly to fall to my death.

"Scarlet!" Ivy gasped behind me.

Finally my fingertips grasped the metal handle and I tugged on it, pulling the window shut again.

I looked back at my twin, breathless.

She didn't have any words for a moment. "It's just weather," she said eventually.

I nodded, but the timing of it had shocked me. My heart was still beating a little too fast.

"We should go," I said as I remembered what we'd been talking about. Even as I said it, part of me was protesting. Deep down, I just wanted to climb under my warm covers and sleep until the storm faded. But I couldn't do that. "I think we might just have to face the possibility that she's put some sort of curse on Ariadne and Muriel."

Ivy sighed at me and went to sit down on her bed – although she immediately got up again, after discovering it had been rained on. "There's no such thing as curses, Scarlet! But maybe Ebony's doing *something*."

"Like what?" I asked, folding my arms across my chest.

"Perhaps..." Ivy stared at the floor. "Perhaps she's somehow persuaded the teachers to tell them off all the time. They don't tell *her* off, do they?"

"Hmm." That was a good point. "She's definitely doing something, that's for sure. I think we need to go and meet her and try to get to the bottom of it. We can't be out of the loop for this. And if we ditch Ebony now, we could be her next targets."

Ivy looked out of the window, where the glass was being battered by the rain. The room was filled with the smell of wet and cold from outside. "But what about Ariadne..." she started.

I filled in the gap in her sentence. "Ariadne will be fine. She knows we're going to investigate Ebony."

*Without her*, my brain added.

*And she's not happy about it.*

My muscles twitched as I tried to fling the thought away.

"She knows," I repeated.

Ivy didn't meet my eyes.

We were curled up with our heads on our (still slightly damp) pillows when Matron came along to check we had our lights out. I could have sworn I heard her muttering something about "blooming cats" out in the corridor as she pulled our door closed.

We waited what I hoped was long enough for her to have made it to every room. I sneaked up to our door and peered out, only to see Matron heading back into her apartment and locking the door behind her.

Ivy's eyes appeared from underneath her covers.

"Coast is clear," I whispered. "But we should give it a minute." We needed to make sure Matron was asleep and not about to go on patrol any time soon. We couldn't risk getting caught again.

The sun had set, but the rain was still pounding on the windows. The thunder had eased off, now only the occasional distant rumble.

Ivy and I slipped out of room thirteen and headed

down the corridor towards Ebony's room, where we found Agatha waiting, bouncing on her tiptoes. Down the hall I could see some of the other doors creaking open and girls peeking out. "You have to knock three times," she whispered.

With a quick glance at Ivy, I reached out and rapped on the door three times as gently as I could.

The door swung open, but there was nobody behind it.

I blinked into the darkness and then my eyes adjusted. Ebony was sitting at the back of the room, her black hair hanging down over her face as she focused on something on the floor in front of her. It was fairly dark, but there was a moon outside casting the walls with a bluish glow.

"How did she open the door?" Ivy hissed, but Agatha just gave her an impatient look – and I knew straight away that she believed it was magic.

I grabbed my twin's hand and pulled her into the room. From the looks of it, we were to be the audience. So I sat down on the carpet and others began to follow, forming a circle. I tried to peer more closely at what Ebony had laid out before her. It appeared to be a series of cards with pictures on them, but I couldn't quite make out what they were. I wondered if they were the same as those she had used in her classroom trick.

"Where's your roommate?" I asked Ebony, looking at the empty bed, the one with the teddy bear perching on it. But she completely ignored me, not even looking up. I rolled my eyes at Ivy.

Soon we were all inside – Ivy and I and Ebony's hangers-on.

"Welcome, sisters," Ebony said. "Are you ready to face your fortunes?" She leant forward and lit a candle, illuminating the cards.

They all had strange paintings on them, with names in bold type underneath like:

**THE EMPRESS**

**THE MAGICIAN**

**THE MOON**

It sparked a flicker of recognition in my memory. *Tarot.* I thought I'd seen a set at our Aunt Phoebe's house once. I think she'd thought they were for playing poker.

Ebony swept them all up in her hands with her long fingers. "It's time to deal the cards of fate. Who will go first?" she asked.

"Me," I said suddenly. I said it so fast that I wasn't sure if the words had even come from my mouth. Ivy looked at me in horror.

Ebony held out her hand and gestured for me to move in front of her. I got to my feet and walked at a snail's pace to the middle of the circle while I wondered what I was letting myself in for.

I sat down in front of her and she began to shuffle the cards. Then, very quickly, she dealt them before me in some sort of order. She reached out and tapped her nail on the card nearest to me. "The Present. Turn it over."

I did as she said.

**THE TWINS**

I laughed. *Obviously!* Ebony looked up at me sharply, shocking me into silence.

She stared into the card. "The Twins. Perhaps someone new will come into your life. Or someone old." She tipped her head to one side. "Or... you may have to choose between two paths."

Agatha raised her hand. "It can also mean that someone is being two-faced!"

"Shut up, Agatha," another girl said, whacking her on the arm.

"Another," said Ebony, tapping her finger on the next card. "The Future."

I turned over the next.

**DEATH**

Everyone gasped. The grim reaper on the card grinned up at me ghoulishly.

"Actually," said Ebony quietly, "Death merely signifies an ending of—"

She was interrupted by a frantic rapping at the door.

Everyone went silent. I gripped the threadbare carpet beneath my hands. Was it a teacher? Someone else? Something else?

Ebony wasted no time. She jumped up, put a finger to her lips and went to open the door. (I noticed that this time, she didn't use any sort of magic trick to do so.)

She gently touched the door handle and twisted it.

Only for it to swing open, and reveal...

*Ariadne.*

## Chapter Twenty-six

## IVY

Ariadne stood in Ebony's doorway. She was holding the cat.

For a moment, I thought she wouldn't be able to see us, but then I remembered the candle.

"Oh," Ariadne said. Her eyes passed over us all, and met mine. They flashed with hurt and I felt a sudden panic in my heart. "I... I brought your cat, Ebony."

She held out Midnight, who climbed into his

mistress's arms and stood up on her shoulders, before curling round her neck.

"Where was he?" Ebony asked. I noticed her voice became much softer, more loving. She obviously did care a lot about the cat.

Ariadne seemed to choke on her words. Her eyes didn't leave mine, but I could see the battle in her mind. She'd known our plan was to infiltrate Ebony's gang and if she spoke out now, everything could come tumbling down. "H-he was scratching at our door and then when we opened it, he kept climbing on Muriel's bed and he wouldn't leave, and I... I just thought..." She took a deep breath. "I'm going back to bed," she finished.

Before I could say anything, she had turned on her heel and dashed away down the corridor.

A smile twitched on Ebony's face, and I realised then that she must have thought Ariadne was afraid of her. Which I suppose she was, but I was certain that wasn't the reason she was acting so strangely.

No. It was because we'd betrayed her.

After that, Ebony ignored Scarlet and began telling other people's fortunes. But my mind was swimming – or more like drowning, it felt like.

*What had we done?*

We'd lied to Ariadne. Well, we'd omitted the truth, but that felt just as bad. From her point of view, we'd told her nothing was going on, while at the same time secretly fraternising with this girl who had been terrorising the school and had probably injured her friend. The hurt on her face was more than I could bear.

I almost didn't notice when Ebony apparently grew tired of reading tarot cards and began putting them away. She'd only done a few people, but she'd seemed unsettled from the start. I did notice that Mary in particular looked relieved not to have been included this time round.

We all left and crept back to our rooms and into our beds. Scarlet and I didn't say a word to each other.

I think both of us were afraid. We'd been caught out, and now we would have to face the consequences.

After a night fraught with worry, I finally woke early on Sunday morning and the sun seemed to shine a new light on things.

*We'll talk to Ariadne. She's* Ariadne. *She's our best friend. Everything will be fine.*

A quick glance at the clock told me it was about six and nobody else was awake – the morning bell had not yet rung. Scarlet was still fast asleep in the opposite bed, her head buried under her pillow. But I was too wide awake to go back to bed, so I decided to beat the morning rush and head for the bathrooms.

But what happened on the way changed everything.

As I was walking there, I was taking my time, enjoying the quiet hallways. The rooks were cawing from the trees outside and the sun was shining brightly. I went past the staircase to the mostly abandoned third floor – and that was when I heard it.

Voices.

Someone was up there. I paused, listened. No, *two people.*

They were talking so quietly that I could barely make out any words, but I was suddenly intrigued. It was rare for anyone to be up on the third floor, let alone at six in the morning.

I began to creep up the steps, craning my neck to see if I could identify whoever was talking. As I neared the top, I caught a momentary glance of two girls.

One had black hair and black boots. The other was tall and blonde.

*Ebony and Muriel!*

I tried to hide my sharp intake of breath as I ducked down on to the stairs. I prayed they hadn't seen me.

*Ebony and Muriel? What were they talking about*

*and why were they talking to one another?*

It certainly hadn't looked as though Ebony was threatening Muriel. It looked like they were having a secretive chat. I could still hear the faint murmurs of from the bottom of the stairs.

My heart was pounding in my chest. I climbed up from the steps and hurried back down the corridor. It was really strange. I had to tell Scarlet.

I shook my twin awake, to which she responded by groaning at me angrily.

"What? What do you want? It's too early!"

"You won't believe what I just saw!" I said.

Her eyelids fluttered open. "It had better be the Holy Grail if it's worth waking me up for."

I went over and perched on the windowsill. "Well, it's not, but it's certainly interesting. I just saw Muriel talking to Ebony."

Scarlet yawned. "What are they doing up at this hour? Were they arguing? Or was Ebony bullying her again?"

I shuffled on the cold sill. "Nothing of the sort. They had their heads bowed together and they were having some sort of quiet discussion. But I couldn't really make out anything they were saying, not without going up there."

That got her attention. She sat up straight in bed. "Hang on. Are you saying that they might have been plotting something? *Together?*"

I nodded this time, feeling the cogs whirr in my mind. There was no sort of confrontation that I could see and they must have planned to meet up that early. How long had they been doing this, out of sight of everyone else? Maybe their conflict was not what it seemed.

"Or maybe," Scarlet said, peeling off her covers and swinging her legs out, "maybe Ebony is controlling Muriel in some way." Now I could see my twin's mind working like my own. "I mean with everything Ebony has done... Doesn't it seem like she could have the power to do that? She doesn't get in trouble with the teachers. She *cursed* Muriel. Ariadne spends time with Muriel and suddenly Ariadne's the one getting into all the trouble. I think Ebony's pulling the strings here."

"Hmm," I said. I wasn't so sure. But there was one thing I was certain of. "Whatever is going on, we need to talk to Ariadne. As soon as possible."

Scarlet nodded her agreement. "Let's just hope she wants to talk to us."

*

We hurried to Ariadne's room and knocked gently on the door. I hoped that Muriel was still occupied elsewhere.

A few moments later, Ariadne came to answer. She was yawning and her mousy hair was sticking up at odd angles where it had recently been pressed into the pillow.

"Oh. Morning," she said when she saw us. It sounded like a normal greeting, but the way she said it was heavy with hidden meaning.

"Look, we're really sorry," Scarlet said, beating me to it. "We need to come and explain. Is Muriel there?"

Ariadne looked back into her room. "No," she said, puzzled. "Her bed's empty. She must have gone to the lavatories or something."

I gave my twin a quick glance, but said nothing. That explanation would wait.

"Quick, let us in," Scarlet said and Ariadne stood aside wordlessly. We both filed into the room, the door shutting behind us.

Scarlet looked back at me and then took a deep breath. "Look, again, we're really sorry. We're idiots. We should have told you that we were going to Ebony's room."

"Have you been going about with her this whole

time?" Ariadne asked in a small voice.

"Yes," Scarlet said. "Well, no. Only since we said we were going to infiltrate her. But then we didn't talk to you about it."

"Because we knew you were unhappy at the idea," I said. "And we thought it would upset you." Even as I said the words, I felt awful about them. How could we have been so foolish?

"You should have *said*!" Ariadne protested. She flattened the back of her hair with an anxious hand. "That's what friends are for. And what if she had done something to you? I'd never have forgiven myself!"

"We're fine," Scarlet insisted. "She did some spooky tricks, that's all. No curses. She thinks we're on her side."

"And are you?" Ariadne asked.

I froze for a moment, shocked by the question. "No!" I said, but the pause might have been a little too long.

We had been drawn into Ebony's world and I had to admit that we found her interesting. But we weren't on her side. We wouldn't support her hurting anyone.

"Of course we're not. We're just trying to get to the bottom of what she's doing," Scarlet explained. "And she hasn't tried to hurt anyone so far. At least, not in front of us."

"But now we've hurt your feelings," I said.

Ariadne's lower lip quivered. "It's not only about my feelings. What about Muriel? You know what Ebony did to her."

"Do we?" Scarlet asked. "We don't even know for sure what happened."

I glanced back at the door, concerned that Muriel was about to return at any moment. I had to explain what I'd witnessed that morning. "There's something else we came to tell you. I just saw..." My words trailed off, like they'd flown from my mouth. I didn't know how to say it. Was I just about to make Ariadne even more upset?

But Scarlet had no concerns about picking up my sentence. "She saw Muriel talking to Ebony in secret. On the third floor."

Ariadne's brow wrinkled in confusion. "What? Are you sure?"

I winced. "Certain."

"What if Ebony was picking on her?" Ariadne's expression became a little frantic. "Should I go and help?"

Scarlet looked at me. "I was concerned that Ebony might be controlling her in some way. But Ivy says it looked friendly."

"Um, yes, it did," I said. "They looked like they were... plotting something, honestly."

Now Ariadne frowned. "That's not possible. Ebony's been *ghastly* to her. Ebony attacked her! There's no way she would be talking to Ebony of her own volition."

"I just think..." I stared at the floor. I knew this would be hard for Ariadne. "There may be more to this than we're seeing. What if they're both up to something?"

Ariadne folded her arms and there was a look in her eyes that I didn't recognise at all. It almost frightened me. "Why would they be? It just doesn't make sense. They'd never even met before the start of term. And Ebony's done nothing but be cruel to her."

"I know, but it's what I saw. Don't you believe me?" I was almost pleading with her now. Could this get any worse?

My best friend bit her lip. "I... I don't know."

Scarlet's mouth dropped open. "You don't believe Ivy? How could you say that! Why would she lie?" She moved closer to me, linked her arm through mine.

There was a flicker of something on Ariadne's face. And then it got worse.

"Maybe you're jealous," she said.

"I... what?" I gasped.

"Maybe you're jealous," she repeated, staring at the floor. "Perhaps you should just leave."

## Chapter Twenty-seven

## SCARLET

Her words hit me like a punch to the stomach. They seemed to come almost from nowhere.

I thought for a moment that I must have heard her wrongly. That my ears were lying to me. Ariadne had never been angry with us before. Never!

Neither Ivy nor I said anything. We just stood there and gaped at her.

"Muriel hasn't done anything wrong!" she squeaked. "It's all Ebony! Can't you see?"

"We know Ebony's up to *something*," Ivy protested. "But I'm just saying that we think there's more to this than meets the eye. Especially now that we've seen Muriel talking to her and—"

Once the shock had worn off, I couldn't hold my tongue any longer. I unlinked my arms from Ivy's and spread them out wide. "We're *not* jealous! Why would we be jealous?"

"Because I'm friends with Muriel now," Ariadne said, "and you don't like it! Maybe you've picked a side!"

"Nonsense," I snapped. It was nonsense. I didn't care a jot who Ariadne was friends with, as long as she was still friends with us. But suddenly our friendship seemed to be rapidly disappearing down the plughole.

"I'm not just your sidekick!" Ariadne squeaked again. "I don't always have to follow you both around. I can make my own friends. I was so afraid of her before, but I've worked hard at getting her trust and now we get along fine. You should be supporting me, not trying to undermine everything!"

"We're not trying to—" Ivy started, but she was cut off by the bedroom door swinging open.

It was Muriel. "Oh, hello," she said pleasantly, unaware of what she'd just interrupted. "You're all up early."

"As are you," I said, with perhaps a bit of a sneer. "Where have you been?"

"Just to the lavatories," she said.

I raised my eyebrows in a way that I hoped expressed the word *Aha!* But Ariadne was no longer looking at me.

I felt the anger bubbling away in my stomach. This wasn't fair. Maybe we should have told her about everything with Ebony, but we weren't lying about Ebony talking to Muriel. Why didn't she believe us? Ariadne was supposed to be our best friend. "Come on, Ivy," I said quietly. We had to leave before my anger boiled over. "Let's go."

At breakfast I gulped down my porridge and I think Ivy did hers too. We weren't keen to have another confrontation with Ariadne. There were tears in my twin's eyes.

I couldn't stop my mind from fizzing with fury. It wasn't really directed at Ariadne, though I did think she was being unfair. She was still our best friend, no matter what. No, it was Ebony and Muriel I was furious with. Now that Muriel had lied about where she had been, I felt certain that she was up to something. And whatever it was – they shouldn't have got in the way of our friendship with Ariadne.

Ivy and I headed for the library, hoping it was somewhere we could cool off.

"Morning, girls," Miss Jones said as we walked in. "I'm only here for a couple of hours and then Jing is taking over." Jing smiled at her.

"Morning," Ivy said, but I could see that her heart wasn't in it.

"No books for us today, Miss," I said, unable to keep the glower off my face. "Serious business."

Miss Jones just looked a little puzzled, shrugged and walked away. Jing, on the other hand, leant forward over the desk.

"Is this about the witch girl?" she whispered.

That was unexpected. I moved in closer. "What do you know?" I asked. "We're investigating."

Jing didn't seem to find that odd. "I saw you with her. I see a lot of things, in fact. People don't tend to notice me." She looked over her shoulder to check no one was eavesdropping. "She's in here a lot with those spell books. I don't know where she gets them from. They're certainly not in our collection."

"Have you seen her with Muriel too?" Ivy asked. "The very tall girl with the blonde curls?"

Jing nodded. "A few times. Always hiding away in

the corner, talking to each other. Just yesterday, in fact, I saw one of them go into the stacks, then later the other. Over there." She pointed far in the distance, over to one of the oldest sections of the library, one that hadn't been destroyed by the fire.

I looked at Ivy. Things were getting weirder and weirder. "Hmm. Maybe they're leaving notes?"

"Could be." Ivy turned to Jing. "Thank you!"

She smiled and leant back, picking up a pile of returned books. "Sundays in the library are not very exciting. I have to do something!"

I grinned at her. Suddenly we had a lead. The chase was on!

We hurried over to the corner where she had pointed. It was in the history section where two bookcases met, along with a third that ran alongside and hid anyone standing there from sight to the rest of the library. The shelves were heavy with thick books.

"If you were Ebony," I said, "where would you leave a secret note for Muriel?"

Ivy paused to think. "Maybe up high, since Muriel's tall."

We began searching the higher shelves, looking at books that I had spent most of my time at school trying to ignore. Books with titles like *Beaumont's History of*

*Britain* and *The Battle of Hastings* and *Stories from the Americas*. Rookwood had been collecting books for longer than it had been collecting students.

I flipped through several and turned them upside down, feeling glad that Miss Jones couldn't see me. But then a title caught my eye.

*The Salem Witch Trials: A History*.

"Ivy, look! This has to be it!" I snatched the book off the shelf.

The book was black and heavy, with gold titling that glinted in the light. I held it out and rifled through the pages, until something gave a soft rustle and floated gently to the floor.

Ivy snatched it up and we both took a look at it. It was definitely a note, written in block capitals.

MEET TOMORROW 6 O'CLOCK
USUAL PLACE
BE THERE

There were no further details, no names. But a secret note, left in a book about witches, after Jing had seen the two of them going into this corner yesterday? It sounded like Ebony and Muriel had arranged the meeting that Ivy had witnessed them having.

"*Usual place*," Ivy muttered under her breath.

"This *proves* it," I said. "It proves that they've been arranging to meet each other, and more than once as well!"

Ivy peered more closely. "And I don't like the sound of the last line. It seems a little threatening, doesn't it? Like Ebony's ordering her to be there, or else."

"Hmm," I said. "It does." I placed the note back inside the black book. "And I don't like that one bit."

## Chapter Twenty-eight

## IVY

We were stuck in a terrible position. Our note didn't prove our suspicions that Ebony and Muriel were up to something. It was too vague, too lacking in details. It lined up with everything I'd witnessed, but nothing more. What if Ebony was forcing Muriel to meet up with her? What if she was blackmailing her in some way? It was entirely possible.

There was no handwriting to speak of, nothing about the paper it was written on to give anything more away. I suggested we take it to Ariadne, but Scarlet thought she needed time to cool off. And besides, if we removed the note from the book, Ebony or Muriel might well realise that someone was on their trail.

It was hopeless. I felt heartbroken and guilty, and I couldn't stop seeing Ariadne's hurt face in my mind. Her angry words played over and over in my ears.

We ran into Ethel on the way out of the library. "Oh, hello," she said. I blinked at her. Ethel usually avoided talking to me at all costs. "I was just speaking to Ebony and I've come to get some books," she said. "But now I've found you two, I can pass on the message. Next Friday night, in the graveyard at midnight. You need to be there. Ebony has plans for us."

She grinned as if this were the most exciting thing in the world, and then slipped away into the library.

I looked at Scarlet.

"Why not?" she sighed. "It's not as if we have anything to lose now."

As the week passed, I began to remember just how horrible it was being at Rookwood without Ariadne. Everything seemed darker and colder. And somehow, it was even worse knowing that she was beside us, but just out of reach. She stayed polite, greeting us, making the odd bit of small talk. But you could tell she hadn't forgiven us and that hurt more than I could say.

It was hard as well to watch her getting into trouble, without knowing why. She kept falling asleep, getting things wrong, causing accidents. It was always minor things, but they were building and it worried me. How bad was it going to get? Ariadne had already been expelled once before, and now Mrs Knight was trying to crack down on trouble... I didn't even want to think about how wrong this could go.

"If this is a curse," Scarlet said, "we need to find out how to break it."

I still didn't believe in curses, but anything was worth a try. Still, I couldn't think of any way we would find out how to break a curse without asking Ebony.

On Friday, at the end of our ballet lesson, Scarlet and I ended up being the last to leave. Miss Finch was in the cupboard at the back, tidying things away. I don't know what compelled me, but realising we were nearly alone, I decided to talk to Madame Zelda.

"Miss..." I said quietly to her. "Do you believe in curses?"

She started, but then turned and fixed me with a curious eye. "Why do you ask?"

Scarlet was nearby, of course, and she piped up,

"We think our friend might be in trouble. Possibly of the magical variety."

Madame Zelda thought for a moment. "Where I come from, people used to speak of curses. They would say if a witch had cursed you, she would leave an onion in your bed."

"That's... rather odd," I said, lost for words. I wondered, not for the first time, exactly where it was that she had come from.

Our eccentric ballet teacher waved her hand. "We had many beliefs."

"Did any of them tell you how to stop curses?" Scarlet asked.

"Eat the onion," Madame Zelda replied.

We both stared at her.

She burst out laughing. "No, no, not really. There is only one way to break a curse. Everyone knows this."

"And what is that?" I asked.

"You kill the witch," she said.

That night, I think Scarlet and I were both trying our best to put Madame Zelda's words out of our minds. We were not going to do anything to hurt Ebony. Scarlet had started a sentence with, "What if we just knocked her out for a—" but I had swiftly cut her off before she could go any further down that route.

"Even if she were a real witch," I insisted as I brushed my hair, "which she *isn't*... we wouldn't *kill* her."

"No, you're right," said Scarlet. "That's far too medieval. There must be another way."

For a moment, I caught myself turning to ask for Ariadne's opinion. But there was no third person in the room, just a disappointingly empty space.

Scarlet noticed. "We're going to have to think this one through by ourselves."

I looked back at the mirror. There were no answers there, just my blank face staring back.

Now my twin started pacing. "Maybe... maybe we can't stop the curses that she's already put on people. But if she's going to attempt one tonight, we can sabotage it. Make it look like an accident so that she doesn't suspect us."

"Scarlet..." I put the hairbrush down. "This isn't magic. Us sabotaging her spell won't stop her doing... whatever it is that's affecting people."

"Oh, but it will." My twin stopped still and grinned at me. "If we sabotage it well enough, if it's all just a trick – her trick will fail too. She can't go through with it if we've clearly ruined the spell."

"Hmm." The hairbrush our mother had left us stared up at me. I suddenly felt like she was watching us, waiting for our next move. I wanted her to be proud. "Perhaps we shouldn't get involved in this." I stood up and faced my twin. "Why don't we just stop talking to Ebony and go down the hallway right now and apologise to Ariadne and Muriel? Wouldn't that make everything better?"

Scarlet nearly laughed in my face. "What? No! Ebony would continue to terrorise the school and we'd still have no idea what was really going on. This is no time to go cowardly on me."

Affronted, I decided to explain my thought process. "I just... I thought of our mother. I want to do the right thing. To make her proud."

Scarlet put her hands on her hips. "Our mother stood up to bullies. When she was here, she ripped this school apart from the inside out to discover what was going on, no matter what it cost her. I don't know about you, but *I'm* going to make her proud. By stopping Ebony."

And that was why, on a wet and windy night, when the clock struck twelve, we were sneaking out of Rookwood School once again and heading for the graveyard.

I wrapped my coat tightly round me. The rain was light, but it made the night even colder and blacker than it already was. The moon was hidden behind endless clouds.

Only this time, our trip to the graveyard wasn't to spy on Ebony's curses. It was to join in.

I'd tried everything I could to talk Scarlet out of it, but it was no use. We were going. And we intended to sabotage Ebony in whatever way we could.

After checking that the coast was clear, we ran down the steps and along the drive. I thought, not for the first time, how we never would have attempted this when Miss Fox was headmistress. She'd always seemed to have eyes everywhere.

But even now, I felt as though there were eyes watching me in the night. Something fluttered past my head and I squealed and grabbed hold of Scarlet.

"Bats!" she said.

She was right. As we stood on the drive and looked up, a dark shape would occasionally flap past, like a bird's shadow.

"Ebony probably summoned them," Scarlet muttered, though only after looking around to check she wasn't being overheard.

I let go of her and shook myself. Bats didn't mean

anything. I'd seen them when I'd lived at Aunt Phoebe's and they'd just been like little mice with wings.

As we neared the churchyard, I saw some of the others lurking beside the gate.

"Where is she?" one of them asked, her hands tucked under her arms in the cold. Her pockets were full of candles. "I thought she'd be here by now."

"Just wait," Agatha snapped, seemingly having been appointed Ebony's spokesperson. "She knows what she's doing."

Ebony's group of disciples seemed to have grown. I saw Ethel was there, her hair in its usual tight bun beneath a dark cap. And there were others too. How long would it be before the whole of Rookwood wanted to join in this madness?

Scarlet jumped up and perched on the rough stone wall of the graveyard, gaining a series of tuts from the assembled girls. "What?" she asked, folding her arms. "If we have to wait..."

I shrugged and climbed up beside her, sitting close for warmth. The wind blew my hair over my eyes and I kept having to pull it back.

After what felt like far too long, Ebony appeared, walking down the driveway. She appeared to be in no hurry – she made everything seem so effortless, as if it was exactly as she meant it to be. She stood in front of us as everyone waited with bated breath for instructions.

"Hmm," she said. "This weather will put the candles out. We'll have to go inside."

"In... in the church?" Mary stuttered through chattering teeth.

Ebony frowned. "No. Not there." She turned her eyes back to where she came from. "In the school."

"*That doesn't seem very magical,*" Scarlet whispered loudly to me.

I saw the whites of Ebony's eyes as they flicked over to us in the darkness. She'd heard.

"The library," she said with an air of finality. "Words have power."

I glanced at my twin, not that I could see much of her in the dark. Part of our plan had been to knock the candles over. In wet grass, that would be no problem. In the library, which had already burned down once in our time at Rookwood... now that was a different story.

Ebony began striding away into the darkness. Scarlet and I hung back for a moment. What were we going to do?

"Coming?" Ethel called back to us. "Or are you *scared*?"

## Chapter Twenty-nine

## SCARLET

Reluctantly, we followed the other girls. We crept along the dark corridors – but with the growing numbers of Ebony's followers, even creeping was noisy. It was like a herd of elephants trying to be as quiet as possible. When we reached the library doors, Ebony tried them, only to find they were locked shut. I hadn't attempted to break into the library at night since last year, so I was surprised to see that a lock had been fitted. But it made sense, given everything that had happened.

And, of course, Ebony somehow had a key. Again. Where did she get it from? The sound of Miss Fox's jangling pockets flashed through my head, but I swatted the thought away. I needed to be concentrating if we had any chance of disturbing Ebony's ritual, whatever it was going to be.

With the grand doors pulled open, Ebony led us inside to the largest empty space, just in front of Miss Jones's desk.

Agatha began lighting some candles and placing them in holders in a circle, without even having to be asked. "Careful," I said with a wince. I only had to close my eyes for a moment to see the whole place alight again, flickering flames and smoke filling my nose.

Agatha ignored me. I rolled my eyes at her. Obviously Ebony was the only one who would be listened to around here.

Ebony leant on the desk, like some sort of overseer. "Make the four corners," she said.

I remembered her saying that from... when was it? *The curse. The curse on Muriel.*

Ivy grabbed my hand and squeezed it. I caught her eye. She was clearly thinking the same as me. We had to stop this before it went too far.

I had to act as casually as possible. As everyone shuffled into position in the circle that Agatha had begun drawing in chalk, I found the spot nearest to Ebony. "So then," I said. "Who are we cursing this fine evening?"

Ebony frowned at me. I think I was ruining her moment. "Mrs Knight," she said simply.

My mouth must have dropped open.

"Close it or you'll catch flies," Ebony said and turned away. She pulled a folded picture of Mrs Knight from her pocket, which looked like it had come from the school newsletter, and placed it on the library desk.

I couldn't find the words, but thankfully Ivy leant over and found them for me. "Why Mrs Knight?" she asked. "What has she done?"

Ebony put her nose in the air. "She wants to take away my cat. This spell should change her mind."

"Oh," I said. "So not a curse then? More of an enchantment?" Whatever it was, spell or curse, I was certain this sort of thing shouldn't be messed with.

Now she stared at me, straight in the eye. "If you know so much, Scarlet Grey, why don't you try the spell?"

Ivy stepped forward. "Why should she have to? And how would she know what to say?"

I turned, once again surprised by my twin. You

would think I'd have got used to her confidence, but after so many years of shyness, it was still new to me. I realised everyone in the candlelit circle was staring at us now. The smell of melting wax filled the air.

Ebony began to laugh. "Both of you, then. Stand in the middle. I'll tell you what to do."

Ivy looked at me desperately. I shrugged. "In for a penny, in for a pound," I said. If we were the ones who had to carry this out, we could do everything in our power to sabotage it.

I strode into the centre of the circle. Ebony stood up straight, putting her black boots on the chalk line. After a few moments, Ivy took a deep breath and stepped in after me.

"So you're going to teach us?" I asked.

"Isn't that why you're here?" she retorted. "To learn?" I wasn't sure whether she meant *here* as in Rookwood School or here as in inside a magic circle in the library after midnight. But I had to admit the answer to either of those would be 'No'.

So I did what I had to. I lied. "Yes," I said. "Show us how it's done." I hoped I seemed sincere, but I heard faint giggles from behind me as I said it.

"All right, then. Stand back to back." She waved us together.

"How will this help?" I whispered to Ivy, only to find myself getting shushed by a circle of would-be witches.

"Silence!" Ebony called out, and the silence fell quicker than a thunderclap.

I almost shuddered. A cold chill swept across my face, though my feet were warmed by all the candles.

"Close your eyes," Ebony ordered. "Both of you."

I did as I was told this time. I couldn't delay any further without them all sensing that something was up. Now everything descended into blackness, with nothing but the temperature and my twin's back to tell me where I was standing.

Ivy tapped her finger against mine, questioningly. I didn't respond. I didn't know what we were going to do.

Perhaps I just wouldn't say it. I wouldn't say Mrs Knight's name, or whatever was required to target the spell.

"Repeat after me," Ebony said. "I will speak slowly and quietly. You must say the words loudly."

"Won't someone hear?" Ivy asked, and I felt her head turn towards Ebony's voice.

"Never mind that!" came the snappy reply. "Keep still. Now..."

And then she began to speak in that strange,

unearthly sounding voice she had used before. She said a few words, words that didn't mean a thing to me, but I could copy the sound. Ivy and I said them together. It was mesmerising, almost. But inside, my mind was racing, racing for a way to stop this.

Something fluttered past my face in a rush of air. I tried to ignore it. It felt like butterflies. Or something worse.

Ebony said more words and we repeated them. "Keep going," she whispered and then said the same words a few times. It was a chant, clearly. I repeated it and Ivy repeated it too, for what seemed like a long time, until...

"WHAT ON GOD'S GREEN EARTH IS GOING ON HERE?"

My eyes snapped open.

Everyone had gone. Ivy and I were alone in the library.

Except for Miss Bowler, who was now standing in the doorway.

## Chapter Thirty

### IVY

Scarlet and I dived apart and faced Miss Bowler. The candles were still burning all round us, but all the other girls had disappeared! I could see no sign of Ebony or any of the others. Even the photograph of Mrs Knight had gone. There were playing cards scattered at our feet.

"Did we do this?" Scarlet hissed.

Miss Bowler was already striding towards us. "OUT OF YOUR BEDS AT SILLY O'CLOCK AND BURNING

CANDLES IN THE LIBRARY!" Her booming voice echoed off the walls. I thought she might wake the whole school.

But as I stared down at the cards, I noticed something.

They were all face down, except for the Jokers.

We'd been set up. It was a trap.

As I raised my eyes again, I found myself face to face with Miss Bowler.

"Explain yourselves!"

I fought the urge to clap my hands over my ears at her deafening volume.

"Sorry, Miss, we, um... we couldn't sleep... and..." I stumbled over every word. How on earth were we going to explain this?

"We thought we'd play cards," Scarlet said suddenly.

I looked at her. Well, that was one way.

"CARDS?" Miss Bowler roared at her. "In the middle of the night? With all these candles?"

We both stayed completely silent. I felt that we were at the point where saying anything else would just make everything much, much worse.

"Right," Miss Bowler said, when it became clear that we weren't answering. "I don't know what you two are up to, but I know I don't like it. I will *personally* be escorting you back to your room and then I will *personally* escort you to Mrs Knight's office, first thing on Monday morning!"

She strode behind us, put a big hand on each of our backs and began walking us forward. There was no use protesting. We kept walking.

Miss Bowler turned and I heard her blowing out all the candles. The library fell into darkness once again.

We were marched all the way back through the corridors. Miss Bowler was muttering angrily about how she had been staying overnight to clean the swimming pool early in the morning, and how she'd heard noises and then someone knocked on her door and ran, and she thought there had been a break-in...

Still, we said nothing. I was barely taking in what she was saying because the consequences of what had just happened were still racing through my mind.

There was no spell on Mrs Knight. Ebony had designed the whole thing to get *us* into trouble. It wasn't magic, just pure skulduggery. I even found myself wondering if she'd somehow caused it to rain, so that we'd have to go inside and be caught.

And that wasn't all. Mrs Knight had already warned

us about getting in any further trouble. What was going to happen?

A horrible vision appeared in front of me as we trudged up the staircase. The two of us, sent home to live with our wicked stepmother... and not even a chance to make up with Ariadne. I couldn't imagine anything worse.

"Which room?" Miss Bowler asked, pausing at the top.

"Thirteen," Scarlet replied.

Miss Bowler marched onward.

"It's the other way, Miss," I said.

She turned round without a word, as if she'd always been going the right way.

Soon we arrived at our room, where Miss Bowler wrenched our door open. "In!" she ordered. "I'll see you both tomorrow! I hope you will have some better excuses by then..." She trailed off into angry mumbling and stomped away.

With a shared glance and a sigh, we went inside and shut the door behind us.

"What just happened back there?" Scarlet asked, once we'd regained our wits enough to talk.

We were sitting on our beds in the pitch-black

night, the clouds papering over the moon and the rain whispering at the window. "Did the spell do something? Did we make them disappear?"

"No, Scarlet, it was a set-up. Don't you see?"

I heard her shuffling and I imagined it was the sound of her mentally readjusting her position. "Oh," she said eventually.

"Exactly." I thought back through everything that had just happened. "Ebony must have planned this. She made us do that 'spell' so that we'd be standing there unawares with our eyes closed, then they must all have run away and alerted Miss Bowler."

"But what about the cards?" she asked. "I think I felt them fly past us."

I thought about it. "Ebony must have thrown them somehow. Those Jokers... that was a message. Telling us that it was a trick."

"Or that we're the jokers." I could almost hear in her voice that Scarlet's face was scrunched with anger and embarrassment, the way I knew it would be. "But how did she get them to be face up?"

I lay down on my bed, relieved to finally be in it, even if the peace wouldn't last long. "I don't know," I had to admit.

There were a few empty moments before Scarlet

spoke again. "And why now? I thought Ebony believed that we really were her followers."

The idea struck me out of nowhere. I sat back up again. "Muriel!"

"What?" My twin sounded confused.

I put my hands over my mouth. I couldn't believe it, but it had to be true. "Ariadne found out that we'd infiltrated Ebony's group and she was really upset about it. She must have told Muriel."

Scarlet took hold of what I was saying and ran with it. "Then we see Muriel talking to Ebony, and we find the two of them passing notes to each other..."

"They planned this together!" we said simultaneously.

I couldn't believe it. It *had* to be true. One thing led to the other perfectly. Muriel was up to something with Ebony! And if she was, then Ariadne was in even more danger than we'd previously thought.

"But there's a big problem," Scarlet said. "How are we ever going to prove it?"

Once again, we were stuck – stuck between a former bully and a witch, and with no proof of what had happened. The only thing we had concrete proof of was that we were about to face *big* trouble.

We kept our heads down over the weekend while we tried to make sense of what had happened and come up with a plan. But we were getting nowhere. Anything I could think of to say just made it sound as though we were being even more paranoid and jealous of Ariadne's friendship with Muriel. I felt a pang in my heart every time I saw them talking together. As we sat across from them at meal times, Muriel would smile at us. Ariadne would say nothing and stare at her plate. Every mouthful of dinner was hard to swallow.

And in the face of Muriel's smile, I even began to doubt myself. What if she was innocent in all of this? Ebony certainly seemed like the main player here.

But looming over all of that was Monday morning and our impending visit to Mrs Knight's office.

And it was going to be much worse than we'd ever imagined.

Early Monday morning, there was a thunderous knock on our door that could only have come from Miss Bowler. It was louder than the school bell.

We got dressed in a terrible hurry, resulting in me wearing odd stockings and Scarlet having her dress on backwards.

"Time!" Miss Bowler shouted from the doorway, tapping her finger on her watch.

We pulled our shoes on and then breathlessly

followed Miss Bowler down the corridor. She didn't talk to us, which was a relief.

She gave another incredible knock on the door to Mrs Knight's office.

"Enter!" Mrs Knight's voice called from within.

Miss Bowler held open the door and I saw... Mrs Knight, sitting at her desk.

And sitting opposite her, our *stepmother*.

I couldn't help my sharp intake of breath. I felt Scarlet stiffen beside me. *Oh no.*

"Stop dilly-dallying," Miss Bowler said, prodding us both in the back until we were forced to go inside.

We stood there, adrift on the sea of blue carpet that Mrs Knight must have had fitted. Her cheery posters bobbed on the walls above us like life rings, just out of reach.

I tried not to look at our stepmother. I didn't want to see the expression on her face. I could hear her quietly seething.

"Girls," said Mrs Knight, taking her glasses off. "I'm sure you can appreciate that this is very serious. I told you that we needed everyone on their best behaviour, and then Miss Bowler finds you playing cards and burning candles in the library in the middle of the night! Would you care to explain yourselves?"

"Well, actually..." Scarlet started, but her sentence trailed away from her. What could we possibly say? *In fact, Miss, we were trying to put a curse on you because a witch told us to, except it was actually all a trick to get us into trouble?* It sounded like madness.

"We're very sorry," was all I could manage.

Mrs Knight shook her head in disappointment. "That's not good enough, girls. I've had to bring your stepmother in to talk about your behaviour, to show you how serious this is. Now, I want to make it very clear that this is your *final* warning."

I gulped. The room seemed to spin around me.

"I have been lenient before," the headmistress continued, "but no more!" She stood up and waved a finger at us. "This is it, do you understand? If it continues, I will be forced to expel you."

I stared down at my feet. Scarlet was shuffling hers. We were both speechless.

"Do you understand?" Mrs Knight said again.

"Yes, Miss," we replied.

"Now," she walked out from behind her desk and put a hand on my shoulder. "I'm going to leave you to have a little talk with your stepmother. I want you both to think very hard about how you will behave from now on." She patted me gently and then left the room.

Left us alone with Edith.

Our stepmother pushed her chair back and stood up.

"Well," she sneered. "Isn't this nice?"

## Chapter Thirty-one

## SCARLET

I couldn't believe our stepmother was actually here, at Rookwood. It made me feel sick. I wanted to lash out at her, to scream and run away. But I was so shocked that I just stood there next to Ivy and said nothing.

Edith put her hands on her hips. Her nostrils flared, her cheeks flushed with anger. "Have you got something to say to me?"

*How about, 'Leave us alone forever, you nasty old cow'?* I thought the words, but I just felt tongue-tied.

"You two are despicable," she spat. "Worthless. Less than nothing. Why are we paying for you to go to this school when all you do is disrespect us?"

"We didn't—" Ivy started, but Edith held a hand in the air to stop her, clearly not interested in anything we had to say.

"This is how it is going to be," she said. "You're going to be on your *absolute best* behaviour for the rest of the year. If you so much as put a toenail out of line, I will hear about it; do you understand?"

"Yes," I muttered. I felt uncomfortably like I was being lectured by a shorter, dumpier version of Miss Fox.

"Hold your tongue! I don't want a word from either of you brats!"

"You never wanted anything from us," I said, finally finding my voice. "You never wanted us at all." Ivy squeezed my hand.

Edith turned to me, her eyes fiery. "You're right, *Scarlet*." She said my name like a curse word. "I don't want either of you cluttering up my home. And that is why YOU WILL STAY AT THIS SCHOOL."

I bit my lip. There were angry tears prickling at the corner of my eyes.

"And if you get expelled," she said, leaning far

too close to our faces, "then you can always be sent *somewhere else.*"

With that, she marched out of the office, slamming the door behind her.

My legs gave out from underneath me and I sank on to the sea-blue carpet.

"Somewhere else?" Ivy whispered in shock from above me.

"She means the asylum," I said eventually. Echoes of night-time sobs and bars on windows flowed through my mind. The one place I would rather die than set foot in again. "She'd put us in the asylum."

The week that followed was dreadful – quite literally filled with dread. It hung over us like a cloud, and just the threat looming on the horizon made us quiet and scared.

There was no more spying on Ebony. She had put an end to us doing that with her *prank*. If I had been myself, she wouldn't have got off lightly. I was dying to scream at her, to wipe the smug, knowing smile from her face.

But maybe we were to blame too, as much as I didn't want to admit it. We'd been spying on her, pretending to want to get involved in her witchcraft.

Ivy and I spent what felt like days sitting in mostly silence, afraid to cause the slightest bit of trouble. I had no doubt at all that Mrs Knight was serious about expelling us if we did anything else wrong, and even less doubt that our stepmother would be true to her word and make our lives worse than hell.

On Saturday afternoon, I decided I was sick of being so miserable.

"We *have* to go and talk to Ariadne," I said, jumping to my feet from my bed.

Ivy looked at me over the book she was reading. It was the first thing I'd said in hours.

"I've had enough of this!" I insisted. "I'm fed up of walking on eggshells. If we're going to spend our lives being terrified of getting thrown out of school, I at least want to do it with a friend."

Ivy put the book down. "That's a good point," she said, her voice a little quiet with disuse. "But what about Muriel?"

I couldn't help but sigh. Muriel was the problem. I *hated* her. I liked her. I didn't know how I felt. Even though I was sure she was involved with Ebony somehow, I had no idea how and no way to prove it. And now you couldn't get to Ariadne without going past Muriel. She was always there.

"If we just confronted her..." I started.

"No!" Ivy said. "I'm not doing it. If she's innocent, Ariadne will never forgive us."

"Ugh." I kicked my bed in frustration. "We can't win."

Ivy sat in thought for a moment, but then she said, "I think you're right that we should talk to Ariadne, though. What if we wait until Muriel leaves their room?"

I nodded. "That could work."

So we took it in turns to wander along the corridor, past their room, pretending to be perfectly innocent.

As I was taking my fifth wander towards the lavatories, I saw Muriel step out and head off down the stairs.

*Going to meet Ebony and turn people into toads I bet*, I thought.

This was our chance. I ran and grabbed Ivy and together we knocked on Ariadne's door.

"Oh, hello," she said when she opened it. I might have been imagining things, but I thought she looked a little pleased. Perhaps she guessed why we were there.

Ivy nudged me and I realised I wasn't saying anything.

"We're here to apologise," I said. "Again," I added.

Ariadne had the ghost of a smile. "Come in," she said.

I had a brief glance around their room. It looked like a whirlwind had hit it. Ariadne and Muriel's bedsheets were in piles that Matron was sure to throw a fit about, their clothes tossed on the floor, school work spread out haphazardly all over the desk. One of Ariadne's jars of midnight-feast sweets was spilling on to the floor below her bed, and there was a chocolate-bar wrapper on the windowsill.

I wanted to mention it as I awkwardly found a place to stand that wasn't covered in discarded school uniform. The words threatened to jump from my throat, but I pushed them back down. This was not the time to start criticising Ariadne's unusual untidiness. But I did make a mental note of how strange it was.

"Ariadne, we..." Ivy started.

"Before you say anything," Ariadne said suddenly. "I'm sorry."

Ivy and I looked at each other in surprise. I was thrown from the script.

"*You're* sorry?" I asked.

She nodded meekly. "I shouldn't have been so cross with you. It was awful of me. I was just... not feeling myself. I felt left out and upset and I was terribly rude!"

She took a deep breath. "I really am sorry!"

"This was supposed to be *our* apology," I said.

"I know, I know." Ariadne went red and stared at her feet. "You can go next, if you like!"

That was when I started to laugh. "We missed you so much, Ariadne!"

She grinned sheepishly.

"We've got ourselves in a total mess," Ivy said.

"You won't believe it!" I put my head in my hands. "You were right to tell us to be careful of Ebony. She tricked us into doing this 'spell' with her at night in the library, and the next thing we knew, Miss Bowler was marching in and carting us off to Mrs Knight's office. We're in deep trouble."

Ariadne gasped and grabbed my arm. "No! I'd heard rumours, but I also heard that you'd been expelled for stealing Miss Bowler's knickers, so—"

Now Ivy laughed as well. I nearly spat out my tongue. "*What?*"

Ariadne shrugged. "I have no idea. You're not going to be expelled, are you? That wouldn't be any fun."

The thought flashed into my mind that the only reason Ariadne had been expelled last year was, in a strange way, because of Muriel. After all, the fact that Ariadne had burned down the shed that Muriel's bully-gang had hung around in was the reason why she'd come under suspicion for the fire at Rookwood.

Had Muriel *really* changed that much? Or was she still that same rotten apple underneath?

"I'm sure we'll be fine," Ivy insisted, snapping me back to reality. "We just need to stay out of trouble."

"Me too," Ariadne sighed. "Mrs Knight gave me a warning as well. She said I've been getting too many detentions."

I gave Ivy a fleeting glance. But I don't think either of us wanted to say anything. I derailed the subject a little. "Our stepmother turned up at school and threatened us. We're as good as forgotten if we get kicked out of Rookwood."

"I can't believe all this has happened," Ariadne said, sitting down on a bare corner of her mattress that the sheet had peeled away from. She twiddled her fingers. "I hope we can all be friends again." Now she grinned up at us. "Us and Muriel, all together!"

I didn't say a word. Because I had just noticed a playing card sticking out from under Muriel's pile of books.

It was a Joker.

## Chapter Thirty-two

## IVY

In the time that followed, it felt as though things were almost back to normal. Ariadne was our friend again. We went to lessons. We did all our work on time.

But it felt as if there was this great spectre breathing down our necks. I felt it every time I saw Muriel smile. Every time I saw Ebony, her cat curled round her neck, doing her card tricks for her followers. Every time we walked past Mrs Knight, and I remembered that morning in her office.

One Monday, though, I saw Mrs Knight and Miss Pepper as I was on my way to take a letter from one teacher to another, as we were often sent to do. I froze for a moment, wondering if I was doing anything that I could get into trouble for. When I was certain that everything was all right, I moved on again.

And that was when I saw the poster.

Mrs Knight was pinning it to the noticeboard and it read:

*Rookwood School*
*First Ever All Hallows' Eve Celebrations!*
*October 31ˢᵗ*
*On the playing field*
*All welcome*
*Bonfire – bobbing for apples –*
*turnip-carving – fancy dress*

It was decorated with a border of tiny bats and owls. My curiosity got the better of me. "Miss?" I asked her.

She turned and saw me standing beside her. "Oh, hello, Ivy," she said.

I smiled. People didn't often get it right on the first try when I wasn't standing beside my twin. I pointed at the poster. "We're having a party?"

Mrs Knight nodded. "It was all Ebony McCloud's idea. We've never celebrated All Hallows' Eve here at Rookwood before, and of course I'm trying to keep up our school spirit. I thought it seemed like a jolly good plan."

"That sounds nice," I said weakly. A sliver of ice had formed in my heart at the mention of Ebony's name, but I was trying my hardest to ignore it. Perhaps a party would be fun. Perhaps it was just what we needed.

Scarlet and I had never really joined in with any All Hallows' Eve celebrations before. When we'd lived at home, the end of October had been a time for cowering inside the house, with the rain and wind battering at the windows, hoping that any witches or spirits that were abroad would stay that way.

Miss Pepper was holding another sheaf of posters. I supposed she must have drawn them up. "Mr McCloud has been very supportive," she said.

That pricked up my ears. "Is he Ebony's father?" I asked.

"Oh yes," said Mrs Knight. "A most interesting man. And very generous too," she added, though I wasn't sure whether she was addressing me or Miss Pepper. Anyway, hurry along now, Ivy."

"Yes, Miss." I did as I was told, and quickly. But as I was scurrying through the corridors, I thought of what she'd said.

*Very generous.* That was interesting.

Was Mr McCloud giving money to the school? And what could that mean?

At lunchtime, I told Scarlet and Ariadne about the poster and what I'd overheard about Ebony's father (which unfortunately meant telling Muriel as well).

"A party!" Ariadne gave an excited gasp and nearly dropped her sandwich. "Whatever am I going to wear?"

"We need to make costumes," Scarlet said. I could already see the ideas forming in her eyes.

"I think I have something," Muriel added eagerly.

I looked at them all in disbelief. "The party wasn't the point!"

All three of them went quiet and stared at me.

I took a deep breath. "Did you hear what I said? Mrs Knight described Mr McCloud as interesting and *generous*. If he's been donating extra money to the school, then..."

Realisation dawned in Ariadne's eyes. "That could

explain why the teachers are so lenient with Ebony!"

"Hmm." Muriel frowned. "Are you sure? She might not have even been talking about money. Perhaps he's just generous as in nice. Anyway, Ebony's proved she has dark powers – that's what all the teachers are afraid of." I watched her carefully as she said this. Muriel always seemed to lean away from any discussion of the fact that Ebony's mischief might not be magic. Was she really a true believer, or did she just want *us* to believe it?

I still thought Mrs Knight's comments might be important. "Don't we need to investigate further? What if Ebony's father is mixed up in this as well somehow?"

Scarlet leant forward. "Maybe he's a witch too."

Ariadne's face wrinkled in thought. "Wouldn't he be a wizard?"

I wasn't sure whether to laugh or cry at this point.

"It seems unlikely that he would be involved," said Muriel, her lips twisting. "He's not even here."

"But it doesn't mean he can't have an influence," Scarlet said. "I think we need to go to that party. And we need to talk to him."

It wasn't long before the end of October. The nights were drawing in, slowly clawing away at the daylight hours. The leaves were a cacophony of reds and oranges and yellows. The school grounds were littered with conkers and pine cones, and everything crunched underfoot.

Scarlet couldn't stop talking about the party and kept insisting we needed to make something for the fancy dress. This was somewhat difficult, as we didn't own very many clothes. The only costumes that we'd ever owned had been the ones Aunt Sara made us for the ballet the year before, and we'd had to give those to Miss Finch for safekeeping.

But then in art, Miss Pepper announced that we would be making spooky masks from papier-mâché.

"We should match," Scarlet said excitedly.

"But what are we going to make?" I asked, staring down at the pile of paper on our desks. I wasn't sure what you were supposed to have as a mask. "What's spooky?"

Scarlet looked around the classroom and her eyes fell on Ebony, who was at the back, carrying two tins of black paint. "A black cat," Scarlet said.

So we both made black cat masks, with pointy ears and white whiskers, and almond-shaped holes for the eyes. We had black leotards, skirts and tights for ballet, and I thought that would do for the rest of the outfit.

I could stuff some old stockings with paper to make the tail.

Ariadne came bobbing over at the end of the lesson. "Look what I made!" She held up her mask and attempted a roar. It was a lion, with orange wool hair.

I grinned back at her. "Perfect!"

I was so pleased that we'd made up with Ariadne, but things were far from back to normal. She was still getting detentions. In music, she sang all the words wrong and was sent out. Her sewing had to be unpicked; she spilt her paints in art; her numbers didn't add up in arithmetic. She seemed in a daze half the time.

And every time I saw Ebony, I wondered... Was she still casting spells? Still putting curses on people? I swore I saw a smile twitch on her face whenever Ariadne or Muriel got into trouble, as if things were all going to plan. I considered whether we ought to follow her again, or try to sabotage her somehow – but then I would remember our stepmother in the headmistress's office, and I would go straight back to keeping my head down. I couldn't risk any trouble, knowing she would make us pay for it.

There was the matter of the party as well. Scarlet was so excited, and I was a little too, but there was something more pressing on my mind. All Hallows'

Eve was supposed to be a time for witches. When they flew out on broomsticks and cackled in the night air. When they stole away children who misbehaved. When they were most powerful.

Whether or not Ebony had a broomstick, I was certain she knew all about the stories and traditions. She had been the one to suggest this party to Mrs Knight. She was in control. She must have something *planned*.

And that scared me more than anything.

## Chapter Thirty-three

### SCARLET

When All Hallows' Eve finally arrived, it was on an unusually warm day. Mrs Knight called an assembly that morning and told us all what "jolly good fun" the party was going to be as we sat fanning ourselves in the previously freezing hall.

I could barely sit still. A real party! With costumes! It was really going to liven up Rookwood.

*Everything is good*, I thought to myself. *I have Ivy and Ariadne. There's going to be a party. We're going to have lots of fun. And as long as we stay out of trouble, it'll all be back to normal.*

I just tried not to look at Ebony and Muriel.

Mrs Knight, who was clearly over the moon about her new attempts to make Rookwood a Jolly Place of Learning that lots of parents would want to send their children to, then announced that there would be a whole-school photograph that morning instead of our first lesson.

We all trooped outside, where numerous benches had been placed on the fallen leaves. We had to line up, from youngest to oldest, and then get organised into our houses. There was a photographer, who had a well-groomed beard and a camera on a stand. He kept playing with its settings, reminding me of Ariadne's camera, which she had loved, but been told to leave at home after last year.

I realised quite quickly that this was not a good time to be unable to keep still. I kept fidgeting. It didn't help that as we were standing there, a chilly breeze began to blow against us.

"Everyone hold your positions!" Miss Bowler yelled. There were first formers crying and sixth formers braiding each other's hair. "Stop messing around and smile!"

"On three," the photographer called loudly. "One, two—"

"Three!" lots of people shouted, before collapsing into laughter.

Mrs Knight sighed so loudly that I could hear it from three rows back. "And again, please..."

When the photographer had finally managed to get a shot, we were shepherded back into school. I wondered what the photograph would look like. Perhaps we would resemble our mother and Aunt Sara in the old school picture Miss Jones had shown us.

"That's better!" Mrs Knight had called out with a smile. "One for the school newsletter!"

I fidgeted all through our lessons. When we got back to our room, I ran straight to the wardrobe and began putting on my black ballet outfit. Ivy, who was not in quite such a hurry, found the masks that we'd made and fitted them with string. I safety-pinned my tail to the back of my skirt. Perfect.

"Ready?" I asked Ivy with a grin.

She pulled her mask down over her face. "As I'll ever be..."

We headed downstairs, alongside a crowd of witches, clowns, ghosts and a whole menagerie of different animals. It certainly made a change from the usual sea of uniforms. Everyone was chatting excitedly, the sound of it buzzing around our heads. I peered out at it all through the gaps in my mask.

Rookwood's huge front doors were wide open, letting in the evening air. It was pleasant, but still had that chill to it. Someone had lit a selection of torches, which were leading the way out to the playing field.

I couldn't help but gasp when I caught sight of the field. What was usually a boring patch of flat grass had been transformed. It was filled with candles and little stands, and towering over it all in the rough at the back was a huge bonfire waiting to be lit. Girls in costumes and masks were milling about everywhere, along with some taller figures who I thought must be teachers and some parents.

Ivy let out a gasp too, but hers sounded a bit less excited and more... afraid.

I lifted up my mask a little. "What is it?" I hissed in her ear.

"The candles... It's just like my dream," she whispered back, sounding dazed.

I tried not to do a double-take as a skeleton wandered past. I'd never seen so many costumes in one place.

"Come on," I said, grabbing my twin's hand.

Whatever this party held in store, I wanted to experience it. I wanted to take it all in.

"Roll up, roll up!" I heard someone shout as we walked on to the field. It was Mrs Knight, who appeared to be dressed as an owl, complete with feathers all down her arms and a beak strapped to her face. She was standing over what looked like a large cauldron, full of water and apples. "Try the apple-bobbing!"

We watched in amusement as Anna Santos, who was wearing rabbit ears, attempted to pick up an apple with her teeth. She emerged with a soaking-wet face and one of the ears pointing in the wrong direction, but she had actually managed to pick up the apple.

Everyone applauded. Anna finally seemed to have found something she was good at.

I tugged Ivy along again. "This doesn't seem so bad, does it? It's just good fun. Not scary at all."

"I don't know," Ivy said quietly to me. "I feel like Ebony is behind this somewhere... I feel as though she's just waiting to trick us again. This whole thing *feels* like her."

I looked around, but if Ebony was present, there was no way to tell. Most people were disguised or had their faces covered entirely, and it was getting dark.

We neared a row of rough benches, where I caught

sight of a lion that I recognised as Ariadne. She waved us over.

"Look!" she said. "We're carving turnips!"

She dropped a turnip into my hands, which was not something I ever expected to happen. "Carving them how?"

Another feather-covered shape leant over us, with a blue-painted face and a knife. "We're making lanterns!"

I adjusted my mask and saw that it was Miss Pepper. "What are you, Miss?" I asked, a little shocked.

She stepped back into the light. "Why, I'm a peacock, of course!" She turned round and I saw she had a fan of peacock feathers behind her. It didn't seem particularly scary, but it did look pretty. "Be very careful with the carving knives, girls. But you hollow out the turnip, cut a little face and then you add a candle and hey presto!" She waved a knife at us and we all jumped. "A lantern! Isn't it fun? These are traditional in Scotland, you know."

I felt certain that Ivy was wincing behind her mask. Ebony's stamp was definitely here.

Miss Pepper gave me the knife (handle first, thankfully). "Give it a go," she said, before walking jauntily away.

I shrugged, picked up a turnip and started to do as

she had said. Cutting through it was a much tougher task than it looked.

There were several other girls carving turnips round the table, and some parents. I wondered briefly if Father might make an appearance, but it seemed very unlikely. I prayed that our stepmother wouldn't be interested. But she wouldn't need a costume if she did turn up. She was enough of a monster on her own.

"Is your father coming, Ariadne?" I asked.

"No," Ariadne said with a sigh. "I wrote to him, but he said he thought it sounded dangerous and that he would rather I went to a Teddy Bears' Picnic."

I laughed, and with some help from Ivy, carried on stabbing the unfortunate turnip.

"And besides," she continued, "he's not happy with me. The school told him that I've been getting into trouble."

"Was he really cross?" I asked, thinking of our stepmother.

"Not really. That was the worst part," Ariadne winced. "He just sounded so disappointed."

We carried on carving. Eventually we had something that looked roughly like a face. We put a little tealight inside and it lit up with a fiendish orange glow. I hoped I wouldn't smell like turnips for the next few weeks.

Pleased, I put the finished product down next to Ariadne's.

"What are you supposed to do with it?" Ivy asked.

"It wards off evil spirits, I think," Ariadne said.

"Oh, good," I said. That was probably something we could do with.

We went for a wander around the field, looking at some of the other tables where girls were crafting masks and throwing balls at coconuts. There were straw bales scattered around with hordes of girls in various costumes sitting on them, chatting and laughing. I spotted Agatha (who I still refused to call Clarissa) in a tall hat, helping to make toffee apples and hand them out, but there was still no sign of Ebony. It was making me feel a little on edge. I preferred to know where she was, so I could keep an eye on her.

We ran into Rose, who was not really wearing a costume, but appeared to have made herself a crown out of roses. She smiled before looking a little confused as she gazed back and forth between us. I realised she couldn't tell who we were under the masks. I lifted mine again and stuck my tongue out at her, and she laughed.

"Scarlet," she said simply, prodding me in the arm and then heading off, happily chewing on a toffee apple.

I grinned. I hoped Rose would be all right on her own.

"Girls!" Miss Bowler's voice suddenly boomed over the field. You could tell it was her instantly – nobody else was as loud as a foghorn. I turned and located her standing on a box. She appeared to be kitted out as some sort of sea creature, dressed in paper seaweed. It was quite a sight. I had to giggle, wondering if she had got the idea from having seen Ariadne dress us up last year.

"Ladies and gentlemen!" she continued, addressing the parents as well. "Make your way to the back of the field for... the lighting of the bonfire!"

"Ooh!" Ariadne bounced up and down with excitement. "I love a good bonfire. It's like Guy Fawkes Night come early!"

We bustled over there at the same time as everyone else did. It was crowded, but the three of us managed to shuffle to the front. Up close, the bonfire was vast, like a miniature mountain.

Madame Zelda stood beside the fire, and she looked *incredible*. Her silver hair was backcombed to the point that it looked as though she'd been given an electric shock. She was wearing a black dress and when she moved her arms, the sleeves draped out behind her like wings – but they were covered in silver cobwebs.

The caretaker stood beside her, holding a can of petrol. The chemical scent lingered in the air. He must have doused the pile of wood with it thoroughly.

"Ready, Miss?" I saw him say.

Madame Zelda nodded and then turned to the crowd, obviously determined to put on a show. "Welcome, all," she said with a flash of white teeth. "Let the bonfire be lit!"

She pulled out one of the matches she used for her incense, struck it and then stood well back before throwing it on the pile.

The wood must have been dry because the flames climbed quickly. Everyone shuffled back, away from the heat. There were lots of *oohs* and *aahs*.

We stood and stared into the dancing flames, and soon people were moving away again (or dancing away in the case of Madame Zelda), heading back to the stalls and the fun.

And that was when I saw her.

On the far side of the bonfire, in the flickering shadows, there was a girl dressed as a witch. A black pointy hat, a black flowing cloak that shrouded her whole body, and long black hair to match. A mask hid her face completely from view.

My heart squeezed. *Ebony.*

But what was she doing behind the bonfire? Alone?

The witch stepped closer and silently held up a piece of paper. I lifted my mask and squinted, trying to make out what it was.

And then I realised with horror... It was a photograph.

Of Ariadne.

## Chapter Thirty-four

### IVY

I think Ariadne and I noticed what was going on shortly after Scarlet did. I remember feeling my twin stiffen beside me, seeing her lift her mask. I followed her gaze.

And I saw the witch.

Ariadne let out a horrified gasp and I soon realised why. The witch was holding out a photograph of her. I recognised it, even from a distance, as the picture of Ariadne that had been used in the school newsletter to show that she was the photographer on our trip to Lake Seren.

At this point, almost everyone else had moved away from the bonfire, back to the activities. The few stragglers left behind were looking into the fire and didn't seem to have noticed the witch in the shadows beyond.

Ariadne had gone white beneath her lion mask. "What..." I heard her say. "Who's there?"

The fire spat smouldering embers, and a column of smoke rose out of it, waving towards us. I suddenly felt too afraid to move.

But Scarlet started shaking with anger. "Ebony!" she shouted over the crackling flames. "What do you think you're doing?"

The mask on the witch's face remained expressionless. The eyes were dark slits and they gave away nothing.

And then, with a flourish, she dropped the picture into the flames.

The bright orange fire licked at the photograph for only seconds before it crumpled away, falling into ash.

Ariadne lifted her mask. There were tears in her eyes. "Stop!" she called out.

But the witch just took a bow and then quickly slipped into the shadows.

Ariadne turned to us. "W-what was that about?" she stammered. "A threat? A *curse*?"

I grabbed Scarlet's arm. I could feel her shaking beneath my grip, see her clenched fists. I knew my twin, and she was about to run over there and do something we would all regret.

But before I could say anything, Mrs Knight appeared beside us, her owl-cape swooshing. "Everything all right here, girls? Staying out of trouble?" She smiled beneath the paper beak.

Scarlet froze and I could hear her heavy breathing. We all looked at Mrs Knight.

I couldn't do it. I couldn't say anything. We were on our very last warning and if we got involved in Ebony's dark dealings, well... things would not go well for us.

"Everything's fine, Miss," I said. Scarlet nodded.

As the words came out of my mouth, my glance slipped over to Ariadne, and I could see that she was crying now. But I could see the fire reflecting in her eyes. She stepped forward.

"Actually, Miss, it's not fine at all!" she cried. "Someone just burned a picture of me on the bonfire!"

Mrs Knight frowned, turned and looked round us. "Who?"

"Someone dressed as a witch," Ariadne gasped. "Over there." She pointed behind the bonfire. "I'm sure it was Ebony McCloud."

Mrs Knight then turned her neck quickly and darted her eyes across the field, which really added to the owl impression. *She's looking for Ebony's father*, I realised. My guess was solidified when the headmistress said, "You must be mistaken, dear. Ebony's a nice girl. I think you might be seeing things. The twins didn't see anything, after all."

I bit my lip. Scarlet stared at the floor. We should have corrected the headmistress. We should have told her that we'd seen it too.

Mrs Knight put a gentle hand on Ariadne's shoulder. "There, there, dear. I wouldn't worry about it. Perhaps you've just had a few too many toffee apples. Why don't you go and have a sit-down somewhere?" With a smile, she wandered off into the crowds.

I couldn't bear the look on Ariadne's face. "Ariadne, I—"

"Don't," she said, wiping away a tear.

"Sorry!" Scarlet said. "We couldn't say anything. You know we're at risk of being expelled. I'd go and give Ebony a good thumping, I would, but we'd be in so much trouble."

For a moment I thought Ariadne was going to back

down... that she would say it was all fine. But that fire was still in her eyes, as if she were possessed. "*You could have said something*. You could at least have told Mrs Knight that I was telling the truth."

Scarlet shrugged. "She probably wouldn't have believed us anyway."

Now Ariadne stepped closer to Scarlet, who was taken aback, stumbling towards the bonfire. "How could you? I thought we were best friends!"

I tried to take her hand, but she shook me off. "Of course we are—" I started.

"But you won't protect me if it means you two might get into trouble, right?" Ariadne cried.

Scarlet folded her arms, ever indignant. "That isn't what's happening," she insisted.

Our friend stared at us both, looking back and forth, as if she couldn't believe what she was seeing. I felt a rush of shame turning my cheeks red beneath my mask. Suddenly it felt like my tongue was swollen – I couldn't make the right words leave my mouth.

The tears fell even harder from Ariadne's eyes, glinting in the firelight.

"Maybe I'm not your best friend any more," she sobbed. And then she was running across the field, leaving Scarlet and me all alone.

We collapsed on to a straw bale a little way from the fire. For a while we didn't speak. And then the words finally came.

"This is awful," I said. My chest felt tight and there was a horrible sick feeling in my throat. What had we done?

My twin put her head in her hands. "We've really ruined everything this time."

"Perhaps we should just go and tell Mrs Knight right now," I said. "Tell her that we saw it too."

"No!" Scarlet looked at me as if I'd suggested we throw ourselves on the bonfire. "We can't! It could get us into big trouble for lying. And what if she didn't believe us? What would she do about it even if she did? She's been brainwashed into thinking Ebony's some sort of..." She scrunched up her face. "*Little Miss Perfect.*"

I didn't know what we could do. "Then perhaps we have to leave it. Just carry on with the party and try to sort everything out tomorrow." I realised that our friendship with Ariadne was becoming one long string of apologies and it made me feel even more awful. Tendrils of smoke from the fire curled around my feet before rushing upwards, making us cough.

Scarlet pulled a fistful of straw from the bale. "Ugh," she sighed in frustration. "Something just isn't right.

Was that really some kind of curse? Or is Ebony just threatening her? If Ariadne gets hurt, we'll never forgive ourselves. We need to stop Ebony right now!"

"But how do we do that without getting into trouble?" I wailed. The situation was becoming desperate. We were getting beaten at every turn.

Scarlet threw the straw at the fire, but the wind caught it, sweeping it away across the grass. "Perhaps I could just talk to Ebony."

I gave her a look.

"I will! I promise! No hitting or kicking or screaming. If I, or we, just talk to her, maybe we can find out what she really wants."

My twin had a point. I stood up. "All right. Let's look for her. Come on."

We wandered aimlessly through the party, where the candles and turnip lanterns now shone brightly in the growing darkness. I began to realise that it was going to be difficult to find anyone in particular because everyone was essentially in disguise.

There were also quite a lot of witches. Every way we turned, I saw black pointy hats. It was as if Ebony was everywhere and nowhere at the same time.

Some of them were Ebony's followers as well.

I saw Ethel whispering to Mary, both of them dressed as witches. I began to wonder if it was deliberate, to confuse us. But then it also seemed that witches were just a popular All Hallows' Eve costume, anyway.

We must have walked all the way round the field about three times. Just as I was beginning to feel frantic, I felt a gentle tug on my arm. I turned and saw Rose standing behind us.

"Rose!" Scarlet said. "Have you seen Ebony?"

Rose made a confused face and gestured around at everyone in their costumes. I realised what she meant quite quickly.

"We think she was dressed as a witch, all in black," I explained. "We just saw her burning Ariadne's picture, and now Ariadne's gone off upset. We thought if we could talk to her, then..."

Rose's quizzical expression deepened. She waved us nearer so that she could talk quietly. "Then I think I have seen her. She was taking Ariadne."

"Hold on a moment," Scarlet said. "*Taking* her? As in dragging her, kicking and screaming?"

Rose shook her head. "I would have told someone if it had been like that. They were just walking away."

"Did you see where they went next?" I asked.

Rose's head shook again. "Sorry."

"That's all right," I said. "Thank you."

As Rose got back into the queue for the toffee apples, I turned to my twin. "Do you think Ariadne's decided to try and talk to Ebony by herself then?"

Scarlet frowned. "She must have done. Damn!"

I had to agree with Scarlet's cursing. Our best friend had just been threatened by a witch on Halloween and then wandered off into the darkness with her, alone. On the whole, "damn" might have been an understatement.

We had to find Ariadne. And fast.

## Chapter Thirty-five

## SCARLET

The search was really on now. We started asking people if they'd seen a girl dressed as a lion, but they either said no or ignored us. I muttered angrily at them as we moved on past. Didn't they realise how important this was?

We found Miss Finch sitting near the entrance, who had evidently just arrived at the party, since we hadn't seen her on her other rounds. She was wearing a long white dress, with a white-powdered face and dark make-up round her eyes. She had even painted her walking stick white and wrapped it in bandages.

She smiled as we approached. "You look like you've seen a ghost! Well, that was the idea, anyway."

Ivy managed a weak smile. "You make a great ghost, Miss."

"Thank you," Miss Finch replied. "I wanted to come as the scariest thing I could imagine, but I didn't think turning up dressed as my mother would go down too well. So a ghost it was."

"Miss," I jumped in, "have you seen Ariadne? Or Ebony McCloud?"

Miss Finch thought for a moment. "I don't think so. Perhaps you can ask Mr McCloud? He's just over there, talking to Mrs Knight."

I raised my eyebrows at Ivy. Maybe this was our chance to get some information. "That's great, Miss, thank you!"

Madame Zelda was approaching Miss Finch with a mug of tea, but we darted round her and headed for the headmistress and Ebony's father.

As the crowds parted, I could see them standing together near the apple-bobbing tub. The ground surrounding it was muddy with all the splashed water, but Mrs Knight had led him to a fresh patch of grass.

I could tell who he was straight away. He was tall and his hair was as dark as Ebony's, as was his perfectly trimmed moustache and beard. He was dressed in an expensive-looking suit with red detailing that I was certain Aunt Sara would have marvelled over.

We got closer and Ivy was about to approach him, but I suddenly had other ideas and held her back. "Let's give it a moment. We should listen," I hissed.

Mrs Knight was clearly buttering him up. "...You're *so* generous, Mr McCloud, to give us a contribution for all this."

"It was nothing at all," he said with a warm smile. "Nothing's too much for my wee girl. She loved all these traditions back home. Where has she got to?"

"I expect she's off having fun," Mrs Knight said, a little dismissively. I noticed she had discarded her paper beak and looked like she was trying to pretend that she wasn't dressed as an owl. "How are you getting on in Fairbank?"

"Oh, marvellously," he replied. He took a sip of his drink, which looked rather like whisky. "It's always been a dream of mine to own a theatre and the Royal is such a treasure."

I looked at Ivy. *He owns that theatre?* It was where

our ballet recital had taken place the year before. Not that we'd taken part in it, because we'd been busy fighting off an evil headmistress, but that was another story.

"I do *love* the theatre," said Mrs Knight. I thought she was hamming it up a bit. "What have you put on?"

Mr McCloud smiled. "I worked my way up from being a magician in a music hall, but Shakespeare is where my heart lies. So of course, the first play had to be The Scottish Play. They say it's bad luck, but not for us it seems. Sold out every night!"

Ivy gasped.

"What?" I whispered.

"He means *Macbeth*," she replied in hushed tones. "It's bad luck to say the title. But..." Her sentence trailed off, but I followed it. Magic and *Macbeth*. Two things that explained a lot about Ebony.

Mrs Knight put her hand on his arm. "I hope Ebony will be a wonderful young actress, then. Perhaps we shall have her for the lead in the school play."

"Oh yes," Ebony's father smiled again, but it seemed a little sad. "I hope so too; she's grown up around the theatre. It's in her blood."

I was beginning to build up a picture. Young Ebony, growing up around her father, seeing plays and magical performances, taking it all in. Was that where she was getting this from?

"You seem a little unsure," Mrs Knight said gently.

"Well," he said, staring down into the glass of honey-coloured liquid. "I worry about her. I think she wants to be an actress, but she's very shy and reserved."

I blinked. *Ebony? Shy and reserved?* Was he talking about the same girl?

"A lot of the time she won't leave her room, the poor wee thing," he continued. "That's why I got her that cat. It's a companion for her, you see."

At this point the picture of Ebony was becoming a ten-foot painting.

"I expect that's where she'll be," he continued. "She loves All Hallows' Eve, but I expect she'll have had enough by now. I'll go up and find her later."

I grabbed Ivy and began to drag her away.

"What is it?" she hissed.

"We have to go and look in Ebony's room," I said as I pulled her through the crowds. "I'm beginning to think she might not be our witch."

Inside the school, it was deathly quiet. Nobody wanted to miss the chance to have a bit of fun at Rookwood. The hallways were empty and we swept through them and up the stairs like ghosts.

We stopped outside Ebony's door.

"Should we knock?" Ivy whispered.

I shook my head. I had a better idea. The element of surprise and all that. I wrenched open the door...

And there was Ebony, sitting alone, just as her father had said she would be.

But she wasn't sitting on the bed I'd expected, the one draped with black embroidery. No, Ebony McCloud was lounging on the regular bed, reading a book and hugging the teddy bear in the pink frilly dress. Her cat was curled up on her feet, snoozing.

Most importantly, though, she wasn't dressed as a witch. She was just wearing her nightgown.

For a moment, we were too stunned to say anything. And so was she. She just sat there, wide-eyed and white, and soon a flush of embarrassment rushed to her cheeks. She slowly let go of the teddy.

The words eventually came to my lips. "You've never had a roommate, have you?"

Her mouth flapped open and closed as if she were about to argue, but she'd clearly been caught red- (or possibly pink-) handed. "No," she said quietly.

We'd got her. I stepped into the room, pulled Ivy in and shut the door behind me. The window was open a crack, letting in some of the chilly night air. "Right," I said. "We know this is all an act. You're not as confident and self-assured as we thought you were. We just heard it from your father and we can see it quite plainly right here." I gestured at her. "Now I'm going to give you five minutes to explain to us why you're doing it."

Ebony folded her arms, although she was a little shaky. "Why should I?"

Ivy pointed at her. "Because our friend has just been threatened and possibly kidnapped by someone dressed as a witch, and we need to get to the bottom of this mess!"

I nodded, feeling a slight spark of happiness at seeing my twin back me up so brilliantly. "And," I added, snatching the teddy bear from Ebony, "because if you don't, I'm going to parade Mr Fluffy here around the school and tell everyone that you're a total fraud!"

With an exasperated sigh, Ebony sat forward and put her head in her hands. Her cat yawned, stretched and moved to a different corner of the bed, paying us no attention. Eventually, Ebony looked up again. "All right," she said. "Fine. I'll explain."

"This had better be good," I said.

She glared up at me. "I'm no witch. I can't do curses.

I made it all up. Is that what you want to hear?"

I waved my hand, telling her to go on. We needed more.

I could tell she was biting the inside of her cheek. "I've never been to school before. I used to travel around with my papa, while he played in different places in Scotland. He taught me about acting and magic, how to read, how to count numbers and sell tickets." She took a deep breath. "And I liked it that way. But since we moved here and he bought that theatre, he decided I ought to get a *proper* education."

I raised my eyebrows. *Now where have I heard that before?* I could understand that much.

"I didn't want to come to school," she continued. "I begged and cried. But he thought it was best for me. I tried my best at the entrance exam because I wanted to make him proud. I thought I had no choice. But then, after the exam... I met someone that day. We got talking. And when I told them I didn't want to stay at Rookwood, they started telling me about this plan they had, and said that all it needed was someone who could perform..." She trailed off, looking unsure.

"Who?" I asked. "Who did you meet?"

She shook her head and ignored the question. "They said they would give me instructions and that if I followed them, the school would soon want to kick me out and I could go back home. Father had told me I needed to make new friends and I felt so lucky to have found someone who wanted me to do what I loved. And at first, it was fun. I got to play this role and it felt right." She moved her hand from her book and now we could see that she was reading *Macbeth*.

I looked at my twin. *How appropriate*, I mouthed.

Ebony must have read my lips. "Father loves books about witchcraft and magic," she said. "He lends them to me. That was another fun part."

Ivy turned back to her. "But then soon it wasn't fun any more?" She knew how this story went.

"Well," Ebony stared at the floor for a moment. "It was still quite fun. But I was beginning to worry that people would get hurt. And more than that... it's tiring, performing all the time. No one here is really my friend. They all just want me to be like a character I made up."

"Not to mention that it hasn't worked," I said, more than a little derisively. "You haven't been kicked out. Quite the opposite, in fact. The teachers don't think you can put a foot wrong."

Ivy nodded. "We thought they were under your spell."

Ebony laughed. "A spell on the teachers? That's a

joke. "That's not what happened. That, at least, is Papa's fault," she explained, reaching out to stroke her cat, who had splayed himself out across the covers. "How was I to know that he'd start making donations? He heard the school was in trouble and wanted to help."

*Aha*, I thought to myself, looking at my twin. So I'd been right about that at least. "So if you're not really a witch," I said, "then who's the one behind this?" I asked. Time was running out. "Who's the one in the witch costume?"

"I can't tell you!" she said desperately. "I can't!"

I racked my brains. Who had been around this whole time? Who had joined the school this year?

And then I saw Ebony's playing cards on her side table and a light suddenly went on in my mind.

Who had previously had a vendetta against Ariadne? Who had been acting suspiciously? Who had a Joker card on them after we got tricked with the very same cards?

"Muriel!" I cried. "It's Muriel!"

## Chapter Thirty-six

## IVY

I could tell from the expression on Ebony's face that Scarlet had hit the nail on the head.

"Don't tell her I told you anything," she said desperately.

"You're afraid of her?" Scarlet asked.

Ebony nodded, slowly and solemnly. It was sad to see her fall from grace like this, from being an elegant enchantress to a shy, scared girl. What exactly had Muriel done to her?

"Look," I said, "I know all about hiding behind a

mask." To make the point, I took the mask off my head. I knew well that sometimes people wore a mask for their own safety. "I had to pretend to be Scarlet once."

"It's a long story," Scarlet added.

I went and sat behind Ebony. I knew we needed to get on her side if we were going to have any chance of finding Muriel and Ariadne. "You don't need to hide any more. I know you don't want to be at this school, but if you're stuck here, then you need to be yourself and make real friends. It's the only way to get through." I felt a pang in my heart as I said that.

"And if you *really* want to go home," Scarlet said, sitting on the opposite bed, "you need to tell your father the truth. That's your only chance. He obviously loves you."

Ebony stared at the floor, but I saw a flush of colour return to her cheeks. I think she knew we were right.

"Tell us what Muriel is up to." Scarlet met her eyes directly. "If we know, then maybe we can find our friend."

"We won't let Muriel do anything to you," I insisted.

Midnight the cat stood up then and padded across the bed back to Ebony. He meowed at her inquisitively.

"You too?" she said with a sigh. "All right. I'll tell you what I know. But *please*, don't tell her."

"We won't." I knew I had to jump on the opportunity. "What is going on?"

"She told me..." Ebony rubbed her arm. "She told me that she'd been expelled from her last school after a snitch accused her of being the ringleader of a gang of bullies. She said that the snitch was expelled too, for burning down their clubhouse."

"Ariadne," I said. "And it was a shed, really."

Ebony nodded and stroked her cat. It seemed to calm her down a little. "Muriel is from a rich and important family, but they were furious with her for having to leave her school. They wanted to disown her completely, called her a stain on their reputation. In the end they sent her to live with some distant cousin in Fairbank. But... she never forgot what Ariadne had done to her. She wanted revenge. So she hatched this plan and she talked me into joining her."

"And you just went along with it all?" Scarlet asked.

I gave her a look. We were supposed to be getting Ebony on side, not upsetting her.

But Ebony seemed unfazed. "I did," she said. "She made it all seem like a big joke, you see. This wonderful prank, convincing everyone that she was a victim of this 'witch', and that we'd be there laughing at how you'd all fallen for it. But the further I got, the more I realised she just wanted to hurt everyone – especially Ariadne." She shut her eyes. "And by that point I was in too deep to stop."

"Did she threaten to do something to you?" I asked. "If you stopped, I mean?"

Ebony gaped for a second, and then she nodded again.

A cold breeze blew in from the open window, bringing a few autumn leaves in with it. One of them fluttered in the air for a second, like a bat.

That was what brought the question to my mind. "If Muriel is responsible for this, then what happened with the curse we saw you put on her? She disappeared and came back hurt."

Ebony shrugged. "Smoke and mirrors."

"What?" Scarlet asked.

Ebony's stormy eyes flashed up to her. "It was all pretend. Acting. Stage make-up. I helped her. She went to a hiding place and then came back when everyone was sufficiently worried."

*A hiding place...* Perhaps that could be where she'd taken Ariadne!

I stood up. "Where was it? Where did she hide?" Scarlet looked at me and I saw the realisation dawn in her eyes. This was our chance.

Ebony winced and the cat jumped before settling down again. "I can't..."

But Scarlet wasn't having any of it. "We need to know! If we don't stop whatever Muriel's up to, Ariadne could get hurt and you'll never be free of her!"

There were a few moments of painful silence before we finally got an answer. "In the crypt."

My twin wrinkled her nose. "Crypt? What crypt?"

"There's a crypt," Ebony explained. "Under the school chapel. I don't think anyone else knows it's there. Muriel found a diagram of it in the school library, in some old book. That's where she was hiding out."

"Have you been there?" I asked. "Can you take us?"

"Unfortunately not." She pulled her knees up to her chest, dislodging the cat.

Scarlet looked at me. "We have to go and look. If she's got Ariadne... that must be where they are."

An owl hooted from somewhere in the trees, reminding us of the time. I looked out of the window and saw a full moon rising out of the clouds. *Of course.*

"Take me with you," Ebony said suddenly.

"What?" we both exclaimed. I'd thought she would be too terrified of Muriel after the way she had been acting.

But she extended her pale legs and stood up, then

went over to her wardrobe. "This is my fault. I need to help, somehow."

"Well," Scarlet said, looking at me. "She does have a point."

Ebony gave a sharp nod. "Give me two minutes."

Two minutes later, we were heading back down the stairs. But this time, the two of us black cats were accompanied by Ebony in her usual dark attire, and the real-life black cat, Midnight. He trotted at her heels like a dog.

But when we got to the bottom, I saw an unwelcome sight – crowds of girls flooding back into the school. The party must be over. As if sensing this too, Midnight slunk away from us. I suspected that meant it would be difficult to get outside.

My suspicions were confirmed when we reached the foyer.

Miss Bowler and Mrs Knight were standing at the doorway, ushering everyone in and waving goodbye to the guests.

With a glance back at me, Scarlet dragged us over to them. And then she tried something that probably only she would do – she tried to walk straight out.

"AHEM!" Miss Bowler didn't clear her throat, but

pronounced the entire word. "Where do you think you're going, Grey?"

Scarlet spun round. "Miss, I... I lost my shoe!"

I looked down at her feet and realised she had quickly kicked her shoe off and it was now resting behind mine. I tried to push it gently out of sight.

"I need to go back and get it!" Scarlet pleaded. "I can't go about with only one shoe!"

I could have sworn Miss Bowler actually rolled her eyes. "No," she said, moving in front of the doorway and blocking our path. "You can find it tomorrow!"

"But, Miss!" we all tried.

"Miss Bowler is right," Mrs Knight called. "You need to get to your beds. Run along, now. It's late enough as it is."

"And besides, there's ghosts and ghouls out there and they'll eat you!" Someone whispered in my ear in a menacing voice. I didn't have to turn round to know who it was.

"Thank you, Penny," I said, not rising to the bait. She cackled as she walked away.

"Looks like there really always was just the one witch around here," Scarlet muttered.

Reluctantly, we moved back through the crowds, Scarlet shuffling her shoe along as we did so.

"We can't give up now," I said. Knowing that Muriel was out for revenge against Ariadne had made everything so much worse. Now I feared our friend was in real danger.

"Who said anything about giving up?" Scarlet pushed us both towards the doors. "Come on…"

She dragged us further down the corridors to a place that was empty and quiet. Our footsteps echoed off the walls.

"Right, Miss McCloud," Scarlet said, leaning down to put her shoe back on. "I *know* you have ways of getting out of the school. So what is it? Magic? Just a trick?"

Ebony looked at the floor sheepishly. "I stole some of the caretaker's keys," she said.

"Do you still have them?" I asked.

As an answer, she pulled them out of the pocket of her black dress. "He still thinks he's lost them."

"You should give them back," I said.

"…after we've saved Ariadne," Scarlet said. "Right. The teachers will probably be keeping a close eye on the front doors for a while. We can't let them see us." She didn't elaborate, but I knew she was thinking about how we were on our last warning. They couldn't know we were involved with this. If we could get Ariadne back and talk Muriel out of her plan, then everything would be fine. "Do you have a key for the back ones?

"I think so." Ebony jangled the keys to select the right one and Scarlet winced at the noise.

We headed for the back door, keeping an eye out for the teachers. When we reached it, Ebony slipped the key into the lock and wrenched the handle. It opened out on to the dark All Hallows' Eve night.

As Scarlet and Ebony peered out, I imagined I could see two paths in front of me. On one, we would walk through that door, throw ourselves into inevitable trouble and be expelled from Rookwood. On the other, we would give up, go back to the safety of our beds...

And lose Ariadne forever.

I took a deep breath, and I chose my path.

## Chapter Thirty-seven

## SCARLET

Of all the things I had expected to be doing on All Hallows' Eve, sneaking out of the school with my twin sister and Rookwood's resident witch was not one of them.

It was quite a walk round the huge building, across gravel paths and grass that was crunchy with fallen leaves. It was lucky that we were all wearing black because we seemed to fade into the shadows.

The playing field was now empty of people, though the stalls had yet to be taken down. Most of the candles had been extinguished, but I could still see a lone grinning turnip glowing at the entrance.

I jumped at every noise, every flicker I spotted out of the corner of my eye. I told myself it was because it could be teachers, but the truth was I felt on edge. It was much colder than it had been at the party and the full moon was casting everything in an eerie light.

When we reached the front of the school, I could see the chapel looming out of the darkness. I turned to look at the doors, but now they were locked shut. Everyone must have been back inside. There were still a few cars in the driveway, presumably because some of the parents hadn't yet left.

We crept towards the graveyard. "How do you get inside?" Ivy asked.

Ebony stopped in her tracks. "I don't know," she said, her brow wrinkling with concern. "I don't think I have a key for the door here."

"Let's try," I said. It was worth it. "I'll keep a lookout."

So we stood at the dark-stained wooden doors of the chapel, while Ebony tried every key she had. Nothing worked. I was beginning to feel twitchy. What if Muriel and Ariadne weren't even here? I pressed my ear to the doors, but I couldn't hear a thing.

"I'm not even sure if this is the way into the crypt,"

Ebony said with a frown. "It's underneath the chapel."

I turned to Ivy. "Have you ever noticed any stairs in there?"

She shook her head. "I don't think so. But then I've never been in the vestry."

I looked to the side of the chapel where the small extension jutted off it. There could be stairs in there, but there was no way into it either.

"There *has* to be an easy way in," I insisted. "Otherwise how would Muriel be getting in and out all the time?"

Ebony stared up at the moon for a second and said something in the strange language that she'd spoken before.

"What is that?" I asked. "I thought you must have been making it up."

She went a little red. "Oh, sorry, it's Gaelic. A rare tongue now, but my mama spoke it to me. I still think in it sometimes. I was wondering... what if the way in is outside?"

Ivy's face lit up. "I think I have an idea. Follow me."

She led us round the side of the chapel, into the graveyard. As we reached a small clearing, she said, "I remembered when you were doing the curse, Ebony. You were in front of these doors."

And sure enough, there were those two wooden doors in the grass beside the chapel wall that looked as if they were leaning into a stone pedestal. They looked ancient.

I glanced at Ivy and Ebony. Ebony was shaking a little, though whether it was from the cold or the thought of confronting Muriel, I didn't know. Ivy looked determined and I knew it was because she had to be.

Without saying anything, Ivy and I knelt down in the grass and pulled open the doors, which were thankfully unlocked. A strange scent swept out, dusty and old, like a forgotten tomb.

And in the moonlight, I could see stone steps. They went down under the chapel, spiralling into the darkness.

I hated being confined in tight spaces, hated not being able to see. It brought back so many bad memories. But this was for Ariadne.

I stepped on to the stairs. It was time to save our friend. I just prayed we wouldn't be too late.

I took each step slowly, holding on to the walls as I went. There were no handrails and they were covered in soil and dust. The others followed me and I could hear their breathing.

I saw a warm light below and a familiar smell filled my nose. It was a burning torch, like the ones we'd used in the cave on the school trip.

And, faintly, I heard voices and then the sound of someone crying.

I stopped as we reached the bottom and took in the sight. It was a fairly small room, with the light from the few lit torches dancing over stone-vaulted ceilings. There were a pair of open iron gates halfway across, and behind them was a dais with what looked like a stone coffin lying on it. The final resting place of another of Rookwood's long-dead lords.

And there, in front of the coffin, was Ariadne. She was sobbing and I could just about make out that her hands were tied behind her back, and attached to an iron ring in the dais.

I would have run to her, set her free, but right in the middle of the crypt...

Was the witch.

I shoved the others back behind me so that we could just see out.

"You see, Ariadne?" Muriel was saying. Her mask lay on the floor, a discarded face. So did a black wig. But she had kept the witch's hat and cloak, and that was all I could see of the back of her. "It's just the way the world works. You ruined my life, so I'm ruining yours."

"I-I don't understand!" Ariadne sobbed. "I thought we were friends now."

Muriel gave a theatrical sigh. "Were you even listening? All of it. *Everything* that's gone wrong in my life. *It was all your fault*." She was speaking so coldly, so matter-of-factly. "You made me do this."

Tears were running down Ariadne's face. I gripped Ivy's hand, feeling Ebony's breath on the back of my neck.

"But you bullied me!" Ariadne cried in a moment of bravery, tugging on the rope that tied her to the dais. "That's why I had to tell on you back then."

But Muriel seemed to be in a trance. She ignored Ariadne and carried on talking. "I didn't see it coming when the school expelled me and my parents disowned me. So I didn't want you to see it coming either. I had to tear you down slowly. I kept you up late. I wanted you tired, so you'd trust me and make more mistakes. I helped those mistakes along in whatever way I could. I had everyone fooled, even the school nurse was stupid enough to believe that I was hurt." She laughed, and the sound was horrible. "I made you believe I was a friend and that Ebony was the one you had to watch out for."

"But Ebony—" Ariadne started.

"Ebony was just a distraction." I could hear the smile in Muriel's voice.

*She thinks she's so clever.* I felt the anger welling up inside me.

"She said it to me herself." Muriel put on an imitation of Ebony's accent. "*It's classic misdirection. You make the people look where you want them to. You hide the cards in plain sight.*"

I couldn't help glaring at Ebony, who shrank back against the wall. She must have known what she was getting involved with, at least on some level.

"You know what the best part is?" Muriel asked, while Ariadne sobbed quietly. "You did most of the work for me. You pushed your friends away. They don't care about you any more, if they ever even did. They don't listen to you. They have each other. You have no one. I could leave you down here to rot if I wanted. Nobody knows this place is here."

Ariadne said nothing now. I prayed that she might be able to see us so that she wouldn't be so scared, but we were in the shadows and her eyes were glued to the floor. She was hunched over, almost curling into a ball, but still standing.

347

"Everything you cared about, gone, just like that."
Muriel clapped her hands once, sharply. "No school.
No friends. No mummy and daddy. How does that
make you *feel*? You. Have. No one."

It was at this point that I couldn't take it any longer.
"You're wrong! She has us!"

I ran into the crypt and squared up to Muriel.
Ariadne gasped through her sobs and I looked up at the
witch. She towered over me already and the tall black
hat and boots only added to her height.

Ivy and Ebony skidded in behind me. Muriel turned
to look at them. "Oh," she said, a quizzical expression
on her face.

I put my hands on my hips. "It's over, Muriel. We
know everything that you've done. And we've come to
get her back."

"No," Muriel said. "You can't do this. All my plans—"

"You shouldn't have used me!" Ebony cried at her.
"I thought you were my friend too, but you're nothing
but a... a... wicked *witch*!"

Muriel's face seemed to crumple and she shrank
down. "Fine," she said. "Have your friend back. See if
I care."

Ivy glanced at me and then together we all ran to
Ariadne.

"Are you all right?" Ivy asked.

"I... I... don't..." she sobbed, her eyes wide and afraid.

Ebony began tugging at the rope that bound Ariadne's hands, but it was tied too tightly. "Ssh, it's okay," I reassured her.

But Ariadne's expression became more frantic. "Don't trust her!" she gasped.

I turned, just in time to see the iron gates shut behind us with a heavy *clang*. There was the click of a key turning in a lock.

"See?" said Muriel from the other side of the gates. "I told you they didn't listen."

## Chapter Thirty-eight

## IVY

We were trapped! Scarlet ran to the gates and shook them furiously. "Muriel!" she yelled. "Don't you dare!"

But the cowed look had gone from Muriel's face and she stood as tall and straight as ever.

"Well, what a show," she said. "I didn't expect to have all of you attending, but here we are. And for my final trick..." She waved her black-gloved hand with a flourish. "I'll be making you all disappear. Happy All Hallows' Eve!"

With that, she dropped her hat to the floor, turned and fled up the spiral staircase, leaving us locked in.

"No, no, no..." Ebony sank down to the floor beside the gates.

"We're stuck," Scarlet said in disbelief. "No one knows we're here!"

I turned to Ariadne, who had half collapsed against the dais. She looked up at me, her face streaked with tears. "It's all my fault!" she wailed.

"How can it be your fault?" Scarlet asked.

Ariadne squeezed her eyes tight shut. "I didn't see all this coming. I pushed you all away! I've done badly at school and you two have almost been expelled, and –" she gulped – "now I've got us into this mess! She's right, I'm worthless!"

"You're not—" Scarlet started, but Ariadne was crying too hard to listen.

"Why did I ever burn down that shed?" she sobbed. She pulled against the rope on her wrists. "Why did I listen to Muriel? I'm so *stupid*!"

"Ariadne!" I put my hands gently on her shoulders. "You have to listen to me. Don't pull, you'll hurt yourself."

She was panicking, her breathing shallow.

"Ariadne," Scarlet said. "You're our best friend. You

always have been our best friend. None of this matters!"

Ariadne shook her head, gulping back sobs. She couldn't wipe her tears away, since her hands were tied, so they just fell from her face like rain. "You'd be better off without me," she whispered.

I had to get her out of this. It was as if she'd fallen into a deep pit and somehow I had to reach her. "No! Just think of everything you've done," I cried. "Without you, Scarlet would still be locked away in an asylum. The school would still be run by Miss Fox and we'd be suffering for it every single day! And goodness only knows what would have happened to Rose. We needed you all those times and we need you again now!"

Ebony stared up at me wide-eyed as I said all this.

"B-but..." Ariadne gulped. "I should have believed you! I should have known I was being taken for a ride!"

Scarlet stepped closer. "We all make mistakes. Maybe you should have, but we weren't honest with you. We got so caught up in ourselves that we didn't talk things through properly." I couldn't tell whether the flush of anger in my twin's cheeks was at the thought of what Muriel had done or what *we* had done, but I thought it was probably a bit of both. "We're twins, it's easy for us to forget that other people don't live in our bubble."

Ariadne's sobs started to get quieter and her eyes

raised a little. "I just feel so worthless," she said. "I've led you into this mess."

"You're not worthless!" I insisted, feeling my voice crack with sadness and guilt and fear. "We need you! *I* need you."

I was trying to push down the panic that was rising in my own chest as I looked at the cold stone walls, dripping with damp. I imagined the darkness that lay behind the last flicker of the torch. *I don't want to be stuck forever*, I thought. *I don't want to die down here.*

"You're our brains, and our heart, and our courage," Scarlet told her. "Muriel's the one who's nothing. She's just an act. A mask."

Ebony stood up then. "And so am I."

Scarlet turned to her. "Ebony, I—"

"No," she said, waving my twin away. "This whole thing is half my fault." She looked at our friend, whose face was crumpled with crying. "I'm so sorry, Ariadne, I really am. I didn't even know you. I was so busy being selfish and thinking about my own life that I got swept up in this whole deception." She came closer and put her hands gently on the rope before closing her eyes. "I might as well have tied you up myself. I don't know what I was thinking. You're none of the things Muriel said you were. You're clearly so much more."

Ariadne bit her lip. Her sobs had slowed to a halt. "Do you mean it?"

"We all mean it," I said. Scarlet threw her arms round our friend and I joined in. Ebony stood looking a little uncomfortable for a moment before she joined in too. Ariadne gave a quiet, mouse-like laugh.

We moved back to stop her running out of air. "Remember our first day at Rookwood, when you cried in the toilets because you thought people might be staring at you? Look how far you've come."

"All the way to a dusty damp crypt," she said, but there was a cheeky glint in her sadness and Scarlet immediately started to laugh. Soon we all did, though I deeply wished we were laughing for a better reason. But if we didn't laugh, well...

It didn't bear consideration. I had to get everyone thinking. "The only way we're going to get out of here alive is if we put all of our strengths together," I said.

Scarlet nodded.

I felt a sharp pain in my chest as I stared at my sister and my best friend, trapped down here forever. This may have been someone's tomb, but I didn't want it to be ours.

Ariadne took a deep, shaky breath. I could see a shimmer returning to her eyes. "Ivy," she said, "can you take a closer look at the gates?"

I went over and shook the bars of our iron prison. They were quite solid.

"C-can you look at the lock? Does it seem simple?" Ariadne said, her voice gradually regaining its steadiness.

"Yes," I said. "I think so." It was a regular keyhole and the gates were very old.

Now our friend's face brightened. "I think I might be able to pick it!" *Of course!* Ariadne had always been skilled at lock-picking, thanks to a governess who would lock her in cupboards. "Oh," she said. "But how am I going to get out of this?" She twitched her tied-up hands.

Ebony tipped her head on one side. "I think I can do it," she said. "Papa used to do some escapology. He taught me a lot of knots." She knelt down on the stone floor of the crypt and peered more closely at the ropes. "Hmm. Muriel was good at these. But... I think I'm better." She began pulling at various bits of the rope, her hands working quickly. And after a few different tugs, I could see the knot getting slacker.

"It's working!" Scarlet cried.

Seconds later, with one final pull, the knot slid out and the rope coiled to the floor like a dead snake.

Ariadne shook her hands out, her wrists burnt red. "Thank you!" she said to Ebony.

"It was the least I could do," Ebony said with a shrug.

Once Ariadne had the feeling back in her hands, Scarlet led her to the gates. "Come on, Ariadne," she said. "You can do this! We believe in you!"

Ariadne grinned nervously. She began patting at her hair round her lion mask, which was still perched on top of her head. "I know I used some pins to keep this on... aha!"

I watched as she pulled out a couple and inserted them into the lock. Scarlet started pacing and I knew what she was thinking. *If this doesn't work... we're done for.* I started composing prayers in my head, to anyone who would listen.

I wasn't sure how long it took, but it felt like an age. And then, suddenly, we heard...

*Click.*

"Yes!" Ebony said, clapping. "You did it!"

Ariadne pushed at the gates and they swung open.

Scarlet ran over and hugged her. "See? We needed you."

Ariadne said nothing, but her cheeks flushed.

"Come on!" Scarlet ran up the stone steps and the rest of us swiftly followed her.

But I began to realise that something was wrong. I could see no moonlight above us. And that meant...

"The doors are shut!" Scarlet shouted.

I leant back against the damp wall, feeling the rough stone beneath my fingers. I should have known that Muriel wouldn't let us get away that easily.

"Oh no," Ariadne whispered.

Scarlet pushed on the doors, threw all her weight into it, but they didn't budge. I went up and stood beside her on the narrow steps and we both tried pushing together. It was no use. Muriel must have wedged them shut.

"It's probably a bad time to admit this," I heard Ebony say, "but I'm actually afraid of the dark."

"I'm not fond of it either," Scarlet retorted a little snappily. "Now what—"

But an idea was forming in my mind. "Then maybe what we need is some light."

I squeezed past the others and dashed back down the steps. And there, on the wall of the crypt, was what I was looking for. The flaming torch, propped in an iron holder where Muriel had left it.

I lifted it out. It was fairly weighty and the heat made me flinch for a second. "Please stay lit," I begged it. Carefully, I made my way back up the steps.

When Scarlet saw me, her face paled. "Oh no," she said. "I had enough of fire last year."

"I think this will work," I insisted, looking up at the ancient doors. "If I can get them to light..." I knew it had been a dry day and that the All Hallows' Eve bonfire had caught easily. It was our only hope.

Ariadne bit her lip. "That doesn't look safe," she said.

"Everyone stand clear, then. In fact, you all go back down. I'll light it and then as soon as it seems to be going, I'll run after you."

"Ivy..." Scarlet warned. It was usually my twin who put herself in danger. I don't think she liked the idea of me doing it. But it was what had to be done.

"I'll be fine," I insisted and hoped I was telling the truth. The doors were set in stone, and the crypt was entirely stone too. I just hoped that the grass round it wasn't too dry.

Reluctantly, the others descended. I heard Scarlet instructing them to cover their mouths in case there was a lot of smoke. I steadied myself, stood on tiptoe and held the flaming torch up to the doors. It licked at the wood, as if it were trying out the taste, and then, slowly, it began to take hold.

I coughed as the smoke trailed into my mouth.

"Be careful!" I heard Scarlet yell from below.

The heat spread. I felt it on my face and pulled my mask down to try to shield myself. The wood was catching, but I wasn't sure it was enough. Would it burn properly?

But then there was a *crack* and the flames spread across both doors. That, I prayed, was enough. I ran back down the steps and skidded to a halt at the bottom, just about managing to keep the flaming torch aloft.

The others looked at me wordlessly, their arms across their faces. Ebony had something black wrapped round hers.

I could hear the crackling of the fire above and then more cracks as the wood splintered. And then, suddenly... there was a cascade of sounds all at once. It sounded a lot like many pieces of burning wood falling on to stone steps.

We ran up, dancing over the smouldering remains on the stones, until we came to the hole where the doors had once been. And together, we emerged, coughing and laughing all at once, into the moonlight.

## Chapter Thirty-nine

### SCARLET

We stamped out some of the small flames that had begun eating away at the grass and then fell into a tangled heap.

"We did it!" I cried, grinning up at the full moon. I waved some of the smoke away and took some gulps of fresh air.

The night sky spun. There was a flurry of dark shapes above and I soon realised why.

"Bats," Ariadne said. "We disturbed the bats."

They flitted between the trees and the chapel roof,

like strange birds. They suddenly didn't seem scary to me any more. They meant we were free.

I heard a commotion then and looked over towards the entrance of the graveyard, where a group of people were coming through the gate.

"Girls! Oh, girls!" It was Mrs Knight. She hurried over. "Are you all right?"

Madame Zelda was close behind her. "What is all this smoke? We saw it from the school. We were searching for you."

I sat back and looked at the others. I didn't know where to start. Ariadne was leaning on Ivy, panting. Ebony was half-lying in the grass, looking a little sheepish. She had a pile of black items clutched in her hands.

The third figure, I realised, was Ebony's father. He reached down and scooped her up. She hugged him, dropping the items to the ground. "What's happened?" he asked, his handsome face wrought with worry.

Mrs Knight looked back and forth between us and realised that we didn't know how to answer. "It's all right," she said. "Take your time."

"Have you found Muriel?" I asked, a little breathless.

"Yes," said Madame Zelda, with a frown. "Miss Bowler caught her sneaking back into the school. She is being *dealt* with." That meant an ear-splitting lecture from Miss Bowler, but I knew Muriel deserved worse. "Why? What on earth is going on here, girls?"

"Miss, I tried to tell you," Ariadne said. "I was threatened by someone dressed as a witch at the party! It was Muriel, and she locked us down here! She's been causing trouble for months!"

Mrs Knight's face wrinkled. She turned to Ivy and me. "I thought you said you didn't see anything?"

Ivy stared down at the grass. "We were being cowardly. We thought we'd be expelled if we got involved in any trouble." It all seemed so far away now, having just run for our lives from a burning crypt. But it reminded me that we weren't out of the woods yet. We were *deeply* involved in the trouble now.

The teachers didn't look very impressed with her explanation. "So Muriel was this witch?" Madame Zelda asked. "Are you sure?"

"Certain," we chorused.

Ebony reached down and I soon realised what it was she'd been carrying – Muriel's disguise: a flattened witch's hat, a black wig and a mask. She held them all out for everyone to see.

"I'm sorry for sneaking out, Miss. We had to. We went looking for Muriel because we realised she must have taken Ariadne," I explained. And we found her tying Ariadne up in the crypt. Then when we tried to rescue her, Muriel locked us in as well. She said she was going to leave us to rot."

"I see," said Mrs Knight, frowning. "I think we need to get everyone back inside..."

I held Ivy's hand as we walked up Rookwood's front steps, suddenly feeling small again. The frown hadn't left Mrs Knight's face and my heart was sinking with every step. This couldn't be good. We'd broken our last warning.

Despite the school's huge doors being shut, I could hear Miss Bowler from outside. She was really laying into Muriel for sneaking out. I almost expected the doors to be quivering on their hinges.

Mrs Knight led us and the teachers back into the front hall.

"THERE ARE RULES AT THIS SCHOOL FOR A REASON, YOUNG LADY, AND I FOR ONE—" Miss Bowler came to a halt in the middle of her tirade, noticing that we'd come in. Muriel was standing, blank-faced, giving nothing away.

"We've found the others," Mrs Knight explained to her.

Miss Bowler went a bit red as she saw Mr McCloud standing there, his fee-paying and generous arm wrapped round his daughter's shoulders. "Ah. Good."

I glared my fiercest glare at Muriel. I almost hoped we *were* going to be expelled because I wanted to tell her *precisely* what I thought of her. But then images of our stepmother and the asylum flashed into my mind. *No*, I thought. *It's not worth it. She's not worth it.*

"I'm afraid we have a bit of a situation, Eunice," Mrs Knight said quietly to Miss Bowler as she headed towards her.

It was a little bizarre seeing them together while they were still wearing fancy-dress costumes, and that went for the rest of us as well: two black cats, a lion, a pretend witch and a real witch.

Muriel said nothing. She just blinked. I wondered if she was going to run away.

"There's been trouble?" Miss Bowler asked.

Mrs Knight nodded. "We found these girls escaping from some sort of basement beneath the chapel."

"It's a crypt," said Ariadne helpfully.

"A crypt," Mrs Knight said. "They burned their way out of the doors."

Miss Bowler turned her lethal gaze on us. "And WHAT, pray, were you lot doing in a *crypt* when you should have been in your beds?"

"I..." I started to protest. "We..." The words just wouldn't come out. Where could I start? "We had to go because..."

Miss Bowler's nostrils flared like a bull. "Did you lie to us about the missing shoe, Miss Grey?"

I looked down at my shoes, which were very much in a pair. "Yes, Miss. Sorry, Miss."

"Well, this is unacceptable." She waved an angry finger back and forth between Ivy and me. "Weren't you two on your last warning? Mrs Knight, don't you think they've caused enough trouble?"

I bit my lip so hard I thought I might draw blood. Ivy was still gripping my hand.

Thoughts raced through my head. *We won't go back to our stepmother. We won't. We'll run away. We'll live on the streets if we have to. Anything but her. Anything but the asylum.* I squeezed Ivy's hand in return, hoping that the thoughts would somehow jump out of my head and into hers.

But Mrs Knight didn't say anything for a moment. She looked conflicted. "Well..." she started. "These girls said that Miss Witherspoon here tied up Miss Flitworth and intended to keep them all trapped down there. Is that so, Miss Witherspoon?"

"No," said Muriel. She folded her arms. "I have no idea what you're talking about."

"We might have to consider expulsion..." Mrs Knight said quietly, and I felt the hairs rise on the back of my neck. I had to do something.

But just as I was about to go and shake the truth out of her, something amazing happened.

Ebony stepped forward.

"Papa," she said. "I have to confess something."

His dark brows narrowed in concern. "What is it, lassie?"

"I didn't want to come to this school. I wanted to get expelled, and Muriel was supposed to be helping me. She persuaded me to pretend I was a witch. I've been causing trouble all term." She winced at Mrs Knight. "Sorry, Miss, but there's more. We are telling the truth. Muriel has had a vendetta against Ariadne because Ariadne got her expelled from their old school for bullying, and she thinks it ruined her life. So she's been trying to ruin Ariadne's life in return. That's why she locked her in the crypt and then tried to lock us in too. Then she dropped her costume and ran away." Ebony let the pieces of Muriel's disguise fall to the floor.

"You're lying," Muriel snapped, her gaze only

momentarily flicking to the costume pieces. "She's lying, Miss—"

"Don't you dare!" Ebony stepped forward and her black hair whipped out behind her. There was lightning in her stormy eyes. I saw Muriel take a sharp breath. The teachers stared in a strange awe. Suddenly, there was something real in Ebony's magic. "I will NOT let you get away with this. You were going to kill us!"

Muriel spoke again, but it came out smaller and quieter. "I was only trying to scare you."

"So you admit it?" Madame Zelda asked from behind us, her arms folded and a quizzical eyebrow raised.

Muriel's eyes darted around the room, panicked. "I... no, I... I didn't mean..."

But the teachers were ignoring her now and had started muttering amongst themselves. I gave Ebony a quick smile. She had done it.

Muriel leant back against the secretary's desk, her face pale and drawn. Miss Bowler marched over and took hold of her arm. "Don't be going anywhere now," she said.

"Ebony," her father called and she went back over to him. "You wanted to be expelled? Why?"

I saw her lower lip quiver, but her determination was still there. "I just wanted to be with you, at the theatre. I'm so sorry, Papa. I just got caught up in it. I shouldn't have listened to her."

"A bit of amateur dramatics, aye?" he said. "Taken a step too far?"

She nodded. He looked down at her and I could see he was making a decision.

"Mrs Knight," he called, striding over to her. "Don't expel these girls. My daughter will promise to be a model student from now on –" He turned – "won't you, Ebony?"

"But, Papa," she protested quietly. "I want to come home."

"And you will," he replied. "In the holidays. And you can have a part in the next production, if you behave well. You've proven yourself a good actress. But you need an education."

Ebony sighed, but then a slow smile spread across her face. "And you'll teach me more tricks?"

"Of course," he said. "And these three," he pointed to Ivy, Ariadne and myself. "It sounds like they've been the victim of this girl's scheming. Shouldn't they have another chance to prove themselves?"

"Well, I don't know..." Mrs Knight began.

"If the girls hadn't disobeyed you and sneaked out, then what would have become of their friend? Haven't they shown bravery and ingenuity? Those sound like important parts of the school spirit to me." He turned and winked at us. It seemed as though he'd been paying more attention than he'd been letting on.

"He makes a very... *valuable* point," Miss Bowler said.

Mrs Knight didn't seem to notice the inflection. I thought she was actually considering what he'd said.

I grabbed Ariadne's hand as well. We all held our breath.

"I think you're right, Mr McCloud. I think the girls should be allowed to stay."

"Thank you, Miss! Thank you!" We all ran forward.

The headmistress was getting increasingly flustered. "All right, all right!" She waved us away. "But Muriel Witherspoon..." She turned to her. "What are we going to do with you?"

"Well," Madame Zelda piped up, "there's only one way to get rid of a witch."

"NO!" we all yelled at her. Mrs Knight blinked at us.

"You don't want to know, Miss," I said.

## Chapter Forty

### IVY

In the end, the only person to be expelled was Muriel. I almost felt sorry for her. She cried and protested when Mrs Knight said her parents would have to be called.

"This is all your fault," she hissed at Ariadne as she was led away.

Ariadne ignored her and turned back to us. "It isn't," she said with confidence. "I know it isn't."

Scarlet hugged her. "Muriel tried to ruin your life, but all she's done is ruin her own all over again."

"She destroyed her second chance," I said. "We've got to be grateful for ours."

"I think we're on more than two now," Ariadne said with a smile. "Nine lives, like a cat."

I grinned back at her. "Or a lion."

As if on cue with all the feline talk, Ebony's cat strode into the foyer.

"Midnight!" she cried. "There you are!" She scooped him up in her arms.

"Ahem." Her father cleared his throat. "I wondered where the theatre's best mouser had gone..."

Ebony turned to him, red-faced. "Sorry, Papa. Here, you take him." With clear reluctance, she kissed the cat on his forehead and then handed him over. He slung himself over Mr McCloud's shoulder like a pelt scarf.

"He'll be waiting for you," her father said, giving Ebony a matching kiss on the forehead.

As they said their goodbyes, I looked back at Scarlet and Ariadne and stifled a yawn. "I'm exhausted."

Scarlet agreed. "That's enough adventure for one night."

"At least there will be more to come," Ariadne said, looking a little embarrassed. "My life would be frightfully dull without the both of you."

"And ours without you," I said.

And for a moment, we all just grinned at each other. Everything was back to normal.

We watched as Mr McCloud left with the black cat. He winked over his shoulder, and then they disappeared into the night.

So Muriel was gone from Rookwood. We heard that her parents had turned up to collect her, so that was something. If her family were willing to take her back, perhaps her life wouldn't be so ruined after all. Maybe she did have a chance at normality too.

Things didn't quite go back to normal for Ebony, though. By Monday morning, the whole school had heard the rumours about what she'd been up to with Muriel. And now they all knew that Ebony was a fraud.

The first thing I noticed was that nobody was sitting with her at breakfast. They had all moved their chairs as far away from hers as possible.

"Do you think she's all right?" Ariadne asked as we watched her despondently clear her plate away and trudge out of the dining hall.

"She does deserve it," Scarlet said, through a mouthful of porridge. "She tricked everyone." She swallowed. "Including us. She nearly got us expelled, don't forget."

It was as if Ebony's power had evaporated overnight. I saw Penny shoving her and laughing on the way into Latin class. Once Ebony, red-faced, had gone to her desk, everyone shuffled away from her.

At break, I went to the library to get some more books out. I saw Ebony sitting alone in the corner and I almost went over to her, but Scarlet pulled me in the other direction.

When we got to the desk, Agatha and some of the other girls were talking to Jing.

"I thought you said your name was Clarissa?" Jing said, frowning. She scribbled something out in the library book.

Agatha sighed. "No, sorry. We don't do all that any more," she said with a sideways glance over to where Ebony was sitting.

"Aren't you her friends?" I asked.

The girls all looked at each other. "Friends don't lie," Mary grumbled quietly.

"She didn't have any real powers," another of them moaned. "It was all a trick."

"So you're not witches any more?" Scarlet asked.

Agatha glared at Ebony. "There's no such thing as witches," she said.

It seemed everyone was embarrassed to have been taken in by Ebony. Everywhere we went, I heard people whispering about what she had done. Some people laughed at her. Some went quiet and solemn when she walked by.

I could understand the feeling, because I felt it too. How had we been so swept up in everything she'd done? Even if Muriel had been behind it all, Ebony had been the one to convince us. She'd lied to everyone, invented a whole personality that she didn't really have. How could anyone trust her again?

After our ballet lesson had ended and the other girls were traipsing back up the stairs, Scarlet hung around the *barre*. I could see that there was something on her mind.

"You're lurking, Scarlet," Miss Finch called out from the piano. "Is there something you want to ask?"

Scarlet went over to her and I followed. "Miss..." she started quietly, before glancing behind her to where Madame Zelda was stretching in the office. "There's something I've been wondering. Why did you forgive Madame Zelda?"

"Scarlet!" I said, shocked. That didn't seem like an appropriate question to ask. Madame Zelda had admitted to being responsible for breaking Miss Finch's leg due to her jealously, many years ago. I didn't think it was something Miss Finch would really want to talk about.

But Miss Finch just blinked and then exhaled deeply. "Forgiving people isn't about what they need, Scarlet. It's about what *you* need."

My twin wrinkled her nose. "What does that mean?"

"It means you have to decide for yourself whether to forgive someone. We..." she turned and looked into the office. "We work together now because I needed a friend and a colleague, and you girls needed a good teacher, more than I needed to hold a grudge for what happened years ago."

I tried to pull Scarlet away, but she was still going. "But Miss," she hissed, "it doesn't make what she did to you okay, does it? She pushed you off the stage and hurt you for life!"

"No, it doesn't," Miss Finch smiled a regretful smile. "It was still wrong and it still hurts. I don't think I had to forgive it, by any means. But I spent enough years hating her. It didn't make me any better." She shrugged. "Forgiveness is up to me. It's nice to do things on my own terms." I wondered if she was thinking of her mother, Miss Fox. "You have a lot of questions today, girls."

"It was just on my mind, Miss, that's all," Scarlet said.

Miss Finch looked up at us both questioningly. "If you have someone to forgive, Scarlet, it's going to be hard. But you won't know if it's worth it unless you try."

A few days later, Scarlet, Ariadne and I were passing Ebony's room after breakfast, when we heard crying from inside.

I looked at the others and they both nodded silently. No matter what she had done, we weren't going to leave her to cry. I knocked gently on the door.

"C-come in," came the muffled reply.

We peered round the door. Ebony was sitting on her bed, holding her teddy bear. Her face was streaked with tears. "What's wrong?" I asked.

"Why weren't you at breakfast?" Ariadne added, closing the door behind us.

"Oh, it's nothing," she said, sitting up straighter and wiping her cheeks. When she saw our expressions, she clearly changed her mind and decided to answer. "It's my birthday," she explained solemnly. "And I'm alone and everybody hates me. I don't even have my cat. This is the worst birthday ever."

"Ebony..." Scarlet began. "We don't *hate* you."

"But I did terrible things," she said with a sniff. "It's no wonder people don't want to be my friend. I brought it all on myself."

Ariadne went over to her. "Did you do terrible things? I heard it was a witch."

Ebony looked perplexed, but I realised what Ariadne was saying. "You weren't being yourself," I explained. "It was bad, but it's over now. Nobody has met the *real* Ebony. Why don't you introduce her to people?"

The realisation dawned on Ebony's face and her expression brightened. "Perhaps I should," she said.

Suddenly, I heard a commotion out in the hallway. People were gathering, numerous voices floating into the room.

Curious, I got up to look and the others followed me.

Someone had arrived at the school. I saw a trunk on the floor. Together we pushed through the small crowd of gossipers that had gathered, just in time to see...

Violet, hugging Rose.

I had never seen Rose look so delighted. Her best friend, the person who had saved her from the asylum, had returned!

"Violet?" I said in disbelief.

She turned and saw us. "Oh, hello," she said, looking

considerably more cheerful than the last time we'd seen her.

"You're back!" Ariadne exclaimed, gaping at her.

"Well," she said sheepishly, "I've been trying to persuade my guardian to let me come back for months. He heard that the school is better now and he finally agreed, but the term had already started. But then Mrs Knight telephoned us to say that a place had become available."

Rose bounced up and down beside her, grinning from ear to ear.

"Who's this?" Violet asked, pointing to Ebony.

"Oh," Scarlet said. "This is Ebony." She looked back and forth between them. "Ebony McCloud, Violet Adams. I have a feeling you two will get on well."

Ebony hesitated for a moment, but then stepped forward. "Shall I help you with your trunk?"

"Yes, please," said Violet brightly.

We left them to it and headed for the stairs. Lessons would be starting soon.

"It's like they're completely different people," Scarlet whispered.

It was true. A light had been switched on in the darkness, and now two of our former enemies might become good friends.

"If we're stuck here, we might as well make the most of it," Ariadne said, hopping down the stairs. It was an echo of something we'd said many times.

I thought how I'd felt when we started the year, how I'd hoped nothing bad would happen to us again. But perhaps bad things were inevitable. Perhaps there would always be challenges to face, monsters to battle. But with my twin and my friends by my side, the monsters were going to have a fight on their hands. And that was what mattered.

Scarlet grabbed both of us in a hug. "And we won't let anything tear us apart again. Promise?"

"Promise," we chorused.

And as the morning bell rang for lessons, I felt as though it was ringing in a better future.

## Acknowledgements

This book is a tribute to my love of spooky goings-on and all the things that go bump in the night. Thanks go to:

All the team at HarperCollins Children's Books – my wonderful editor Michelle Misra; Sarah Hughes, Samantha Stewart, Louisa Sheridan, and everyone who has helped to put me in front of my readers in some form or another. Also to Lizzie Clifford, who had some brilliant witchy ideas.

The legendary Jenny Savill, and all at Andrew Nurnberg Associates – thanks for your support.

The illustrators of these editions, the great Kate Forrester and Manuel Šumberac, and to Elisabetta Barbazza for working so hard on the designs.

My overseas editors, illustrators, translators, and everyone who brings these books to a worldwide audience. You are stars!

As usual, everyone at r/YAwriters, #UKMGchat, Bath Spa Uni and the fabulous MA Writing Group of Wonders. Thank you for all your wisdom and chatter. You are writing lifesavers. And to all my online followers, for sticking around.

My friends and family, and Ed – with love, always. Thanks for indulging my spooky side.

And of course, thank you for reading. There are still some final secrets to uncover . . .

# Have you read them all?

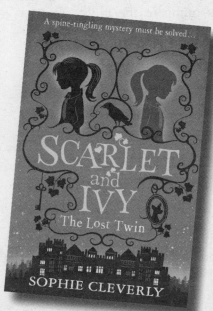

## The Lost Twin

A creepy boarding school.
A sudden disappearance.
A secret diary waiting to
be found.

This is the story of how I
became my sister...

## The Whispers in the Walls

The wind is howling.
The rain is freezing.

But that's not the reason why
pupils at Rookwood School are
feeling the chill...

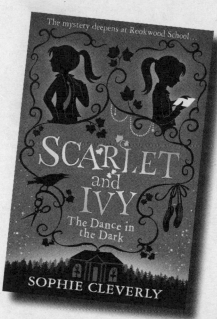

## The Dance in the Dark

Nasty notes.
Frightening dreams.
Rumours running wild.

The girls of Rookwood
School are in danger
once more...

## The Lights Under the Lake

Locals say that at night the
troubled souls buried in the
ancient flooded graveyard no
longer rest in peace...